I0666087

THE ELUSIVE CURVE

A MODERN-DAY QUEST TO DISCOVER ANOTHER WORLD

BILLY ZIG

Copyright © 2019 Billy Zigouras (Billy Zig)

All rights reserved. No part of this publication may be reproduced, distributed, or transmitted in any form or by any means, including photocopying, recording, or other electronic or mechanical methods, without the prior written permission of the publisher, except in the case of brief quotations embodied in critical reviews and certain other non-commercial uses permitted by copyright law. For permission requests, write to the publisher, addressed "Attention: Permissions Coordinator," at the address below.

All characters in this book are fictitious, and any dealings with businesses directly or indirectly mentioned are the work of fiction. Any references to historical events, real people, or real places are used fictitiously. Names, characters, and some places are products of the author's imagination.

ISBN: 978-0-6485968-1-3 (Paperback)

First printing edition 2019.
Revised 2021.

Ziggy Publishing
www.elusivecurve.com

I dedicate this book to my family
and friends... and to the open-minded.

*"It is the mark of an educated mind to
be able to entertain a thought, without accepting it."*

ARISTOTLE: 348BC - 322BC

1

"What do you mean – *the Earth is flat!* Have you lost your freakin' mind, Max?" replied Sam—his rowdy, spontaneous outburst prompting several nearby diners to see what the commotion was all about.

"No! I haven't lost my mind, Sam. But you know, I had a feeling you were going to react like that, mate!"

"Well, Max, what did you expect? Because that's probably the craziest thing you've ever said!"

Best of friends since primary school – spanning over thirty years – there was hardly a topic of discussion that Max and Sam didn't agree upon. But, the last thing Sam expected to hear on that sunny morning before ordering breakfast at the St. Kilda Pier café in Melbourne: was that *the Earth is flat.*

Max's expectation of Sam's response was not unfounded, as it's a common reaction when the words "flat" and "earth" are combined. Whereas typically, people react by instantly dismissing the idea and often resort to ridicule. This dismissal may be due to a psychological phenomenon known as cognitive dissonance, caused by an uncomfortable clash between new ideas and deeply ingrained beliefs. As a result, it often triggers a range of awkward responses and ad hominem attacks.

Whatever the case may be, the fact remains that people have justifiably pondered and hypothesised about their existence within the cosmos for thousands of years; including the shape of the Earth beneath their feet.

Feeling somewhat uneasy at his friend's public outburst, Max shrugged it off; remaining cool, calm, and collected.

"Yeah. Okay. Fair enough, Sam. And you know, I reckon that's exactly how I reacted when I first heard about Flat Earth. It's almost like we've been brainwashed to respond like that!"

Flabbergasted—Sam just stared at Max in disbelief.

Max persevered, "But, Sam, do you really believe that I would say the Earth is flat – if I didn't have the evidence to prove it?"

"Are you freakin' kidding me, Max! What evidence?" Sam heated up. Infuriated by Max's insistence on the matter – the frown on his forehead deepened with concern.

Without waiting for Max to reply, Sam pointed toward the distant horizon that could be clearly seen from the deck of the café and insisted, "Look out there, Max – I've seen ships disappear over that very horizon, and it was due to the curvature of the Earth. Anyway, isn't that how Aristotle proved the shape of our Earth? You know, something like over 2,500 years ago! The ships didn't fall off the edge... did they?" he laughed, while slowly shaking his head; now suspiciously wondering whether his friend was just testing his patience as he waited for Max to end the absurdity.

Knowing he had the upper hand, having conducted countless hours of research on the matter, Max smirked and then replied, "Touché, Sam!" whilst thinking about the axiom, he who gets the last laugh – laughs loudest.

"*Anyway*, of course, ships don't fall off the edge of the Earth. They just disappear from our perspective view. Because a ship vanishing over the horizon is simply an optical illusion – as both linear perspective and convergence, together with angular resolution play tricks with our eyes. And it's blatantly obvious that objects become smaller with distance."

"No way, Max! That can't be right... I know what I've seen – and I've seen it with my own eyes!" stubbornly crossing his arms over his chest.

"Okay... Here's the thing, Sam. One of the first things you need to grasp to see the world around you as intended – are the laws of optical perspective. Because anyone can prove that convergent perspective limits our ability to view distant objects."

"Really? How so?" he curiously frowned.

Max pointed toward the bay and explained. "Well, it's rather obvious that when you look at the horizon, that the sky appears to ramp downward, and the water appears to angle upward: and the point where they converge and intersect at the horizon is defined as the vanishing point."

Sam briefly considered the concept before replying, "Ah, yes... you mean, similar to linear perspective drawing, just like we did in art class at school; is that right?"

"Exactly! You got it, bud. So, in effect – boats disappear out of view due to visual perspective; not vanish over the elusive curve of the Earth. And the same phenomenon also occurs over a flat-level surface. Just test it: and you'll see!"

"You know, it can get rather complex when you delve into it: as there are several factors to consider that can influence our vision across long distances; with inferior and superior mirages, the refraction and diffraction of light, atmospheric compression, and most importantly – the angular resolution of our eyes."

Sam stroked his chin postulating the scenario. "Hmm... okay. That kind of makes sense. But I still highly doubt that boats disappear over the horizon simply due to perspective."

"Yeah, I had my own doubts too. But, please – allow me to elaborate."

"Sure... Go for it... I'm all ears. Even though you're never going to persuade me that the Earth is flat. Never in a million years!" he added with conviction, whilst shaking his head defiantly.

"Never say never, Sam!" Max smiled wryly.

"Anyway, I've been dying to tell you about Flat Earth for quite some time now. But I just didn't want to mention it – until I had all the facts. But the key to unlocking the deception is to understand how our eyes work."

"You see, convergent perspective greatly influences our observations and can be demonstrably proven by simply looking down a long-straight highway, hallway, or even a railway track. Where you can clearly see that all parallel lines appear to converge together.

Just look around you; you'll see it occurring everywhere!"

The sound of water splashing against the jetty's pylons from a passing jet-ski caught Max's attention, where he casually pointed towards the end of the pier. "Hey, don't just take my word for it, buddy. Take a look for yourself; the deck, pylons, and even the light poles all converge to a narrower point in the distance. And the point of convergence at the horizon is defined as the vanishing point."

Sam swivelled in his chair for a better view. "Hmm... very interesting, Max. And yeah, it's kind of obvious, actually."

"Bloody oath it is, Sam! Especially when we're made aware of it."

"And besides, the word horizon is literally derived from the word horizontal – or level! And we need to realise that the horizon is not a physical geometric tangible entity but simply rather an optical illusion. And just like all optical phenomenon, it's subject to multiple variables, for example: observer height (or altitude), terrestrial refraction, temperature fluctuations, and precipitation; as well as other atmospheric conditions including mirages."

"It's far more complicated than we could imagine, Sam. However, when we discard all the variables and stick to the facts: it's evidently demonstrable that we don't live on a spinning ball that's erratically flying through Space!"

"Whoa... Max! You're spinning me out right now – and I'm not even stoned!" replied Sam, whilst imitating puffing on a joint.

"Are you sure it's not from the spinning Earth, buddy!"

"Well... it could be," Sam cheekily grinned.

"All jokes aside, and to finally answer your question regarding boats disappearing over the horizon: it's simply all about visual perspective; inlcuding the angular resolution of our eyes."

"You see, if we expect to see curvature across the Z-Axis – that is, the linear perspective view directly in front of us; then wouldn't you agree that we would also see curvature over the horizontal X-Axis – which is discernibly far greater in distance? Because the fact is, if the Earth is spherical by nature, then we would obviously see curvature across both vectors!"

"Hmm... Yeah... I get it, Max," while lightly scratching the side of his neck. "It makes sense: because if we don't have curvature over both directions, then our Earth would be kind of shaped like a toilet roll," motioning a cylindrical shape with his index fingers.

"It sounds like you're on a roll today, buddy," having a chuckle and throwing Sam a wink – always appreciating his witty sense of humour.

"Hey, Sam... I've got a great idea!"

"Hit me with it, Max!"

"Well, let's take the Sunseeker out for a day cruise. We'll have access to binoculars and a telescope onboard, and most importantly – a fridge full of cold beer! And while we're on the water; we can test the theory on whether boats disappear over the horizon due to the curvature of the Earth," Max enthusiastically suggested.

"Top idea! But in all honesty, you had me at cold beer!" he joked. "You know, I still don't believe that a boat can be zoomed back into view after it has disappeared over the horizon; but sure... let's test it – and while we're out there, maybe we can cast out a few lines!" replied Sam; a keen amateur fisherman.

Max signalled a thumbs up. "Sounds like a plan to me!"

Adjusting his baseball cap – so that the Sun wasn't beaming directly into his eyes; Sam picked up the menu, leaning back into his chair to read the chefs recommendations. Also, taking a brief moment to casually glance around at the other diners of the busy café, feeling slightly embarrassed from his outburst moments earlier.

Waiting patiently, Sam wondered if they were ever going to be served when he was elated to see his favourite waitress – whom he had flirted with on several occasions – approach their table.

Jessica was in her early thirties and looked many years younger, with her long mousy-blonde hair tied back into a ponytail. She apologised for the slight delay, explaining they were short-staffed, and then cheerfully asked if they were ready to place their orders.

Famished after working out at the gym earlier that morning, Max and Sam ordered several dishes from the menu; with Sam kindly asking for his usual: a side of fresh hot chillies.

"How could I forget. You just love your hot chillies – don't ya, Sam?" she kidded; because, as a regular, he always requested the very same on every visit.

"The hotter, the better," he cheekily grinned.

Jessica flirtatiously smiled back, then tapped their selections into her handheld tablet before she daintily whisked away, leaving a scent of perfume in the air – causing Sam to temporarily forget what they'd just moments earlier been talking about.

After the more than pleasant distraction by Jessica, Sam leaned forward resting his elbow on the table while supporting his chin with his fist, and facetiously asked, "But Max, if the Earth is flat, then why can't I see China from the Eureka Tower in Melbourne?"

Max snapped, "Are you for real, Sam! You're not friggin Superman, so you can't see forever! And even if you could, would you just imagine how small the 'Great Wall of China' or 'Chinese people' would appear from here?"

Leaning back into his chair to ponder the scenario, Sam smiled broadly before they both burst into laughter.

Following a hearty chuckle – Max described how numerous environmental factors and conditions such as precipitation, humidity, mist, fog, haze, pollution, air density, and even dust particles influence the atmosphere, limiting our ability to see infinite distances. Together with the optical limits of our eyes, where visual perspective, and not to mention Earth's undulating terrain, demonstrably prevents us from seeing, for example, China from Melbourne. Especially when an object is beyond the distant horizon, where evaporation and humidity can frequently create a lensing or magnifying effect, often manifesting objects (including the Sun) to appear larger; particularly when setting over the ocean. Where humidity is obviously denser at Earth's surface. Therefore, the atmosphere and our eyes play a huge role in how far we can see.

"So, anyway, Sam; that's why we can occasionally see Geelong from over 60-kilometres across the bay, while other days, we struggle to see more than just a few kilometres away. Especially when the weather is crap!"

"Yeah, okay... that kind of makes sense, Max. And come to think of it, I reckon I've seen Mount Macedon from the shoreline of Brighton beach – and that's about 100 clicks away!"

"Precisely! Proving – once and for all – that atmospheric conditions influence how far we can see on any given day. It's not rocket science!"

They looked around almost in sync to see if Jessica was approaching with their order; as by this stage, their stomachs were rumbling with hunger.

"You know what, Sam? I feel like there's so much more to learn about how our eyes work in the grand scheme of things. And we literally have a God-given gyroscope built into our head that can sense even the slightest motion via our vestibular system.

"So, let me tell you something; if we're somehow living on a spherical planet that's spinning at over 1,600 kilometres an hour whilst chasing the Sun at the supersonic speed of around 100,000 kilometres per hour: we would friggin know it!"

Sam momentarily remained quiet as he contemplated Max's profound statement. "Yeah, I suppose we would," he hesitantly agreed but just couldn't resist asking.

"But, Max, if the Earth is flat – then where is the edge of the flat Earth? And why hasn't anyone ever taken a photo of it?"

Max rolled his eyes!

"Really, Sam! Before you ask me for a photo of the edge of the Earth, which I obviously can't provide – nor do I know if an edge even exists: I hope you know that scientists haven't even proven what's at the core of this 'supposed' spherical Earth!"

"Sure they have, Max! Isn't there molten iron at the core?"

"What... hang on a moment, Sam! Let's just question whether there is molten metal at the core before we accept it as fact. You see, scientists claim to have known what's at the core of our Earth since the 1930s. But, the deepest hole drilled to date is the Kola Superdeep Borehole, which the Russians achieved during the late 1980s. And the fact remains that despite their valiant efforts, they only drilled a skimpy twelve kilometres (approx. eight miles) into the surface of the Earth before acknowledging, after many exhausting attempts spanning ten years and breaking countless drill bits, that they couldn't drill any further. It was impenetrable! And well short of the core of the Earth, which is postulated to be 6,000 kilometres deeper than their achievement of only 12 km."

"So, Sam, please tell me... how would they friggin know what's at the centre of our Earth if they haven't even drilled that deep?"

"Well, they must know, Max. It's science!" he praised, raising his palms to the sky – borderline religiously.

Max swiftly replied, "It's more like the religious cult of scientism. And you have to admit that most people these days are blinded by science. Should we just blindly believe everything scientists tell us? Because, if that's the case, then we might as well also believe the fantasies portrayed in movies such as 'Journey to the Centre of the Earth'!" he joked.

"No, Max... we shouldn't! But, the experts must know! Don't they have ground-penetrating radar, seismometers, spectrographs, and those radio-spectrum thingamajigs? You know, all that fancy high-tech stuff that can peek into the Earth to find minerals and stuff," he rambled, trying to sound all knowledgeable on the topic.

"Give me a break, Sam! What experts? How could anyone definitively know what's in the middle of a watermelon if they'd never cut one open to look inside? You could guess, but you wouldn't actually know. Would you?"

"Of course, I wouldn't know. But do you really believe that we are being deceived about the shape of our Earth? Because as you know, I'm all for delving into conspiracy theories like JFK, the events of 9/11, or the moon landings, but this Flat Earth thing is an impossible conspiracy theory to comprehend! It just doesn't make any sense. We live in a modern world amongst some of the smartest scientists of all time who would have told us by now if the Earth was flat!" picking up his glass and taking a sip of water—still in disbelief that he was even discussing the topic.

"Listen, Sam... let's just agree for now that I can't show you a photo of the edge of the Earth – and you can't prove the core of the Earth. What do you say?"

"Okay, sure... fair enough, Max," he reluctantly conceded.

"Anyway, why does a Flat Earth even need to have an edge?"

"Because, if we are to assume that Space is infinite, then isn't it more than plausible that a flat Earth realm could be infinite? So, it kind of got me thinking: what if there's undiscovered land or extra territories to be found across this infinite plane? And who knows, there could even be advanced civilizations; or 'extra-terrestrial life'!"

Sam's eyes widened. "Oh my God! Do you actually believe there could be more land and more people and civilizations on this Earth?" Suddenly fascinated by the concept of unexplored land; forgetting he was just moments earlier resisting the slightest possibility that the Earth could be flat.

"Yeah. For sure. Who knows? There could be! Anything is possible in this crazy world where we live... right?"

Jessica returned, placing their hot meals on the table and remained to chat for a few minutes; before noticing the demanding café manager gesturing to her to get back to work by arrogantly tapping his watch.

Reluctantly leaving their table, she quietly murmured, "What a slave driver!" under her breath – then politely asked if there was anything further they required; with Sam in the spur of the moment, asking for her phone number.

"Maybe later," she blushed in reply – tucking a loose lock of hair behind her ear before strutting away.

Sam was smitten. Once again, taken aback by her charm.

"Well... that was awkward!" Max teased.

"Shut up, Max!" he snapped.

Their fiery discussion about the shape of the Earth came to a pause as they eagerly tucked into their hot meals.

2

Most people would consider that Max was somewhat crazy, for in this day and age, questioning the commonly accepted cosmology of our Universe.

But in fact, he was just an ordinary guy in his late-thirties who was seeking answers to questions about life. And as a seasoned conspiracy theorist for over twenty years, he knew that many of the countless conspiracy theories he'd researched consequently resulted as conspiracy facts.

Max also believed that many historical events were to some extent distorted; where it's often said, the victor dictates history – or 'his-story'. And he could not fathom people who lived their lives by blindly trusting and accepting the indoctrination of the education system, media, pop-culture, or the status quo—without question and with pure blind faith.

But not Max!

He was finally pleased to discuss the Flat Earth theory with Sam and was relieved to see that since disclosing the prospect of undiscovered land on Earth, Sam's feistiness mellowed; now beginning to engage in the topic with genuine curiosity – rather than ridicule.

Quietly enjoying his breakfast, Max gently placed down his cutlery and took a sip of orange juice, and said in a relatively low voice so that the other nearby diners could not hear.

"Sam, could you just imagine the fury of people if they found out the Earth was not a spinning ball that's hurtling through Space? And that society has been misled about the very place we live?"

Gently drumming his fingers on the table before responding, "Max, if what you're saying is true and can be confirmed through the scientific method, then this would be the biggest and the most controversial conspiracy to be perpetrated in the history of humanity!"

Wiping his lips with a napkin, Max slowly nodded his head. "Yeah, I know, Sam... I know!" he replied, with a look of concern that Sam had rarely seen before.

An awkward silence set in as they continued their meals, both contemplating the scale of the conspiracy at hand.

Beads of sweat appeared on Sam's forehead, and it wasn't from the hot chilli's that he added to his food. But, from the sudden realisation of the worldwide implications of such a grand conspiracy; which suddenly hit him like a tonne of bricks.

"Max, are you kind of implying that even the photos of Earth from Space are fake?" asked Sam, whispering to ensure that the other diners could not hear the crazy words coming out of his mouth.

"And what about the other planets in Space? Are they flat too?" leaning back into his chair to reconsider what he just asked.

"I'm not sure what they are," replied Max, then continued to explain that the reality of a flat Earth will virtually change his entire perception of the world around him and life as he knows it.

"You have to unknow what you currently know, Sam. You have to start from the very beginning by forgetting all the bullshit you've been taught. And when you peel through the layers of deception, only then will you finally break free and truly comprehend the beauty of the world where you live; relearn to trust your natural senses; and appreciate nature at a higher level than you have ever experienced in your entire life."

"Sorry for my wild rant, Sam. But please... hear me out, bud."

"Go for it, Max. I have all the time in the world for you. You know that, right?"

"Yeah. I do, mate. Likewise," Max smiled in appreciation.

"And Sam, the way I see it, is that the human race has forgotten how to use common sense. Foolishly and naively neglecting their natural senses whilst trusting advanced mathematical theories devised by eccentric astrophysicists, whose theories do not correlate with reality. And they often admit it. These same 'mathemagicians' derive complex theoretical formulas in an attempt to explain natural phenomena, but fundamentally many of their theories have not, and cannot be proven."

Sam snorted, "Haha... 'Mathemagicians'. That's clever."

Max was a little animated at this point but stopped to sip his coffee, which was now almost stone cold. "Please... tell me if you don't want me to continue, Sam. It's just that I have so much to share with you, mate!"

"Relax, Max! It's cool, man. Go on... I'm rather intrigued," taking another mouthful of his food.

"Thanks, buddy. I must admit it's a big relief being able to discuss the topic with you openly. You know, I was kind of worried that it would compromise my credibility; but I just need to know the truth about where I live."

"Yeah, I get it. That makes perfect sense. We should always question our reality," giving Max a reassuring smile.

"And come to think of it, why the heck haven't we been back to the Moon since the 1970s?" Sam candidly asked. "You know, I've always been kind of suspicious about those bloody moon missions, and just as the lyrics by the Red-Hot Chilli Peppers say, *'Space may be the final frontier, but it's made in a Hollywood basement'.*"

Having a hearty chuckle, "Bloody oath, Sam. A Hollywood basement is as far as they got! You know, they fooled us with that bullshit for far too long. But the good thing is that tens-of-millions of people are waking up to the grand deception of the Apollo Moon landing hoax."

"Undoubtedly!" Sam agreed while briefly excusing himself to answer a phone call from his office.

Max signalled a passing waitress to order two short black espressos, and known to have a sweet tooth: two slices of death by chocolate cake.

"I'll have that out to you in a jiffy," she replied, swiftly walking away to place the order.

After returning to the table, Sam rested his hand on Max's shoulder, and said, "You know what, Max; I gotta admit, that it crossed my mind on more than one occasion today – that you've finally lost the friggin plot!"

Sliding back into his chair, he clarified, "But having said that, you're kind of making sense. So, I promise to conduct my research on the topic, and I'll try to keep an open mind about it."

"I'm thrilled to hear that, Sam. Just be prepared to have your mind blown!" gesturing an explosion with his hands.

"Yeah, well... it kind of already is!"

"Should we get out of here?" after finishing his short black espresso and stuffing down the last bite of cake.

"Sure... let's do it!" Sam eagerly replied, who was more than keen to see Jessica again, as they left the alfresco dining area of the café to settle the bill inside.

Pleased to see her standing behind the counter, Sam casually flirted with Jessica for a few moments, then generously tipped her for the excellent service.

Scribbling her name and number on the back of the receipt, she handed it to Sam, and in a hushed tone so that her nosey manager couldn't hear said, "I hope you don't think I just give my number out to anyone."

Trying to stay composed, Sam replied, "Well, as long as you don't think I just ask anyone. I'll call you soon," snapping her a subtle wink.

A smiling Jessica blushed while watching the two men exit the café.

Slipping on their sunglasses, they strolled the pier towards Sam's car which was parallel parked on the busy main road.

Max grinned while nudging his friend with his elbow as they neared the parked vehicle, and said, "Very suave, Sam... very suave!"

"Hey, don't you worry, mate. I've still got it!" he self-assuredly smiled, grabbing the keys from his pocket and unlocking the car.

3

It was a somewhat quiet drive while they cruised several blocks along scenic Beach Road to Port Melbourne, with just the sound of the Nissan R35 Skyline's custom exhaust humming in the background.

Sam manoeuvred the car into the private U-shaped driveway of Max's apartment building, parking in one of the available bays with the engine still idling.

"Hey, by the way, Sam – I've been thinking; why don't we take the boat out for a cruise this Saturday? How does that suit you?"

Without even hesitating for a moment, Sam replied, "Sounds brilliant, mate. What time should we head out?" knowing that a day out on Max's boat was always epic.

"Let's meet at the Marina... at say, 11 am. I'll also ask some of the fellas to join us, and we'll make a day of it. I'll text you the details."

"Awesome, Max. The more, the merrier. It should be a blast!"

"Sure will," he replied, opening the car door and easing his almost six-foot athletic frame out from the low-riding vehicle.

Max closed the door and crouched down at the open window. "Hey, Sam. Just one more thing, before I go. I'll email you a link to a video called *200 Proofs Earth is Not a Spinning Ball*. So, it should help answer most questions about the heliocentric model and our Flat Earth."

"Are you serious? There are actually hundreds of proofs?" he curiously asked.

"There's way more than that," he said with a Duchenne smile; while reaching over to shake his hand before Sam departed for the drive home.

On approaching the entrance to the apartment building, Max was welcomed by Henry; the charming middle-aged doorman with a bubbly personality, who the residents adored just like a member of their extended families.

"Good morning, Mr Carter! Beautiful day, isn't it?" greeted Henry, in his typical cheerful demeanour – opening the large glass door exposing the elegant décor and the marble-tiled foyer.

"Not too shabby at all, Henry. It's great to see the Sun shining bright. I just hope we don't get four seasons in one day today."

Henry wittily remarked, "Yes, that would be typical of Melbourne weather, wouldn't it, Sir?" where they shared a laugh as Max headed toward the elevator that privately accessed the twenty-second-floor of his penthouse apartment.

Stripping off and throwing his workout gear into the laundry chute, Max quickly showered, then dressed into a finely woven cotton business shirt and tailored trousers – and remaining barefoot, he walked downstairs to his office.

Residing at his desk, he prepared for a video call with Roberto, who was on vacation with his family in the Japanese Prefecture, Shizuoka; visiting Mt. Fuji for their annual getaway.

Max glanced across his desk and was struck by her enchanting green eyes, her warm smile, and beautiful classic facial features, leaving him momentarily breathless. He was looking at his favourite photo of Zoe, portrayed in a slim-line silver photo frame and taken when they had celebrated their first anniversary whilst on vacation in New York.

They had been a couple for just over two years, when Zoe recently accepted a consulting position with a boutique investment bank in London's financial district. She was reluctant to leave, but the chance to advance her career – after being headhunted for the role through numerous recommendations – was an opportunity that was just too good to refuse.

Max adored Zoe's ambitious nature and encouraged her to accept the role, believing it was vital for her to achieve her goals in life, even if it meant that she would be halfway across the world –

and that he would miss her immensely whilst she was away.

Time passed slowly, and it had been a long and lonely six weeks since he last visited her, and he was excited that they would soon be reunited. Luckily her six-month contract was concluding, and Max was looking forward to flying to London to spend the weekend with her, before returning home to Melbourne.

He was lost in deep thought when an incoming Skype alert from Roberto popped up on his monitor, snapping him back to reality.

* * * * *

Battling the mid-day traffic on the bustling streets of Melbourne, Sam didn't even listen to music during the busy drive home.

Somewhat perplexed, he just drove in silence thinking about his conversation with Max; observing life around him as he'd never done before.

Smiling to himself, he thought, "That bloody crazy Max!"

The traffic lights signalled red as Sam geared down to a complete stop.

He looked heavenward through the open sunroof and pondered whether the Earth was spinning.

Lost in deep thought, the car behind him honked the horn to move him along after the lights turned green, where Sam waved to courteously thank the driver in reply.

Arriving home several minutes later, Sam parked his car under the carport, then walked the tree-lined driveway to the letterbox where he noticed that not even a single leaf was moving on the surrounding trees.

In fact, he noticed that nothing was moving.

And for the first time in his life, Sam sensed the apparent stillness – of the motionless Earth.

"Three things cannot be long hidden: the Sun, the Moon, and the truth."

BUDDHA

4

Dusk was setting as Max parked his matte-black BMW M760Li in the underground private car park of his apartment building.

He was looking forward to chilling out after a physically exhausting day volunteering at one of the several charities he supported by assisting in the kitchen and serving dinner to some of the numerous disadvantaged people that were doing it tough in Melbourne.

It was a humbling experience because, although Max donated to various charities; contributing his time at one of Melbourne's largest homeless shelters and witnessing the appreciation firsthand – gave him a feeling of great personal satisfaction.

Happy to be home, he entered the apartment and asked the voice-recognition device to play *"I Can See for Miles"* by The Who, which began to softly play in the background as the elevator doors chimed and slowly closed behind him.

Walking toward the mahogany desk of his home office, he looked outside to soak in the beautiful twilight view of Melbourne's shimmering city skyline.

Lightly exhaling with relief, he slid off his shoes and socks and quietly murmured, "Ahh... that's better!" while making *fists with his toes* in the soft-woven rug under his desk; after remembering the technique from a scene of one of his favourite movies.

Reaching for a pre-rolled joint of quality Kush from the top drawer of the desk, he lit up and took a big puff, then sat down and reclined back into the plush leather office chair. Now resting his feet onto the desk and pondering about his ambitious plan to search for unexplored land.

But not before long, he had a case of the munchies.

Making his way to the kitchen, he grabbed a plate of freshly made club sandwiches from the refrigerator that his considerate housekeeper Elena had earlier prepared for him. And returning to his desk, he slowly munched his food while drifting away in thought, back to the very first moment he heard about Flat Earth.

And just like most people, Max initially ridiculed the concept. Playfully teasing Flat Earther's for their wild eccentric claim that the shape of the Earth is not what we have known for many centuries. However, he just couldn't shake the possibility from his mind.

It was not long after that Max set himself on a mission to find the truth about the world where he lived, as he always believed, that the *truth should not fear investigation.*

During the early stage of his research, he didn't care if the Earth was a spinning ball or flat. Thinking it was not going to change his life either way.

Regardless, Max became somewhat obsessed and relentless in his search for answers as he delved *deep down the rabbit hole*; convinced that it was the duty of our current generation to get to the bottom of the Flat Earth debate – once and for all. But the further Max investigated, the more contradictions and flaws within the heliocentric model were being exposed. And after countless hours of investigation, he could not find empirical proof that he lived upside-down on a spinning ball.

He noticed that people liked to ridicule and laugh at the concept of a Flat Earth, but the truth was far more important to Max than a random laugh. And he was yet to encounter anyone who would bet their career, life earnings – or even a few pints of beer, for that matter – that the Earth was a spherical planet flying through space, and not flat and motionless, just as one's senses and observations would suggest.

Max often wondered why people became so triggered about the topic and whether it was possibly caused by the ridiculous notion presented to us as children: Flat Earth conceptualised and depicted as a pancake-like object floating in Space – invoking the ludicrous suggestion where we would fall off the edge and into the abyss if we dared to travel toward the outer perimeter.

Yet, now as an adult, it was the heliocentric model, that when put under scrutiny, was presenting itself as ludicrous. And a fairy tale – or "theory tale". Where it appeared to Max that society had been hoodwinked to believing they live on a spinning ball without demonstrable empirical proof.

Fortunately, the missing pieces from Max's quest for truth were starting to seamlessly connect after the life-changing realisation that he was not spinning and orbiting at preposterous breakneck speeds through the Universe – as he once blindly believed.

It was a grand awakening: as his *real eyes* were beginning to *realise*, the *real lies* – like finally finding the missing piece to an unfinished jigsaw puzzle.

Max still recalled the days when he adamantly attempted to de-bunk the preposterous Flat Earth conspiracy theory and assumed the easiest way to prove our Earth is an oblate spheroid was via the images of our Earth from Space. So, he searched online to verify that the world is a spinning ball – just like he'd learned at school.

But to his profound disappointment, Max soon realised that the photos of our Earth were not 'photos' after all. But instead, computer-generated images stitched together from composite data – as per the admission by Robert Simmon, a Senior Data Visualization Engineer at a division of NASA, where he acknowl-edged that they take a flat map of the world and wrap it around a spherical surface. The designer further explains how his part was to integrate the surface, clouds, and oceans to match people's expectations on how our Earth would appear from Space; where he gloats that he also adds a specular highlight to show the Sun's hotspot shining on a spherical Earth.

Commenting on the famous Blue Marble image during a 2016 radio interview, the data visualizer made a stark admission by awk-wardly stating (sic), *"It is photoshopped... but its, its... has to be".*

After hearing the comment on a YouTube video, Max was ut-terly astounded, having always believed the photos of our Earth

– that he'd even used as his desktop screensaver – were in fact real, genuine photos!

Bitterly angered and gesturing toward the computer monitor, Max shouted, "Are you freakin' kidding me! What else is fake if the photos of Earth from Space are fake?"

That's when Max began to scrutinise the scientific claims behind the heliocentric model and the Big Bang Theory with a fine-tooth comb.

And following an extensive investigation, he found no empirical proof to verify that our Earth is spinning at almost twice faster than the speed of sound, at 1,666 kilometres-per-hour at the Equator; whilst axially tilted at 23.4 degrees – that disturbingly equates to 66.6 degrees when subtracted from a 90-degree right-angle.

Nor was there empirical proof – either by experiment or sensory evidence – that our Earth is orbiting the Sun at the unfathomable speed of over 100,000 kilometres-per-hour, or 66,600 miles per hour. Neither was there evidence the Sun traverses through the Milky Way toward the galactic centre – or 'the great attractor' – at a breakneck-haphazard speed of approximately 720,000 kilometres-per-hour.

And these exorbitant motions apparently occur whilst Earth's inhabitants purportedly corkscrew amidst an infinite ever-expanding Universe, expanding at over 1,800,000 kilometres-per-hour; or approximately 40 million kilometres per day. Our world and our home: a planet wrapped with many billions of tonnes of water, careering ballistically through the vastness and blackness of Space; encompassing billion and billions of kilometres every year toward a hypothesised final destination – coined by astrophysicists as 'The Big Crunch'.

It's enough to make anyone dizzy – just thinking about it!

In the documentary, *"The Principle"*, the theoretical physicist and futurist, Professor Michio Kaku, confessed:

> *"Usually in science, if we're off by a factor of two, or a factor of ten; we call that horrible. But in cosmology, we're off by a factor of ten, to the one-hundred-and-*

*twenty. That is – one, with one-hundred-and-twenty
zeros after it. This is the largest mismatch between theory and experiment – in the history of science!"*

The renowned astrophysicist Carl Sagan once famously stated,
'Extraordinary claims require extraordinary evidence.'

Max wondered, "Could the lack of 'extraordinary evidence' be
the reason for the resurgence of the Flat Earth momentum spreading across the pond; with countless people questioning modern
cosmography by asking, 'Is the Earth flat'? And if the concept was
so absurd, why is it that millions of well educated, open-minded
people are now Flat Earthers?"

Because it appeared to Max that an apocalyptic awakening was
occurring, snapping humanity out of a deep knowledge coma and
without partiality to a specific demographic, gender, colour, or religious belief. Where the "wisdom of the crowd" was seemingly
beginning to triumph pseudoscience.

Surprisingly, he found that Flat Earthers stemmed from all
walks of life and spanned various professions; such as pilots, engineers, surveyors, professors, ex-USA intelligence operatives – and
even Army, Navy, and Air Force personnel.

Furthermore, numerous prominent celebrities, musicians,
artists, and famous sportspeople (including basketballers, tennis
players, and footballers) were also openly coming forth as Flat
Earthers; and not to forget, the many who secretly remained in
the closet for fear of public retribution.

And why was there a sudden increase in Flat Earth proponents?

Max giggled as he thought, "Well... it was probably because
they all failed to find – *the elusive curve of the Earth*".

Based on Google Trends, online queries for the keyword "Flat
Earth" is soaring at an all-time high. With search volumes climbing exponentially over recent years, due to an increase of people
researching the topic. With thousands of people also sharing their
personal experiments, ideas, life experiences, and even informative
memes that were being widely shared online.

Max was astounded to find that according to a study conducted in France in 2017, one in ten participants surveyed thought that the Earth is flat.

Another recent poll conducted in the United States of America indicated that one-third of 18-24-year-old's interviewed were sceptical about the heliocentric model. Furthermore, 23% of Americans believe the Sun is traversing above them, rather than our Earth spinning towards the Sun in an eastwardly rotation to create day and night: as claimed by the heliocentric model. Over in Russia, 3% of people openly proclaimed to be Flat Earthers. In the UK, a poll conducted by a morning television program in England – after an interview on the subject was broadcasted – indicated that 18% of respondents proclaimed the same belief. And a further poll conducted in Brazil ascertained that 7% of Brazilians believe the Earth is flat – or approximately 11 million people.

Max felt relieved that he was not alone because it seemed that millions of people from around the world were beginning to realise that the mainstream explanation of the cosmos – was pure malarkey.

Modern-day 'celebrity' scientists also weighed into the Flat Earth discussion. However, they did so, not by presenting empirical proof to quash the conspiracy in its track; but by throwing ridicule and outlandish assertions, claiming that a ship vanishing over the horizon is sufficient evidence to prove the Earth is spherical.

However, Max had personally debunked that claim by zooming a boat back to his view with high-powered binoculars and knew that it was just visual perspective that created the illusionary myth – that ships vanish 'hull first' behind the curve of the Earth.

Commenting about the Flat Earth movement that was spreading across America, Neil de Grasse Tyson said (sic), *"The fact that there's a rise of Flat-Earthers is evidence of two things. One, we live in a country that protects free speech. And, two, we live in a country with a failed educational system. Our system needs to train you not only what to know, but how to think about information and knowledge and evidence. If we don't have that kind of training, you'd run around believing anything."*

The inability by mainstream scientists to offer verifiable scientific proof on the matter – combined with their degrading and belittling remarks; triggered Max's conspiratorial switch where further suspicion was seeded into his mind. At the time, tipping him closer to if not becoming a Flat Earther – but a globe Earth sceptic.

Shaking his head in absolute disgust; Max switched off the computer for the night, as he really needed to take a break.

5

Throwing on a casual black leather jacket, Max left the apartment for a walk to the local pub – located less than two blocks from his home – to enjoy a few pints of beer.

Arriving at the pub several minutes later; notoriously renowned as one of Port Melbourne's roughest venues during the times of the Melbourne Water Front Dispute in 1998 but since modernised to a more cosmopolitan setting—Max was greeted by the barman, Marcus, who had already begun to pour him an ice-cold pint of beer.

Taking a swig, he said, "Ahh... cheers, Marcus; I friggin needed that!"

"You're welcome, Max. Good to see you again, my friend," fist-bumping him, whilst acknowledging another customer that was waiting for service with a nod of his head.

"Likewise, Marcus," he replied, taking his beer and walking away to casually mingle with some of the other customers, who appeared to always be there, just like part of the furniture.

After downing a couple of pints, Max struck up a casual conversation with a friendly chap at the bar – and as serendipity would have it – he happened to be a retired Sea-Captain, who had once navigated some of the largest vessels across the Mediterranean Sea, before migrating to Australia during the mid-nineties.

His name was Pierre, and he was a rather dapper looking gentlemen in his mid-fifties, who had European features with dark curly hair, and wore lightly tinted thin-framed glasses.

Following some small talk, Max built up enough Dutch courage to apply the Socratic and Zetetic method of inquiry in the lead up to discuss Flat Earth with Pierre. Feeling it was his obligation to personally inform as many people as possible about his newfound reality.

Max gently placed his pint of beer on the bar, and pointing towards it, he asked, "Hey Pierre, do you reckon the liquid in this glass is level?"

Overhearing the beginning of the conversation, Marcus knew exactly what Max was about to say – as he'd heard it all before – and quietly mumbled under his breath, "The poor bugger!"

Pierre briefly glanced at the half-full pint of beer and responded, "Well... yes... of course, the liquid is level. No doubt about it!"

Max then casually pointed towards the sink behind the bar and asked, "What about that sink full of water? Is the water level?"

Pierre considered the question for a brief moment. "Absolutely! I believe it is."

"Okay. Cool. Then, what about water in a swimming pool: would it be level?" whilst gesturing a horizontal line with his forearm.

He took a sip of his beer, now somewhat bemused and wondering where Max was going with his unorthodox questions, but self-assuredly smiled and said, "Bloody oath, Max! Of course."

"And what about the surface of water across the largest lakes on Earth? Would you say that the water is also level?"

His new friend appeared slightly perplexed; however, he respectfully answered, "Yes. Definitely! It must!"

Just one further question, Pierre. "And do you think the surface of the vast oceans that span over 70% of our Earth would also be level—or does the water somehow curve?"

But before he had a chance to reply, Max excused himself for a brief moment to try his luck on a game of Keno, which also established an opportune break for his new acquaintance to consider a response to the question.

Upon returning from the Keno gaming console minutes later, Pierre looked at Max with a bewildered expression, and asked,

"Max, are you kind of suggesting that the Earth is flat?"

"What made you arrive at that conclusion, Captain?"

"Well, if 70% of our Earth is comprised of water, and water is always level, then how does it possibly wrap around the Earth whilst also seeking level? So it kind of makes sense that the Earth should be flat – doesn't it?" Pierre rationalized.

Max responded, "Precisely. And yeah, it does make sense. So, that's why I'm beginning to believe the Earth is flat, as there is no proof of curvature to be found anywhere. And believe me, I've looked everywhere!" swigging down the remnants of his beer.

They wholeheartedly burst out laughing while signalling Marcus to pour another round of drinks, who was somewhat relieved that Max hadn't entered into another heated debate with a random customer about the shape of the Earth.

Marcus placed two shot glasses on the bar and said, "This round's on me, gentlemen," while filling the glasses to the brim with Ouzo – creating a meniscus effect over the glass.

"You're a bloody legend, Marcus. I wish you could join us," said Max, clinking glasses with Pierre and sculling the drink.

Marcus watched them down the Ouzo and replied, "Trust me when I say... I wish I could too," before walking to the end of the bar to serve another customer.

They spent the next few hours drinking pints of beer and shots of Ouzo, sharing jokes and reminiscing their past into the early hours of the morning.

Pierre even recounted the vast distances he could see during his career as a Captain, including lighthouses that he now realised should've been hidden by hundreds of metres of curvature. And countless stories about the many broken hearts left behind at the numerous ports he visited during his lifetime cruising the Mediterranean and Aegean Seas as a younger man.

"Max.... thinking about my life right now; did you know I spent almost thirty days on a ship when I migrated to Australia from Mykonos. Anyway, my friend, I must say that I never considered the physics behind the precise moment when the ship travelled from Greece to Australia; but now that I do, I don't believe the ship journeyed to the bottom of a globe. The very notion is rather absurd!"

* * * * *

It was 1:55 am and Marcus had already called 'last drinks', as the venue was closing for the night.

But as per usual, he had to practically kick Max and his new drinking buddy out of the premises, who reluctantly exited after boisterously saying their goodbyes to the staff, who were eagerly waiting for them to leave.

A fresh sea-breeze was gusting as they waited outside the venue for the taxi to arrive, where they exchanged phone numbers and promised to meet up again – after acknowledging it was a great night.

The taxi pulled up to the kerb, where Max assisted a rather drunk Pierre into the front seat of the cab, then merrily said, "Takin' my boat out with a few buddies this weekend, and I'd really like you to join us."

Pierre, with a slur in his voice, almost struggling to complete his sentence, replied, "Didn't know ya had a boat. Love to join ya, mate," hiccupping after the last few words.

"Yep, she's only little, but she'll get us around," he chuckled. "I'll send you a text with all the details," closing the door.

Double-tapping the roof of the taxi, Max gave Pierre a thumbs-up as the yellow cab departed.

Merrily strolling along the footpath back to his apartment, Max looked up to the waxing crescent Moon and the twinkling stars in the night sky and mused, "How the heck can I be standing upside down in Australia, spinning almost twice the speed of sound; and not know it?"

Max knew that he wasn't standing upside down and that his senses were correct. And the dizziness he was feeling right now was not from a spinning, wobbling Earth. But from the shots of Ouzo and the countless pints of beer that he just consumed at the pub.

He laughed with vigour thinking about how naive society has been for blindly accepting the nuances of pseudoscience, rather than common sense.

Noisily stumbling into the foyer of his apartment building several minutes later, the night concierge looked up and made eye contact with Max; smiling as he shrugged his shoulders – as a red-faced Max unsteadily staggered toward the elevator, struggling to swipe his access card.

Safely reaching the mezzanine floor of his apartment and entering his bedroom, Max just couldn't wait to be horizontal – where he clumsily kicked off his shoes into the corner of the room before collapsing onto the king-size bed.

And as the ceiling above him spun around, the very last thought on his mind before passing out for the night; was Zoe.

But the fool on the hill
Sees the Sun going down
And the eyes in his head
See the world spinning round.

THE BEATLES

6

It was mid-morning when Max woke up with a massive hangover, where the piercing bright Sun beaming through the floor-to-ceiling windows of his bedroom, made him instantly regret not closing the block-out blinds before passing out for the night.

And from the moment he opened his bloodshot eyes, he knew that he shouldn't have pushed himself so hard on a Tuesday. Because what should've only been a few quiet drinks at the pub, resulted in another big night out. And he had a very strong feeling that Pierre would be suffering, just as much as he was!

Admittingly, he was 'living it up' while Zoe was overseas, but he also missed their usual routine – as she kind of kept his crazy lifestyle in check.

Max's dependable housekeeper, Elena, had just brewed a freshly percolated coffee, where the aroma wafted throughout the apartment and into his bedroom.

Forcing himself out of bed, he rubbed his eyes and thought, "I've gotta give this shit up!" then slowly staggered downstairs from the mezzanine floor to the kitchen.

"Good morning, Max. How's your head feeling this morning? Coffee or paracetamol?" she cheekily asked.

"Both... actually, Elena! I don't even know why I do it to myself," he responded with a croaky voice; reaching into the kitchen cabinet for two capsules, then grabbing the cup of coffee she had just poured.

"Remind me never to drink again... would you!" whilst leaning back his head to swallow the capsules.

"Yeah, right... sure thing, Max!" Elena laughed, jovially shaking her head while exiting the kitchen to continue her chores.

Max slipped on his dark polarised Sunglasses and shuffled out onto the balcony. He slid onto the reclined padded sun lounge and placed his coffee on the side table, laying back and enjoying the beautiful vista of the Bay as the radiance of the Sun warmed his face.

His apartment – situated at the top level of a state-of-the-art building complex – offered an uninterrupted 360-degree panoramic view of Melbourne and Port Philip Bay, and as Max gazed across the bay, he was instantly captivated by the calm tranquillity of the water and the level horizon; once again reaffirming that the Earth is flat.

The spectacular view from the waterfront location, was one of the main reasons he purchased the 4-bedroom penthouse; soon after, the cutting-edge patented software he developed was acquired by a venture capital group for an undisclosed sum. Many in the financial sector speculated that the acquisition was within the range of hundreds of millions of dollars.

Despite his newly attained fortune, Max continued to be just a regular guy with a down-to-earth attitude. And apart from a few lavish toys that he acquired, he chose to live a relatively modest lifestyle; and was always the first to help family or friends unconditionally – whenever in need.

Observing the exoskeleton framework of a nearby high-rise building, he recalled that builders had used water levelling instruments and tools to construct perfectly level structures for many millennia. And he doubtingly wondered how water could convex or adhere to a spherical solid planet, whilst at the same time always seek level – given that approximately 72% of our Earth is covered by the 'vital to life' liquid element called water.

The further Max considered the fluid dynamics and fluid statics (hydrostatics) and the origins of all water on Earth, it became self-evident that water will always find level at rest after beginning its perpetual journey by falling from the sky - or via snowmelt from the mountainous regions spanning the world.

And when droplets of water accumulate on the surface of the earth – whether on a hill, mountain, valley, or across a plain – they trickle together, forming gullies, streams, creeks and rivers. Often cascading over waterfalls as they carve their way through Mother Earth's terrain to seek level into the flat plains, lakes, seas, and oceans worldwide.

Also irrefutable, is that all rivers flow downhill. Such as the Nile River where at almost 7,000 kilometres in length, fails to curve over the Earth's radius as the water gently meanders through Africa to find sea level at the Mediterranean Sea.

In the same manner, the hundreds of rivers and tributaries in the Missouri, Upper Mississippi, and the Ohio regions of the United States of America, all progressively flow to seek level into the Gulf of Mexico; flowing downward – without ascending or descending over an arc – before the waters reach the Gulf.

And at over 2,500 kilometres in length, the Murray River is the longest in Australia, similarly flowing downhill after beginning its long journey from the alpine regions to find sea-level into the Great Australian Bight; again, with no resistance to the alleged curvature of the earth.

In essence, all rivers flow down to the seven seas and never do we witness a Sea flowing into a river.

A great thinker by the name of David Scott once said –

> *"Whoever heard of a river in any part of its course flowing uphill? Yet this it would require to do were the earth a Globe. Rivers, like the Mississippi, which flow from the North southwards towards the Equator, would need, according to Modern Astronomic theory, to run upwards, as the earth at the Equator is said to bulge out considerably more, or, in other words, is higher than at any other part. Thus the Mississippi, in its immense course of over 3,000 miles, would have to ascend 11 miles before it reached the Gulf of Mexico!"*

The mathematical formula for spherical trigonometry specifies and implies that our Earth should curve downward from the
observer's position at an approximate rate of 7.8-inches per mile
squared. Signifying; that across a distance of 100 miles, there
ought to be 6,666 feet (or approximately 2,000 metres) of curvature; but Max amusingly smiled as he thought, "Where is this *bendy water* that curves around the Earth?"

Modern-day digital cameras and smartphones now allow the
average person to view distances well beyond what the ancient
Greek philosophers could have ever seen with their naked eyes.
Raising the question: how did our ancestors prove the Earth is
spherical without the aid of the technology to do so, especially
considering that Hans Lippershey had not invented the first telescope until 1608? Somewhat, two-thousand years later!

During his research, Max encountered the Abyssal Plain; an
underwater plain on the deep-ocean seafloor that allegedly spans
over 50% of the Earth's surface. And according to sonar tests conducted by the United States Geological Survey, concluded that it's
the 'flattest' and the most unexplored region on Earth.

Max reasoned; if the table of the Abyssal Plain is flat, and the
surface of the ocean above is also demonstrably flat and level. There
could only be one logical conclusion:

"The Earth must be flat!"

Reflecting back to a road trip taken in 1998, when Max drove
approximately 3,000 kilometres from Adelaide in South Australia
to Darwin in the Northern Territory – noted as one of the flattest regions of the world. He recalled seeing distant lightning over
200 kilometres away, reinforcing the impossibility that the Earth is
spherical. Because the lightning he witnessed shouldn't have been
visible from that distance, and should have been hidden behind
many kilometres of physical curvature.

Another thought struck his mind; and it was the moment he
crossed the Northern Territory border from South Australia, where
at the time, it was legal to drive at unlimited speeds—remembering
the thrill of putting the pedal to the metal and overtaking a high-
way-patrol car with absolute ease.

Now having a quiet giggle to himself about his wild antics as a younger man; he reminisced about his girlfriend at the time, who shouted at him, "Max! Do you realise you're going over 240 kilometres an hour right now?"

Where he calmly responded – still pedal to the metal, "Yeah... I know, babe. But so are you!"

7

Trying to wash his hangover away under the raindrop shower, Max dried off his lean body and entered his walk-in wardrobe, where he selected a pair of comfortable cargo shorts, a t-shirt, and sneakers to wear for the day.

Making his way downstairs from the mezzanine floor to grab another coffee, Elena surprised him with a hearty breakfast dish of smashed avocado, poached eggs, and diced tomatoes on two-slices of toasted continental bread.

Placing the empty plate and cutlery into the dishwasher, he said, "Thanks, Elena. I really needed that. It was just what the doctor ordered."

"You're welcome, Max. It's my pleasure," she smiled in reply.

Picking up his smartphone, he dialled Alex arranging to meet at the Marina around 3 pm, then texted several friends – including Sam and Pierre, to invite them out for a day on his boat. After where he spent the next few hours brainstorming his mission to find more land on Earth, across what he was beginning to believe was an infinite flat plane.

Although Max enjoyed keeping in shape, he occasionally strayed from a healthy routine due to his sometimes overindulgent lifestyle. So, he jumped on his mountain bike just after 2:30 pm, leisurely riding the 5-kilometre dedicated bike track which hugged the shoreline of Port Phillip Bay, hoping the exercise and fresh air would finally help clear his head.

Powering his mountain bike along the pathway and coming to a sideways skid after arriving at the St. Kilda Marina, he rested his bike against a jetty pylon where his boat was moored.

Max boarded the vessel, where he spotted Captain Alex in the galley, brewing a cup of tea.

"G'day, Skipper, it looks like I'm just in time for a cuppa."

"Hello, Sir. Welcome aboard. It's great to see you again," firmly shaking Max's hand.

"Likewise, Alex. But, hey, just call me Max – as I haven't been knighted yet," he chuffed, although he'd used that joke once or twice before.

"Good one, Sir... I mean, Max," handing him a freshly poured cup of Earl Grey tea.

"Thanks, mate... nice strong brew," almost burning his lips after taking a small sip.

"Alex, I've organised a day trip for a small group of ten, for this coming Saturday. We plan on departing at 11 am. Can you please ensure the boat is in tip-top shape for the day?"

"Consider it done, Max! I'll make sure she's in mint condition and adequately stocked... especially with booze," he assured.

"Thanks, Alex. That's music to my ears. I'll leave it in your capable hands," turning to leave the galley.

"Oh, before I forget... do you know any good fishing locations around the bay? As I'm pretty sure that the guys would love to throw in a line or two."

"I sure do, Max... leave it with me. Luckily we are heading into Snapper season, and I've got some of the best hot spots around the bay. So you can be quite confident of reeling in a few big ones."

"Excellent... sounds great!" Max enthusiastically replied. "And according to the weather forecast, it looks like the weekend is going to be superb."

"There's nothing better than a clear blue sky and smooth sailing, Max. Perhaps we'll even get a chance to push the throttle a little harder this time, as I'd love to see how fast she can go," Alex eagerly replied, grinning from ear to ear.

"Well, let's hope for perfect conditions, and maybe we'll do just that."

"Anyway, I'm going to chill-out, and soak up some sun. I'll leave you to it."

"No problem, Max. She's your boat. Enjoy! Just buzz me on the intercom if you need anything."

"Cheers, Alex," he replied.

Placing the empty cup into the sink and leaving the galley, Max then climbed the stairs to the flybridge, where he lounged on the soft-cushioned daybed reading a fishing magazine until his eyelids became heavy; soon after dozing off for a short siesta.

* * * * *

Feeling refreshed after a one-hour cat nap, Max left the Marina for the ride home.

Clutching the rear brake lever, he pulled up right beside a food truck that was randomly parked along Beach Road for a quick bite to eat.

He ordered a souvlaki wrap and a side of hot chips topped with crumbled Feta cheese and a sprinkle of oregano. Sitting on the bluestone fence, he scoffed down his food – while watching several wind-surfers performing aerial tricks on the bay before courteously thanking the owners for the feed; then continued the ride along the bike track to his Port Melbourne apartment.

Arriving home, Max grabbed a bottle of cold sparkling mineral water from the refrigerator, determined to have an alcohol-free day. He then reached into the top drawer of his desk for a pre-rolled joint before strolling out to the full wrap-around balcony with perfect timing to observe the mesmerising Sunset, where the noble gases colourfully illuminated the sky in a spectrum of orange and purple tones.

Taking a toke, he slowly released the smoke from his lips whilst glancing across the bay. Suddenly mesmerised by the beauty of the glistening lights of Mornington Peninsula that were over 50-kilometres away, and he smiled wryly, knowing that the water was observably level and flat over that distance.

Wishing Zoe was by his side to witness such a spectacular Sunset, he called her phone, realising it was mid-morning in London.

When Max's handsome face appeared on her smartphone screen, Zoe answered the call within seconds, after politely excusing herself from the boardroom, where she was about to commence an important presentation.

Zoe spoke softly into the phone, "Hey, honey bear!" as she stepped out to the reception area for some privacy – the receptionist giving her a warm smile.

"Hey there, sexy lady! Tell me: are you wearing the red Victoria's Secret panties that I sent you?"

"Max! You cheeky bugger! You're lucky that I didn't have you on loud-speaker. Yes, I am... by the way," she confessed. "But I really can't talk right now. I'm about to begin a meeting with the CEO and the Board of Directors. I'll call you back in a few hours or so."

"Oops. My bad. Sorry, babe! Knock 'em dead. Talk to you soon. I'll be thinking about your red panties all day now!" he giggled.

"Oh, Max... stop it! I love you, my darling," blowing soft kisses into the phone.

"I love you too, Zoe. Can't wait to see you," his heart skipping a beat by simply hearing the sound of her dulcet voice.

"I can't wait to see you too, Max. But, I really have to go. The CEO has just walked in, and they are waiting for my report," before hanging up the call and dashing back into the boardroom to re-join the meeting.

Staring at his phone, Max came to realise that "absence does make the heart grow fonder", even though he always thought the expression was just a cliché, as he wanted her home – now more than ever. And the next few weeks until he was reunited with Zoe were going to feel like an eternity.

Although he was a successful man in many aspects of his life, it wasn't always the case when it came to his relationships.

But that was until he met Zoe.

She was unlike any other woman he'd ever met; feisty, kind,

intelligent, funny, and stunningly beautiful – inside and out. And he felt extremely fortunate to have her in his life.

His thoughts were distracted by an email alert from his PC.

After checking his email accounts, Max double-clicked, entering a secure password into his locked word processing document to continue devising his preliminary pipe-dream feasibility plan to form an expedition to find unexplored land on Earth. Acknowledging extensive planning would be essential to accomplish such a perilous mission.

Glancing over at the bar, he wondered whether he should have a drink, and not before long; he was sipping on a glass of Hennessy XO and thought, "So much for not drinking today!"

Pouring another dash of Cognac, he flashed back to when he visited New York with Zoe to celebrate their first anniversary. Now remembering crossing the Verrazano-Narrow Bridge, where a rather chatty and informative taxi driver with a strong New York accent boasted that the Earth's curvature had to be factored for when building the long-spanning bridge.

With nothing planned for the night, Max decided to verify the taxi drivers claim that bridges account for Earth curvature by searching Google and found a photo of the Verrazano-Narrow Bridge that he had crossed—discovering it spans a whopping 13,700 feet or approximately 4,000 metres.

However, Max immediately noted an anomaly with the taxi drivers claim – where he thought, "Well, the bridge may be curved, but the water beneath the bridge in New York Harbour certainly looks pretty flat and level to me!"

It was only fair to ascertain additional information rather than reach a hasty conclusion by researching the dimensions of only one bridge.

And that's when Max located a Wikipedia page showcasing the longest bridges worldwide, including the Jiaozhou Bay Bridge in China, which spans over 25-kilometres in length, and then the Danyang-Kunshan Grand Bridge, also in China. Whereat, almost 165 kilometres in length, is currently classified as the longest bridge in the world – much of it spanning across many kilometres of flat-level water. However, virtually several thousand feet of curvature was mysteriously missing, as not one inch of curvature was accounted for by the engineers, surveyors, or architects during the design or construction stages of the world's longest bridge.

He questioned, "How could the longest bridges in the world not account for curvature – if the Earth is spherical?"

Max concluded that no bridge, railroad, nor canal, including the Suez Canal, which at over 160-kilometres in length – has ever factored for the curvature of the Earth. And surveyors and engineers were beginning to confirm it.

Switching off his computer for the night and changing into comfortable sleepwear, he lay down to relax on the soft white leather couch in the living room, to watch a blockbuster movie on the large LCD television.

But, it was wishful thinking on his behalf.

Because; he was fast asleep and softly snoring within minutes, as the flickering TV watched him instead.

8

Just as the weather forecast predicted, it was a pristine Spring Saturday morning in Melbourne, with not a single cloud in sight; and the calm-still-water created a mirror-like effect across Port Philip Bay.

Arriving slightly behind schedule after eventually finding Max's boat docked at the far end of the Marina, Pierre was stunned as he approached the group gathered alongside the huge 84-foot Sunseeker Predator. Never envisaging for even a moment that such a luxurious grand super-yacht belonged to Max – judging from his casual and unpretentious demeanour, during their first encounter at the pub.

Max was standing port side of the boat wearing a Captains hat and yelled out to Pierre, "I told you she was only little," chuckling.

"Yeah, you got me, Max! She's a bloody beauty, mate. What's her name?" Pierre shouted—still absorbing and admiring the grand exterior design of the vessel with her dark blue and white duo-colour custom paintwork.

"Zenith Star," he called out. "C'mon guys, don't just stand there... come aboard!" signalling his guests to make their way up the gangway.

Sliding open the tinted glass door, Max directed the group into the climate-controlled saloon area.

"Welcome, fellas! Grab a drink, and make yourselves at home. I'll be back in a moment; I'm just going to give Pierre a quick tour of the Sunseeker."

"I can't believe my eyes. She's absolutely splendid," said Pierre, gliding his hand over the smooth-polished mahogany balustrade whilst descending the stairs to the saloon.

"Hey, she gets me around. But I just don't take her out as often as I should."

"Don't worry, Max; my wife says the same thing about me!" Pierre replied, laughing at his own joke.

"You crack me up, Pierre. I'm so glad you joined us today," laughing and gently slapping his shoulder.

Re-joining his guests at the bar, Max asked, "Hey, Pierre – what will you be drinking today; beer, wine, or should we hit the hard stuff?" pointing to the glass liquor cabinet behind him, which was stocked with top label brands.

"Oh, God! Not sure if I can handle a drink right now! I'm still trying to recover from our drinking session from a few days ago. I had Ouzo burps for almost two full days!"

Max chuckled, "Yeah, so did I! C'mon, Pierre – we might as well make a big day of it. What's the worst that could happen?"

Sam reached over to shake Pierre's hand while introducing himself, then cracked open a beer and passed it to Pierre. "Trust me... this will make you feel better," he smiled.

Without hesitation, Pierre took a swig. "Ahh! Cheers, fellas. Here's to Max," as they all held up their drinks and saluted.

The luxury super-yacht departed the Marina – where a nearby crowd of people gathered in awe, staring at the majestic vessel as she left her wake carving through the smooth, calm waters. Where Captain Alex gently pushed the throttle unleashing the roar-power of her perfectly tuned twin Caterpillar engines as he charted the vessel out to sea, now cruising across the water at a comfortable 15-knots per hour.

The crew served Max's guests canapés and refreshments, and approximately 30-kilometres from Melbourne, the Captain brought the vessel to a complete stop, releasing her anchors.

Soon after, Captain Alex announced lunch was ready for service; when the guests who were scattered about different sections of the boat – made their way to the dining area, the crew now serving fresh seafood, a variety of salads, and platters of seasonal fruit.

Gently patting his stomach, Max suggested, "Hey guys, now that we've finished lunch, let's grab our drinks and migrate to the outside deck."

They gathered at the stern of the boat, where Max had earlier set up his telescope.

Max gestured toward the city skyline, and said, "Take a look out there. We're about 30 kilometres from Melbourne right now, and the city is still clearly visible – even with our naked eyes."

"So, let me ask you a question, gentlemen: would you say that the water is curved over that distance, or is it level?"

Pierre swiftly responded, "It's noticeably level, Max. Because, how is it possible that we can see the city right now; if the water was curved?"

"That's exactly my point, Pierre. You catch on rather quickly, for someone who has just recently heard about Flat Earth."

Pierre explained, "Well, I've got to tell you, Max, that I always suspected that something was fishy when I navigated the vast European seas as a captain. And from memory, on many clear days, I could see for miles-and-miles."

"But, what really gave it away for me... were lighthouses. You see, they can be clearly observed in line-of-sight from over fifty nautical miles across the Mediterranean Sea. And I've witnessed that on countless occasions, during my younger days as a captain. And did you know; plane sailing requires making arithmetical cal-culations on the assumption that the Earth is perfectly flat? And when you think about it, even periscopes wouldn't be effective if the Earth was curving, as they say, it does."

They attentively listened as Pierre elaborated, "So, having said that, I've spent nearly every spare moment during the last few days looking into this 'crazy' Flat Earth theory. And it seems to me that the globe model is bullshit – or should I say, 'ball-shit'," the group laughing at his clever wordplay.

"Hey, gents... check out the city through the telescope," said Max, where he offered his guests the opportunity to view the dis-tant panorama.

Max focused the high-powered binoculars hanging from his neck toward the horizon, then eagerly passed them to Sam. "Check that out, mate... look out there! I just zoomed a container ship back into view that supposedly disappeared over Earth's curvature."

Sam focused the binoculars toward the horizon and exclaimed, "Holy shit, Max! So much for boats vanishing over the curve!"

"Exactly! So, can we finally settle the argument that boats don't disappear over the horizon due to the supposed curvature of the Earth?"

"Yeah... you know... it kind of hurts to say this, but I guess we can. Especially now that I've seen it with my very own eyes," Sam conceded—completely astonished by what he'd just witnessed.

Edward chimed in, "Hey, fellas... I can distinctly see the West Gate Bridge from our vantage point. By the way, don't they say that engineers account for the curvature of the earth when they build long-distant bridges?"

Max responded, "It's coincidental that you ask, Ed. I've recently spent some time looking into the design and construction of bridges, and from what I've discovered, even the longest bridges in the world don't account for curvature. And the biggest giveaway for me was that water is always level underneath the bridges."

He elaborated, "Because... I hate to harp on the matter, but water is always level; and will always remain my first principle. It's what we observe in our lives every day. You know, to deny the fact that water is level at rest is equivalent to denying objective reality! Put simply, a sphere does not have the capacity to contain bodies of water!"

Edward, a Professor of mathematics, thought Max had lost his mind, when he randomly called many months ago and mentioned after a casual discussion that the Earth could be flat. However, at the time, Max was simply reaching out, hoping that he would quash the topic within an instant.

But although Edward had taught countless students advanced math during his esteemed career as a Professor at a leading University in Melbourne, having always believed that math had a direct correlation to reality. He, at least, had the integrity to acknowledge that he didn't know it all. And after several months of conducting his research on the topic, he couldn't prove to Max that the currently accepted view of the cosmos was, in fact, correct.

Edward stroked his chin. "Yeah, you're right, Max. Because, the more I think about it, apart from a meniscus effect caused by surface tension – water will always remain level when unmanipulated. It's quite preposterous that I thought otherwise, as water does not bend over vast distances. It's an impossibility," he insisted.

With a look of concern, he said, "I must confess that I never imagined I'd be questioning the shape of the Earth during my lifetime, especially after being a Professor for almost twenty years. But it appears that the formula for applied spherical trigonometry based on the notion the Earth has an equatorial circumference of 40,075 km with an assumed radius of 6,371 km; well, it is fallacious. It's incorrect. The math just doesn't correlate with reality! I feel rather betrayed!" he sighed, feeling slightly despondent; leaning onto the railing, trying to avoid eye contact as he glanced across the bay, pondering his future.

"Yeah, haven't we all! But, don't worry, Ed... I've got something that will cheer you up." Where Max then yelled out, "Who's up for another drink?"

"You don't need to ask me twice," Edward suddenly perked up as the group made their way inside for another round of beverages.

Max called the bridge via the intercom to chat with Alex. "Hey skipper, let's get a move on; the guys are keen to cast out a few lines."

"Too easy, Max... let's do it," immediately restarting the massive engines, then cruising at almost full-speed for approximately twenty minutes toward his secret fishing location before once again anchoring the vessel.

A pod of dolphins frolicking in the distance caught their attention, as Sam, Edward, and Will, watched in awe – as they baited up their hooks to cast out their lines from the lowered swimming platform at the stern of the boat.

Captain Alex was right. The fish were biting. And biting hard.

After catching then releasing half a dozen large snappers over a two hour period, they washed up and re-entered the Saloon area. Where they witnessed Max and his friends in fits of laughter; as a YouTube video playing on the wall-mounted LCD screen showed Elon Musk's red Tesla car – flying around in space. Musk justifying the footage during a media interview by saying, "*You can tell it's real because it looks so fake.*"

Wiping the tears from his eyes after viewing the hysterical video, Max excused himself to visit the bridge, where Alex asked if the guests were enjoying the day.

"They sure are, mate! Thanks a million. Hey, by the way, we're all a bit hungry again, so I'm about to book us a table at Riva's."

"Would you like to join us for dinner tonight, Alex?"

"Thanks... I'd love to. That would be fantastic."

Max dialled Riva's restaurant, booking a table for 8 pm. "Absolutely, Mr Carter. We'll have a table ready for your arrival. We look forward to seeing you," said the maître de as Max hung up on the call.

"All booked, Alex. Let's head back home – and make it snappy!"

"With pleasure," he replied, chuckling at the bad pun, and after placing down his coffee mug, he started up the engines to navigate the vessel back to the Marina.

The Sun, close to setting over the horizon, created a straight-line specular reflection across the calm water when Max suggested to the group that they climb up to the flybridge for an unobstructed view of the glorious spectacle where he asked, "Can a curved surface produce a perfect mirrored reflection?"

Pierre was quick to interject, "Absolutely not, Max – a mirrored reflection requires a perfectly flat surface, and large bodies of water are observably flat. Not to mention that water cannot conform to the exterior of a ball. The very notion of trillions of tonnes of water wrapping and adhering around a sphere-shaped surface is bloody absurd! Because it's a scientific and observable fact that water is level at rest."

"I couldn't agree more, Pierre."

The group fell momentarily silent, marvelled by the revelation, agreeing that such a reflection would be impossible on a curved surface, reconfirming amongst themselves that water must be level, where Sam mentioned that the effect looked like – "*The Sun of God, walking on water.*"

Max's friends encompassed various skills from all walks of life. Many held prominent positions within the community, and he considered them intelligent, high-spirited, adventurous individuals, and he felt privileged to know them.

But Max knew that if he were going to disclose his wild idea to find more land on Earth, then he'd better have a bloody good plan to show them.

He wasn't prepared to announce his mission today, but it had been an excellent opportunity to acquaint his friends with one another, and as far as he thought – the day was a huge success.

9

The Zenith Star returned to the Marina, where Captain Alex expertly manoeuvered the vessel, berthing her into the designated docking bay.

The group disembarked and boisterously walked to Riva's Restaurant, arriving fifteen minutes early, and while waiting to be seated, decided to start with a round of Caipiroska's at the bar. One of Max's favourite drinks.

Since Zoe had been away in London, Max felt like he was just three steps shy from being an alcoholic. Some might even say, only two!

"Good evening, Mr Carter. It is wonderful to have you and your party dining with us tonight," said the maître d', shaking his hand.

"Your table is ready, Sir. Please follow me," leading the small group to an elegantly presented table near the opened bi-fold doors that offered a clear view of the multi-million-dollar boats moored at the Marina.

"For dinner... may I suggest the Chef's special of Whole Baked Snapper – with ginger, chilli, sautéed garlic asparagus, and a selection of seasonal roasted vegetables."

"Sounds delicious, Oliver. Thank you, how could we resist," replied Max, as Snapper seemed appropriate following a day out on the water.

"You're welcome, Mr Carter," said Oliver as he rushed towards the kitchen to leave the order with the Chef.

After Max selected several red and white wine bottles from the sommelier, the rowdy group reminisced about the day out on the boat, where they continued their discussion about the shape of the Earth, with occasional bouts of laughter and uproar emerging from their table.

The majority consensus was that our Earth is unmistakably flat and motionless and should be apparent to all. Especially when the philosophy of Occam's Razor is applied, which implies that the simplest solution requiring the fewest assumptions is most likely to be correct.

"Hey, Kane – didn't you recently go on vacation with your family?" enquired Zach.

"Sure did... best holiday ever... a trip of a lifetime. We travelled around most of South America visiting many ancient cities, including Machu Picchu."

"It's a fascinating continent, and I finally fulfilled my life-long dream to cruise along the Amazon River and also had the opportunity to tour an Amazonian tribal village – deep within the midst of the jungle."

"Sounds bloody amazing, Kane. South America has always fascinated me as a holiday destination, and it's on my bucket list."

Kane implored, "Make sure you do it, as we only live once! And when you do, I suggest you visit the Salar de Uyuni Salt Flats of Bolivia, where the water physically manifests a mirror image of the sky. And from memory, I think it's something like 10,000 square kilometres of flat surface."

"Really, Kane? I didn't realise the salt flats were that big!"

"Yeah, they sure are, Zach. And as flat as! Because they have a variance of less than one metre across the entire distance. One of the locals mentioned that NASA uses the flats to calibrate altimeters. So it's as flat as you can get!"

"Come to think of it: it was friggin awesome; it felt like I was standing on a colossal sized mirror! Hey, check out these photos."

Kane picked up his smartphone and swiped through the photo gallery, trying to avoid any risqué pictures of his wife, and enlarged a photo of the salt flats to show the group. Explaining that the mirror-like effect would be impossible if the earth is curved, as curved surfaces cannot create a perfect mirrored effect.

"What an absolutely brilliant photo, Kane," said Dave, Max's cousin and a well-respected eye surgeon. "You know, I've also been lucky enough to visit those salt flats, many moons ago. But, I never realised that I was viewing a life-sized mirror. It seems that we've failed to see some of the most obvious natural marvels in this world for what they truly are. Truth being, our eyes are far more remarkable than we give them credit. Most people don't give it a second thought, but even the staunchest atheists can't answer basic questions on how the eyes of all creatures on Earth evolved to such precision that still can't be replicated in a laboratory to this very day."

"I wholeheartedly agree, Dave. It's amazing what our eyes can see when the veil has been lifted to reveal the truth," said Kane.

Their banter halted when two waiters approached carrying a large oval silver-platter, with a spectacularly presented one-metre-long Snapper, and centred it onto their table. Where they feasted like kings, with the only leftovers remaining were the large fish bones.

After a giant feed, Edward leaned back, rubbing his stomach; when Sam pointed to Edward's exposed round belly and said, "Hey guys, I think I've finally spotted some curvature!" where they all collectively laughed.

To everyone's surprise, Captain Alex unexpectedly proclaimed, "Of course, the Earth is flat, and the biggest proof is water: as it always seeks level at rest! And there's no certainly no bendy water out there," pointing towards the bay.

Max leaned across the table to high-five Alex. "Knew I liked you... from the minute I met you," slightly slurring his words, as by now he'd been steadily drinking since just after 11 am.

Sliding back his chair, Max headed toward the bar to order another round of beverages; smirking, he turned around and said, "If you can't smell the bullshit of the heliocentric model by now, then your nose must be blocked!"

"Baa, baa... or a sheep!" Alex joked as the group erupted into laughter.

After merrily chatting with the manager and Chef Johan for several minutes, Max returned to the table with a tray of large crystal balloon glasses, each with a double serve of Cognac.

Raising his glass in a salute, he said, "It's Hennessy, gents. Drink it slow!" sculling his drink in one big gulp.

They all did the same.

Exhaling his fiery breath. "Whoooh... Max! That's some good stuff," said Sam, then made a short speech to thank Max for such a wonderful day.

It was late into the evening, and they were ready to wrap it up for the night when almost sequentially, the text message alerts from their wives and partners began to stream in.

Max glanced at his watch. "Well, it looks like we should call it a night, gentlemen," where they agreed and reluctantly exited the restaurant saying their farewells before parting ways in their taxi rides home.

* * * * *

Following an enjoyable day with great company, Max entered his apartment, once again feeling the solitude of his home.

The only other presence of life were his two constantly fighting Murray River short-necked turtles and the collection of colourful exotic African Cichlids hungrily swimming around the large aquarium that divided the dining and lounge areas.

Approaching the tank, they all congregated toward him as if to recognise their master, and when Max sprinkled a handful of tropical fish food and turtle pellets into the water, they scrambled for their feed.

It has been often falsely assumed that fish only have a three-second memory, but Max was beginning to understand that the little creatures swimming in his tank were far more intelligent than most people gave them credit.

But the only thing on his mind, whilst watching his pets devour their food, was that his outing today on the Zenith Star was a total friggin success.

Because Max was elated to finally convince his friends that water is observably level over vast distances.

Whereby they all acknowledged that they shouldn't have been able to see the Central Business District of Melbourne from their distant vantage point earlier that day if the earth was, in reality – curved.

"The fact that water is flat like a sheet of paper (when undisturbed by wind or tide) is my 'working anchor', and the powerful 'ground tackle' of those who reject the delusions of modern theoretical astronomy. Prove water to be convex, and we will once and forever recant and grant you anything you like to demand."

THOMAS WINDSHIP

10

Sam unlocked the front door of his Edwardian style home to find his purring cat Jafina comfortably perched on the window sill—meowing at him with delight as he entered his abode.

After a quick cuddle and a scratch of her belly whilst walking down the hallway, he placed her down on the kitchen floor, filling the empty pet bowl with dry kibble; now watching her prance around with her characteristic lunging and stretching routine – before Jafina crunched away on her food.

He rescued the loveable stray multi-coloured cat only months earlier after she won his heart by hanging around his house nearly every day. And when Jafina one day adoringly circled his legs three or four times – in a strange kind of weird "cat-like" ritualistic practise; well, at that moment, she owned him.

Flicking the switch on the kettle to brew himself a cup of tea, following an exhausting day out on the water, Sam just couldn't shake the idea of a Flat Earth from his mind. And having participated in the long distant experiment to observe whether boats disappear over the horizon due to the earth's curvature, his mind was now perplexed.

Finishing a cup of green tea while reading the latest news on his smartphone, he lay down on his bed and managed to doze off within several minutes as Jafina curled up like a fluffy ball beside him.

Sam awoke early the following morning feeling surprisingly clear-headed and refreshed, immediately wondering where he would take Jessica out for dinner that night – for their first date.

Upon entering the gourmet designed kitchen, he selected the

cappuccino option on the automatic coffee machine. And after sprinkling chocolate powder onto the fluffy foam top, he made his way to his home office and sat down to catch up on his Facebook news feed as he sipped the hot coffee.

Lighting a cigarette, an alert from his computer notified him to an incoming message from Max.

"G'day, Sam. How are you feeling this morning?"

"Feeling awesome, Max. Thanks for a wicked day yesterday," he typed.

"My pleasure, mate. Anytime."

"BTW, it was great to see the guys again. They sure know how to drink... don't they?"

"Haha. Yeah, they sure do, mate."

"Hey, Max. Did I tell you that I'm taking Jessica out for dinner tonight?"

"Congrats, Sam! That's terrific news. Where are you taking her?"

"Thinking about going to MoVida. Apparently, tapas is one of Jessica's favourites."

"It's always a good feast there. She'll love it! Have fun, mate."

"Hey, did you watch the video '200 Proofs Earth Is Not a Spinning Ball' that I sent you?"

"Not yet. But I'll do it today. As I'm planning a lazy Sunday."

"It's a great video. You won't regret it."

"Yeah, I'll definitely check it out."

"That's good to hear, Sam. I was concerned that you thought I was going crazy with this whole 'Flat Earth' thing."

"What do you mean? I already know that you're crazy! LOL," Sam mocked.

Max typed, "LOL. Yeah... good one, ya dag," adding a sideways smiley emoji to his comment, where they then shared several funny memes before logging off.

Sam entered the rabbit hole at full speed in his search for truth, and he was hooked: just like finding the gateway drug to reality.

Dedicating every spare moment of that day to researching and re-educating himself about the heliocentric model of the Universe and the newfound flat Earth theory.

He was in no way convinced that the Earth was flat, but a spark of doubt was already emerging within his mind. And after coming to terms – following his initial shock – that his friend was a Flat Earther, he was now settling into the idea that the shape of the earth was quite possibly not what he had been told.

Sam didn't know everything relating to the Flat Earth theory, with many questions rattling around in his mind that needed answers. But he was beginning to doubt that he was living "down-under" on a spinning ball; as he gradually began to break free from the lies of the heliocentric fairy tale.

And after joining a Flat Earth discussion group online, and from the few debates that he was already involved with, he realised that trying to discuss the topic with globe Earth defenders – was like telling an 8-year-old child that Santa isn't real.

They just throw hissy-fits!

Regardless of who was right or wrong, he found that Flat Earther's were at least using their natural senses, perceptions, logic, discernment, keen observations, and furthermore conducting modern-day experiments using some pretty cool technologies. Including ultra-zoom SLR cameras, powerful laser pointers, and even going to the extreme of launching high-altitude balloons at elevations exceeding 120,000 feet.

Unlike heliocentric defenders who were banking their beliefs on second-hand claims and unproven theories based on hypothesis, conjecture, sophistry and imaginative presuppositions stemming from moot, antiquated experiments—even after their outlandish claims were debunked repeatedly, ad nauseam.

11

Within moments of arriving at the café for their regular weekly meet up, Sam leaned across the table toward Max and asked, "Hey, Max... there's just one big question that's been really bugging me about this Flat Earth thing."

"What's up? Hit me with it!" replied Max, raising his sunglasses to the top of his head.

"Well, mate... if the Earth is flat, there would have to be millions of people involved to keep it a secret! And I just can't see that happening. It's unfathomable! A whistle-blower would have leaked it by now! Don't you reckon?"

Max gently rubbed the light stubble growth on his face and responded, "Actually, it wouldn't require millions of people to be involved; it would just require billions of people to be asleep and to never question the world where they live."

"Hmm... That's a fair point. And regardless of the shape of our Earth, it appears that most people are in some kind of a deep hypnotic sleep these days. Unfortunately, they just go with the flow and never take the time to question anything with an open mind."

"Exactly, buddy! But we can't blame them entirely, as most people have been bamboozled with nonsensical trivial issues including materialism and pseudoscience – for far too long."

"Just like virtuous, obedient sheep, hey Max?" taking a sip of his hot cappuccino, then scooping a spoonful of the fluffy foam into his mouth.

"Well, you know, a flock of sheep are far easier to control than a pack of wolves!"

"Spot on!" Sam chuffed, snapping him a quick wink.

"And they achieved it with endless Space propaganda since we were children; with sci-fi shows such as *Lost in Space*, *Star Trek*, and *Star Wars*. And now with movies like *Interstellar* or *Gravity*, or even bloody worse, those preposterously exaggerated end-time movies about alien invasions like *Independence Day*, and all that other dystopian crap!"

"True... it's non-stop space hype, Max. And yeah, it seems like that crap is continuously promoted everywhere these days."

"That's undeniable, Sam. But what really pisses me off are the fake images of the Earth from Space. And not only in blockbuster movies but also in children's shows, news reports, television adverts, video games, and even on billboards. It's neverending! And most people think the photos are actually real!"

"They sure do plaster that cartoon ball wherever they can. Look, Max... it's even on my phone!" revealing the background wallpaper on his smartphone.

"Yep... it's all just part of the systematic, repetitive, constant brainwashing!"

"Hmm... it could be, Max. And I gotta say, that based on my initial research, I've noticed that every photo of the Earth from Space looks different. So, how is it possible they can differ so significantly over just 20 years?"

"Who freakin' knows, Sam!"

"Max, another anomaly that I've noticed is that some of the images of Earth have repetitive clouds that appear to have been deceptively just copy-and-pasted using PhotoShop – or whatever! And one photo even has weird looking clouds that look like the face of a demon or an alien... or something like that on it! Another one has the word 'SEX' designed or embedded into the clouds. They're all bloody fake! Fake news, fake people, fake science... and now, even fake photos of our Earth! The whole world is friggin fake! Fake, fake, fake!" seemingly troubled by the revelation—Max secretly relishing the moment listening to Sam rant like a madman.

He took a deep breath and exhaled, "Besides, you would think that with the thousands of satellites floating around in outer space like the Hubble Space Telescope, well, that just one of them would take a real photo – or live high-definition video of our Earth. But all we get from them is crappy CGI! The shifty buggers!"

"That's exactly what I've been trying to tell you. All the recent images of our Earth from Space are just computer-generated at the admission of the space agencies. The last photo of our Earth taken by an astronaut in outer space was apparently during an Apollo mission way back in 1972. But even that photo was a friggin fake! Just pure nonsense, at best! And it's not only the images that are fabricated, as I've discovered that even the theoretical science to back the globe model is also pure bullshit."

"Let me share a quote from the brilliant scientist, Nikola Tesla, with you." Max then paraphrased:

> *"Today's scientists have substituted mathematics for experiments, and they wander off through equation after equation, and eventually build a structure which has no relation to reality."*

"Hmm, I see what he means... clever man, that Tesla bloke."

"Bloody oath he was! Probably the most brilliant scientist to ever walk this earth. And did you know that when Albert Einstein was asked how it feels to be the smartest man in the world, he said, '*I'm not sure? You better ask Nikola Tesla*'."

"Fascinating!" smiled Sam, striking a Tesla pose.

They came to agree that humanity had placed far too much faith in theoretical science, and that there is a vast difference between natural science; and scientism.

"So... what now, Max?"

"It's time to take action!" he replied, unconsciously thumping the table with his fist and jarring the cutlery; the nearby diners looked at Max in surprise.

"What do you mean by that? What type of action?" asked Sam, with a look of concern.

"Well, Sam... as I've mentioned before – I've got a big hunch that there is more land across this possible infinite plane that we live on. And I want to conduct an expedition to find out if there's unchartered land beyond the horizon!"

"What! Are you friggin crazy, Max?" charged Sam.

"Yeah, well, we already established that, haven't we?" Max humoured, widening his eyes to impersonate a mad man.

"Remember when I said that I had something big to tell you? Well, this is it! And I want you to help me lead the expedition. You know: so that we can find any new discoveries together! Just like modern-day explorers," replied Max, excited about his grand plan.

"Maybe you didn't hear me properly the first time; are you friggin crazy?" still in shock at Max's outlandish proposal.

Laughing loudly, "Okay, okay... I may be, Sam. But if I know you well enough, then so are you!"

Max hastily changed the subject. "By the way, I forgot to ask you, how was your date with Jessica?"

"It was brilliant, mate. She's a really cool chick! We had dinner, then strolled along Southbank Boulevard, chatting and laughing until well past midnight. We're meeting up again in a few days."

"That's awesome, Sam. I had a feeling you guys would hit it off."

"Hey – I'm flying to London to pick up Zoe next weekend. And did I tell you that you're coming with me? And just a thought: why don't you invite Jessica to join us?"

"What? C'mon, Max! I can't just leave! I have work to do! Customer deadlines! Commitments!" Sam objected.

Looking pleased with himself, "It's all good, mate. It's all been taken care of. I've bribed your boss and have arranged a week off work for you. So, there are no excuses. We leave next Friday."

"What the heck do you mean by you 'bribed my boss'?" raising his voice.

"Whoa! Chill! Don't stress, Sam! Take it easy! Let's just order breakfast because I'm starving. And I'll fill you in with all the details later," as a waiter approached their table to take their order.

12

"Wow... that's one heck of an aircraft, Jeremy!" remarked Max, as his eyes absorbed the enormous dimensions of the plane; being significantly larger than he expected from the photos that he viewed online.

Max excitingly enquired, "What's the maximum duration that one of these babies can stay airborne?" as they stepped onto the tarmac, which showcased one of the largest aircraft Max had ever seen; the Odysseus High-Altitude Unmanned Aerial Vehicle.

Max had taken a last-minute flight to the township Manassas, Virginia – situated approximately 50-kilometres west of Washington DC, to visit Aurora Flight Sciences. A Boeing company specialising in Unmanned Aerial Vehicles (UAV's) and bespoke High-Altitude Long-Endurance drone-style aircraft—otherwise known as High-Altitude Pseudo-Satellites – or HAPS.

Jeremy, the Sales Director at Aurora, replied, "Well, it's more than just an aircraft, Max. You see, she's a highly advanced UAV, and we believe she's the best in her class," in his southern-style American accent.

"And flight time largely depends on the payload. However, with an average load, Odysseus's elaborate configuration of solar panels, which constantly recharge the onboard lithium batteries, can be customised for ultra-long endurance missions with global reach. So in effect, she's capable of staying aloft for many months, even years – whilst flying hundreds-of-thousands of miles, or kilometres, as you refer to them in down under Australia. Our aeronautical engineers have been working on her design for decades."

"That's super impressive, Jeremy. And can I just ask, how is the Odysseus controlled once in flight?"

"In fact, that's a great question, Max."

"You see, our sophisticated software will allow your mission-control centre to guide Odysseus. And she can persistently maintain a constant altitude in the stratosphere – whilst relaying voice, data, video, as well as other forms of communication to mission control in real-time. And the greatest advantage is that it can fly to designated locations autonomously above controlled airspace, even without a ground-based operator. It's basically set it and forget it. And we offer full training for your operators."

"Again... very impressive. Oh, and can I just ask about the type of video recording capability and the quality of the footage we could expect to receive from its onboard cameras?"

Jeremy pointed to the exterior cameras installed at various sections on the Odysseus. "Max, we've installed multiple 16K ultra-high-resolution cameras with night-vision capabilities to deliver the highest quality video recording. And that's also relayed back to mission control in real-time. So, it makes high-resolution recording a breeze."

"And with our specially developed sensors, she also offers the capability to measure ground moisture, vegetation, and even ice coverage. Not that you guys would get too much ice in Australia," he chuckled.

Max smiled then stroked his chin, seemingly impressed with Odysseus's capabilities to execute stage one of his plan.

"Oh, I almost forgot to mention that the onboard spectrometer can measure various wavelengths using infrared radiation by reflecting beams off ground surfaces, and our engineers can even install a laser-operated altitude measuring device."

"To be honest, that's way over my head, Jeremy. But having said that... I love it."

"What's the price tag on one of these bad boys?" double-slapping the UAV's large tyre.

"Well, Max, it's part of my obligation and duty to inform you that these UAV's are highly classified for specific use. So, I'm sure you'll understand when I say that we don't sell them to just anyone.

You know, for national security reasons, and all. And therefore, before we proceed – I would need to ascertain further information for your reason for ownership."

"Oh, yes... I perfectly understand, as there are many individuals with nefarious motives walking this Earth. However, my motive is pure business. Please. Allow me to explain:"

"You see, my newly founded company in Australia has clientele signed up to conduct satellite geo-mapping services to ascertain the impact of climate change on rural farms and cattle stations in outback Queensland and far north in the Northern Territory. And based on our due diligence to date, after considering all available options, we found that a HAPS is far more cost-effective than launching a traditional satellite into the thermosphere."

"Yes, that is correct, Max."

"Well, without wasting your time, as I know you've travelled a long way for this presentation, the price-tag largely depends on the configuration. But as a ball-park figure, the Odysseus pseudo-satellite will set you back approximately twelve-million dollars."

Jeremy elaborated, "That's U.S. dollars... of course. But, hey, as you said, it's a far more cost-effective solution than launching a geostationary satellite into LEO – or Low Earth Orbit."

"Yes, we've investigated the use of geo-sats, and it just wasn't a viable option for us."

"By the way, Jeremy... when could we expect to receive delivery of the Odysseus?"

"Max, we could have one ready within 3-4 months from receipt of an official purchase order. That is, of course: on the proviso that your company meets criteria for ownership and that everything checks out okay."

"That sounds perfect, Jeremy. My Board of Directors will also require further information, including detailed specifications. But from what I have seen to date, you've got yourself a new customer," leaning forward to shake Jeremy's hand.

"Please forward me a proposal and the necessary paperwork by email so we can proceed," handing Jeremy a business card to the shelf company Max created just months earlier to disguise his real motive for the acquisition of a high-altitude pseudo-satellite.

"I certainly will, Max," shaking his hand again, then escorting him through the reception area to an awaiting taxi.

Sitting in the back of the taxi on the way to the airport, he affirmed that the Odysseus was the safest method to execute a stage-one exploratory mission to discover more land, eliminating the risk of losing human life by wandering off into the abyss on a speculative crewed mission.

13

Questioning the shape of the Earth was possibly the most isolated journey that Max had ever undertaken in his entire life.

Where he soon discovered that raising the topic for discussion would often result in confrontational heated debates – or even destroy relationships with family and friends – something he'd witnessed firsthand.

In fact, daring to question the shape of the Earth and our ultimate position within the cosmos: that is, whether geocentric or heliocentric – has remained a contentious topic of discussion for many centuries on end.

And that is what the philosopher and astronomer Giordano Bruno discovered over five hundred years ago—having been brutishly burned on a stake on the streets of Rome during the Roman Inquisition for simply questioning the accepted cosmological model. With his tenacious and unorthodox beliefs that Space is infinite and that the Earth is not geocentrically positioned within the cosmos, as was commonly believed at the time. In what was considered by the ruling elites as heretic philosophies.

Although Max was considered a smart-successful man, with numerous connections worldwide and more money than he knew what to do with. Most of his family and friends just didn't want to hear Max rant on about the wild conspiracy theory that Governments across the world were wilfully collaborating to deceive humanity about the shape of the Earth.

In a speech about world politics, J. Edgar Hoover publically declared, "*The individual is handicapped by coming face to face with a conspiracy so monstrous he cannot believe it exists.*"

And Max believed the insightful statement still holds true to this very day. Whereas humans ordinarily appeal to authority and consensus rather than reaching a conclusion through honest, unbiased research.

Max couldn't help to occasionally wonder if his deep obsession with the Flat Earth topic was the reason why Zoe accepted the temporary role to work overseas. Because she was resistant to the concept of him researching flat Earth, even triggering minor arguments between them.

* * * * *

Zoe also enjoyed engaging in conversations about various controversial conspiracy theories with Max, and they had spent many nights discussing numerous historical events that appeared to be smeared with conspiracy.

However, growing up as the daughter of an Australian Ambassador stationed in Europe for many years had provided Zoe with the privilege to travel across the world on several occasions. So she found it impossible to believe that the Earth could be flat.

Being away from Melbourne and desperately missing Max, Zoe felt that she owed him to look into the theory, no matter how crazy it sounded. And after delving into the topic during her spare time from her cosy London-based apartment, she had a change of mind and couldn't wait to tell Max in person.

Zoe was astounded to witness first-hand that the Flat Earth topic was even being discussed in London. And would often hear her work colleagues talk about the subject, sharing funny memes around the office – with images of 'cats pushing objects off a Flat Earth'; and even one of her junior assistants proclaiming herself as an advocate.

Surprisingly, Zoe wasn't alone in her epiphany. Just like many of Max's family, friends, and colleagues, who initially laughed and ridiculed him, she soon enough became accustomed to the fact that Max was right all along – and that he was not so "crazy" after all!

✷ ✷ ✷ ✷ ✷

Several weeks had passed since Sam was introduced to the concept that the Earth may be flat, and Max could sense that Sam was gradually accepting the idea that the shape of the Earth was not what he once believed.

Like many, Sam had never given a second thought that the Earth was not a spinning ball. And Max knew that if Sam was going to see the world around him for what it was, then he needed to shake off his biggest objection. Whereas he just couldn't fathom that a conspiracy of such magnitude could be perpetrated on the masses without their knowledge.

Max both wanted and needed Sam to be part of his mission, which he coined "MissionX" – the "X" signifying his belief that there was "extra" land across this infinite water-world that we live upon. Because Sam was a senior logistics analyst with nearly 20-years of experience managing large-scale multi-million-dollar operations and a meticulous planner to the minute detail; and Max knew that Sam would be an advantageous asset to accomplish the mission.

But, Max still had a long road ahead of him. Because he still had to convince Sam of two crucial facts.

That the Earth is flat.

And that he was not going insane!

14

Elena didn't even flinch when Max told her about his belief that the Earth is flat and geocentric.

She just nonchalantly shrugged her shoulders and stated, "Max, it could be flat; shaped like a banana; or a pizza, but it makes no difference to my life. My husband and I are just trying to live a happy life, pay our mortgage, feed our kids, and get them through school!"

Her brash honesty was one of the reasons Max cherished Elena.

She just appreciated life for what it was. And as a devout Greek Orthodox Christian, she would often cross her chest three times with her trident pointed fingers whilst she whispered, "Doxa to Theo" – or praise God, in English. Whilst she silently prayed that Max would one day settle down with Zoe and finally have a family of their own.

Elena's Grandmother taught her a mysterious ancient Greek tradition that she believed could detect and rid the presence of evil spirits. So before Max departed on his trip to London, she half-filled a bowl with water, then drizzled in a few drops of olive oil and whispered a barely audible secret ancient Greek prayer. Instantly suspecting that he was hexed by an evil eye, judging by the odd separation of the oil with the water.

"Oh my God! Look at this, Max. Someone tried to hex you. Please be careful on your trip!" Elena suggested with a look of deep concern.

The supernatural was not Max's thing. "Objective reality" was his new keyword, but he was not about to ignore her advice – as she had been right before.

"Don't worry, Elena – I will," he reassuringly replied. "I'll be back home in a few days. Why don't you take some time off until I return? Just relax and enjoy yourself."

"Thank you, Max. I so appreciate the time off, to be honest. My sister is in town from Sydney at the moment, and it will give us some extra time together. I'm taking her to the theatre tomorrow night to see Aladdin, the musical."

"Oh, Elena. That's actually one of my favourites. Zoe and I had so much fun the last time we went to see the show. We laughed all night long."

"I can't wait to see it, Max. I'm so excited," she said, happily dancing around with joy.

"Anyway, have fun while I'm away, and say hello to your sister for me," giving Elena a warm hug and kissing her on each cheek.

Before walking away to the master bedroom, Max discreetly placed an envelope with the word 'Elena' handwritten in cursive – that contained a generous cash bonus – beside her handbag that was resting on the kitchen bench.

15

Snapping closed his lightly packed suitcase, Max rode the private elevator down to the underground car park of his apartment building. His vehicle automatically unlocking the driver's side door – after remotely detecting the sensor built into the key fob – as he approached the car.

Missing the morning peak hour traffic, Max arrived at Sam's house approximately twenty minutes later and hopped out of his car to welcome his guests.

Max mimicked a posh British accent whilst shaking Sam's hand, "G'day, old chap. Are you ready for our trip to London?"

"Sure am, buddy," Sam cheerily replied as he shook his hand, then walked toward the trunk of the vehicle to load the suitcases.

"Cheerio, Max. It's such a pleasure to see you again," smiled Jessica, putting on one of the best fake English accents that he'd ever heard from an Aussie chick.

Continuing with the English accent and politely shaking her hand. "Likewise, Jessica. It's great to see you too. I'm glad you could join us today."

Sam shook his head and laughed while loading her large travel case into the trunk of the car as he briefly wondered, "What the heck is in this bag!" then climbed into the rear passenger seat of the car with Jessica.

Suddenly feeling like a chauffeur but happy to see the two lovebirds comfortably nestled in the backseat of his car, Max cruised his black BMW 7-Series along the Nepean Highway, setting the cruise control to 80-kilometres per hour to avoid any further fines by the strategically placed and corrupt speed cameras – or 'robocops', as he would refer to them. Where they excitingly chatted behind the subtle ambient sound of Sade's "Smooth Operator", playing through the surround sound system.

Max always preferred waiting until the morning traffic would dissipate before contemplating making his way on the roads. Dreading rush hour, where he would often find himself driving no faster than snail-pace, with the constant stop-and-go of Melbourne's ever-increasing traffic.

His personalised "666-247" number plates frequently triggered the flashing lights of the Highway Patrol, who would unjustifiably pull over his vehicle, where Max would find himself explaining that the plates were just a play on the heliocentric model: which suggests that we orbit the Sun at 66,600 miles per hour – every single day. Hence the 24/7.

It was a beautiful sunny morning with not a cloud in sight as they arrived at the local airport in Melbourne's South Eastern suburbs. And after parking his vehicle within the designated area in the hangar, the trio walked to the tarmac, where the pilot and flight crew were waiting to greet the passengers.

The pilot, Andy, warmly welcomed Max and his guests, "Good morning, everyone. What a great day for flying," shaking Max's hand and giving him a man-hug whilst lightly slapping his back.

"G'day, Andy. It sure is! It's good to see you again, mate. You're looking mighty sharp as usual," replied Max.

"Thanks, Max. You're too kind," slipping his Ray-Ban aviator sunglasses into his shirt pocket.

"How's life treating you, champ?" asked Max.

"Busy as usual with the family. But loving life, Max. The kids are growing fast; and driving me crazy," having a chuckle.

Max smiled. "Yeah, I can just imagine."

Turning to greet Sam and Jessica, Andy asked, "Hey there, Sam; it's been a while since I've seen you, buddy. It's great to have you flying with us today," warmly shaking Sam's hand and welcoming Jessica; before they all climbed the steps to board the Gulfstream G650ER chartered private jet.

Andy was Max's life-long friend since they sported the same daggy 1970s style haircuts at primary school in a middle-class Melbourne suburb. Being somewhat rivals, having scuffled many times in the school playground as young children; as fate would have it, they rescued a kitten stuck in a tree on the last day of primary school before the summer break – and since that day, remained close friends through thick and thin.

Although Andy was now relishing his lifestyle crisscrossing the world as a privately contracted pilot flying multi-million-dollar private jets, he previously patriotically served the Australian Defence Force for several years. Receiving multiple commendations during his military career in the Royal Australian Airforce, electing to serve his country during the second Gulf War in Iraq – whilst many of his friends were drinking and partying in bars and clubs within the safe borders of Australia.

Andy's time in service was not glamorous by any means, having witnessed countless atrocities that he now wished he had no part of – and was elated to have his feet back on Australian soil. Vowing like many others that he would retire from military service upon completion of his tours of duty.

"Wow! This is the life!" exclaimed Jessica. "I could really get used to this," she joked, walking into the luxurious cabin area, which boasted cream leather seats, contrasting polished timber-lined walls, with an interior configuration fit for both business and pleasure. Sam assisted Jessica into her seat; then, sitting beside her, buckled up his seatbelt to prepare for take-off.

It was a routine trip that Max had ventured several times while Zoe was in London. A 16-hour flight with a brief stop-over in Dubai to refuel.

"Tower, this is Gulfstream GS650Z, requesting to taxi to Romeo two, for north-west departure with information Zulu," Andy communicated to air traffic control through the VHF radio.

"Roger, 650. You are cleared to taxi to runway two," beamed the traffic controllers voice into the plane's cockpit radio, as the ground traffic controller signalled by waving his paddles for the pilots to proceed to their designated runway.

"Roger, tower. Proceeding to runway two for take-off," the younger co-pilot James replied to the control tower, after verifying the inputted data on the flight management system, then reconfirming that the planes gyroscope had successfully recalibrated its datum point to sea level.

Max quickly exited the flight deck, joining Sam and Jessica in the Aft cabin, tightly buckling himself into the adjacent facing seat; as the plane waited on the runway to receive final clearance from the control tower.

"650Z, you are cleared for take-off at six-zero-zero, flying straight out. Over."

After rechecking all flight systems, Andy levered the throttle forward where the twin-jet-engines on the multi-million-dollar jet roared as the aircraft launched down the runway.

The sudden acceleration pushing the passengers back into their seats, as the aircraft smoothly ascended into the air, climbing rapidly towards its designated cruising altitude of 43,000-feet; where the Gulfstream achieves maximum fuel efficiency by flying within the jet-stream – at Mach 0.9, or almost the speed of sound.

16

Soft ambient, modern jazz music filled the cabin as the trio settled in for the long-haul flight.

Jessica gazed out of the large oval panoramic windows of the aircraft, feeling like the luckiest girl in the world when the seatbelt notification sign chimed. And within minutes after take-off, the friendly flight attendant served freshly brewed coffee, orange juice with an assortment of quarter-cut sandwiches and pastries.

"Thank you, Sonya. Looks delicious," Max complimented.

"Would everyone like coffee?" she asked, where Sonya received a chorus of, "Yes, please!"

The trio watched Sonya pour the hot steaming liquid into white gold-trimmed porcelain cups, as they relaxed into their electronically operated leather seats; casually chatting about life in general – where Jessica asked Max a million questions about Zoe.

Having answered her bombardment of questions, and giving Sam and Jessica a brief outline of their itinerary, Max was eager to demonstrate a simple experiment.

Reaching for a glass tumbler, Max stood up and placed it onto the polished wooden credenza adjacent to a three-seater sofa spread with soft, plump pillows.

"Hey, guys! Let's try a little experiment. I'm going to half-fill this glass with water and leave it here while we fly from Australia to England."

After half filling the glass with bottled water and returning to his seat, Max said, "You can clearly see that the water has already levelled out."

"Can we all agree?" Max confidently asked.

"Yeah, it has, Max. No doubt!" replied Sam.

"For sure. It definitely has," Jessica concurred, taking a sip of her coffee from the fine China cup while resting the saucer in her palm; eyeing off the selection of fresh pastries and quarter-cut sandwiches.

"Cool. So my question is: will the surface of the water adjust its level to follow the supposed arc of the earth and find a new level as we fly to London?"

"Hmm, I'm not quite sure," replied Sam, lightly stroking his clean-shaven chin.

Placing her lipstick-stained cup and saucer onto the polished centre table, Jessica leaned back into her slightly reclined leather armchair, now just listening attentively to see where the conversation was going.

Max pressed ahead, "And what will happen to the liquid at the equator? Will it be sideways? And what about when we reach England; will it then level out at another angle?"

"Well, I believe the scientific consensus is that the surface of the water is going to adjust to Earth's radius due to gravity. Don't they say the force of gravity pulls everything to the centre of Earth?" asked Sam.

"That's what they say. But it defies all logic! Because, unless we use the overly–hyped justification of gravity, there is no reasonable explanation, except that we must be currently flying over a flat and level Earth with no curvature. You see, I believe that the water in the glass will remain level on this aeroplane – just as water remains level at rest on Earth."

Sam glanced at the glass tumbler on the credenza, thinking about the fluid dynamics of the water before his eyes, then leaned closer to Jessica to briefly look out the window to view the expansive waters below.

Turning to face his friend, he said, "You know... maybe you're right, Max. It doesn't make sense when I think about it!"

"Exactly, mate. And the only way theoretical physicists can explain the conundrum is via a complex mathematical equation, which Einstein coined as Special Relativity, then General Relativity. Because even he couldn't explain the theory on his first attempt!"

"Man, I have to admit that it's been quite a while since I've sat in a science class. Give me a quick refresher, would you, Max? What do they mean by relativity again?" asked Sam.

"I've got this," Jessica interjected. "Well, in layman's terms, and in relation to our Earth: Einstein postulated that gravity – through the warping of Space and time – commands that 'up is up' for everyone, regardless of where they are standing on Earth. So in effect, the theory suggests that people who are down under in Australia, or anywhere in the Southern Hemisphere, for that matter, are standing up. Even though they are upside-down. In essence, they say that up and down on planet Earth are both relative to the observer!"

She elaborated, "You see: they say that it's all relative to your position on Earth. Because apparently, everything is being pulled to the centre of the Earth by the force of gravity," gesturing quotation marks with her fingers after the word 'apparently'.

"Wow, Jessica! Impressive explanation," replied Sam, looking at her admiringly and thinking – this woman may be the one.

"Thank you, Sam – you're so sweet," fluttering her eyelashes.

"Max teased, "I know... he's so cute, isn't he," mischievously fluttering his eyelashes at Sam, where they all laughed at his silly antics – with his friend now shaking his head.

"Anyway, I agree; great explanation, Jessica – couldn't have said it any better myself. However, in my opinion: the theory is rather ludicrous, as relativity makes a mockery of our natural senses! Because if this plane was flying sideways over the equator right now, we would all know it!"

"Yes. It is rather silly, the further I consider it, Max," replied Jessica, crossing her eyes in jest. "As nature commands that there can only be one up – and only one down, for all on Earth. Any other claim without empirical proof, well, it borders lunacy!"

After laughing at her hilarious facial expression, Max said, "It sure is silly, Jessica. And to top it off – they make a further mockery of our senses by telling us that we live on a ball suspended in space that spins at a supersonic speed, at almost twice faster than the speed of sound."

Sam nodded in agreement while taking a bite of a sandwich.

"And when you consider that Issac Newton, who after an apple supposedly fell on his head – as they taught us in school – suddenly postulated the theory of gravity. Well... it's even more absurd! Because, didn't he even consider for just a moment that the twig could no longer support the weight of the apple and therefore fell to the ground due to the apple being heavier than the air it displaced? Otherwise known as the natural laws of relative density— or specific gravity."

"So, in other words, the twig just couldn't handle the weight of the situation anymore," Max smirked – taking a bite of a Danish pastry, then wiping the blueberry jam from the corner of his mouth with a cloth napkin.

"He's just lucky he wasn't sitting under a coconut tree," joked Sam, as they laughed at his witty segue.

"But in all seriousness, Max. That's quite fascinating," replied Jessica.

"Hmm... and come to think of it – why don't butterflies or bumblebees get pulled to the ground if the force of gravity is so powerful that it can hold all the oceans to this Earth as it spins?" she asked.

"And what about the clouds, mist, and fog... for that matter? Why do they miraculously avoid the magical force of gravity?" as she playfully dropped her napkin onto the table.

"Precisely, Jessica. Gravity seems to be rather selective! Almost magical!"

"However, the laws of relative density and buoyancy explained the phenomena of why some objects fall whilst others float, well before Isaac Newton postulated his theory. Who never in his wildest imagination – while working under candlelight – contemplated the possible effect of electromagnetic attraction. Where he even crafted calculus to validate his hypothesis, which was formulized from an assumed radius of the Earth, derived from Eratosthenes's prior assumptions of the Earth's circumference."

"What! Who the heck is Erato... or whoever you just said? I've never heard of him," asked Sam.

"Don't worry, Sam. Neither did I, until I started investigating this topic."

"Anyway... he was an ancient Greek dude who was a scholar, mathematician, and geographer. And Eratosthenes conducted an ambiguous experiment to calculate the circumference of the Earth. From memory, I think it was circa 200 BC, or something like that."

"Ah, yes, of course... I remember him now, Max. That's the guy who did that dodgy 'stick and shadow' experiment thousands of years ago in Egypt."

"Yeah, yeah... that's him. Let's call him 'shadow-man' because his name is kind of hard to say," as they giggled.

"And the claim is that Erato... I mean, shadow-man recorded a measurement of Earth's circumference within only ten percent of the currently accepted circumference, which they say is approximately 40,000 kilometres at the equator. All by simply measuring shadows!" Max explained.

"Pardon the pun, guys, but 'shadow-man' sounds 'shady' to me too!" said Jessica. "Because wouldn't the topography, as well as other factors, influence the results? And how was he so certain that the elevation was the same at both locations? As any discrepancy would surely cause a variation in the results – wouldn't it? And by the way, has anyone since reproduced his experiment – because you'd think it would be easy, in this day and age?" she rhetorically questioned.

"Yes, I believe it would, Jessica. And yeah, Eratosthenes does sound rather shady. The experiment has multiple flaws and essentially necessitated many assumptions right from the very get-go. It's as if they always wanted the Earth to be a spinning ball. As it kind of models their Kabbalistic religious beliefs, which stemmed all the way back to the Sun worshipping ideals of Pythagoras!"

"But what concerns me, even more, is that there are conflicting stories about how the experiment was conducted."

Max placed down his glass after sipping some orange juice. "You see, some academics claim that Eratosthenes placed sticks in the ground to measure the shadows. The astrophysicist Carl Sagan claimed that he used obelisks. And others speculate that he used wells. Hey, it gets even crazier, because some claim it was via a combination of both obelisks and wells. And it obviously can't be all of them. So, the entire experiment oozes a strong stench of bullshit to me!"

"Sure does, Max. It seems that the only evidence for Earth radius is by dodgy experiments, mathematical theories, and suppositious constructs. And we all know that math is not reality," Jessica confidently replied as Sam stared at her in absolute awe.

They attentively listened as Jessica continued, "And I don't even think that they knew about the refractive index of light, terrestrial refraction, or the exact distance to the Sun. Besides, did they even know about parallel and divergent sun rays way back then? As surely that would also skew the results, now that I come to think of it!" slightly tilting her head.

"Brilliant points, Jessica," replied Max.

He then looked at Sam and said, "Far out, mate... she's a friggin brainiac! Good catch," he cheekily teased, as Jessica leaned across giggling while lightly slapping his arm.

"Yeah, definitely. I reckon she's a keeper, alright!" Sam smiled as she wrinkled her nose – then nudged closer to Sam to give him a soft peck on the lips.

17

Millions of people from across the pond – who were now questioning the heliocentric model; were beginning to dispute the Eratosthenes experiment, as many factors could have skewed his findings.

Especially given that the distance to the Sun from our Earth was only recently agreed upon; thus, any rational person would have to acknowledge that determining triangulation of the Sun without this prior knowledge – would be near impossible.

Most people didn't know that Max's ancestral heritage was European, but having been brought up by parents who migrated to Melbourne from Greece during the 1960s, he unofficially changed his name from Max Cartopoulos to Max Carter in the latter years of life. Opting to use the nickname that he adopted on the sports field from his schoolmates many years ago.

Max treasured the Greek language, history, philosophy, literature, art, and science; and would proudly acknowledge it if Eratosthenes was correct with his findings. However, even the astrophysicist Neil de Grasse Tyson made a stark admission on his TV show, 'StarTalk'; acknowledging the experiment would deliver the same outcome on a spherical Earth with a distant Sun millions-of-miles away; or on a flat Earth with a localised Sun, just a few thousand miles of distance.

"Anyway, Jessica – I wholeheartedly agree with you that math isn't reality. And many people are finally beginning to see through the plethora of sophistry within the heliocentric paganistic Sun-worshiping model," said Max.

"Yeah, I get ya, Max," Sam earnestly replied. "I can't believe that I never questioned it all before. But, mate – I still don't get why it's so damn important to you. You've got everything one could ever desire and a beautiful lady who adores you. So please, whatever you do, don't mess that up now... with this crazy idea of *finding more land!*"

Max swiftly rebutted, "Oh, don't you worry, buddy. That's never going to happen," smiling confidently, then reclining his seat into a more comfortable, laid-back position.

"Anyway, I'll tell you why this is so important to me. Well, let's just go back to the time you discovered that Santa Claus wasn't real. Did you try and tell your friends and everyone you knew?"

"I guess I did, Max. And come to think of it, I may have even teased them a little, including you – if I recall correctly!"

Max smiled, briefly reminiscing the event, which now seemed a lifetime ago. "Ha-ha... very funny, mate. So, then I'm sure you'll understand when I say that I'm doing the same about Flat Earth because the truth is that we are not living on a spinning oblate spheroid that's careering through space. And I feel like it's my obligation to open people's eyes about it!"

"Okay. That's fair enough, Max. But can it be proven without a doubt?"

"Yes, it can, as there isn't a scintilla of empirical evidence to support a spherical Earth. But there's a preponderance of evidence to support a flat, motionless Earth. But first, we must stop resisting our God-given senses. Because does it really fuckin feel like the Earth is spinning faster than a speeding bullet?" asked Max.

"Oops. Sorry, Jessica. Pardon my French," Max endearingly apologised.

"No fuckin worries, Max," she cheekily laughed.

"No, it doesn't, Max. But it's not that easy. As we wouldn't feel the spin," Sam insisted. "Just like we can't feel this aeroplane moving right now, as we're moving at a constant velocity, and so is the Earth. It's Newtonian physics, isn't it?"

"It's more like just good old-fashioned brainwashing and shifty pseudoscience if you ask me," replied Max, taking a sip of his freshly poured coffee.

"Because in fact, no one can prove that the Earth spins: since the Earth simply doesn't spin!"

"And, Sam, did you know that according to the heliocentric model, that Earth's motion around the Sun is not at a constant velocity? As our alleged orbit around the Sun is elliptical and not a perfectly circular orbit. So, therefore, Earth's motion supposedly accelerates, then decelerates, by millions of kilometres per hour during our rumoured annual orbit. Once and for all, quashing the schoolyard theory that we are moving at a constant linear rate."

"Hmm. That's rather interesting, Max. I didn't know that," replied Sam.

"But I still can't fathom how, and more importantly, why, worldwide Governments would unite together to perpetuate such a grand conspiracy! Many don't even like each other, for God's sake! And I'm quite confident that they would love to disclose the propaganda of their most hated adversaries. You know, to pull the curtain on them. Especially if they had the opportunity to do so!"

"What if all the animosity is just smoke and mirrors, Sam? I mean, just another method to manipulate our minds. To keep us in constant fear, if you like."

"I've gotta admit that it's quite possible, Max. But I can't help but wonder; why they would lie to us about the shape of the Earth? As it seems quite trivial, and kind of meaningless."

"You're tripping me out right now, Sam! Do I need to remind you that you're the person who introduced me to conspiracy theories? It taught me how to think critically and be sceptical in this tainted world we live in, and it was one of the most important life lessons I've learnt to date. And I need you to do the same for me right now. I know it's a difficult concept to accept, but Flat Earth is the granddaddy of all conspiracies. The grandest of all!"

"It sure is difficult to comprehend, Max. As it kind of changes everything about our understanding of the Universe. And you know, that's a big thing to grasp," Sam acknowledged.

"I get ya, buddy. It does change everything. And don't worry, I had the same resistance as you when I first heard about Flat Earth.

I think everyone does. And that's why I held back from telling you until I was absolutely certain. I knew it would hit you hard, Sam. Especially knowing how much we enjoyed watching science-fiction movies when we were younger."

"Man. That sure feels like a lifetime ago."

"Sure does, Sam. And do you remember those times when we'd smoke a few joints as we chilled out to watch the science documentary Cosmos by that American astrophysicist? But you know, never in my wildest dreams did I question if what I was viewing was actually real. But now that I do question it, it's barely even a documentary. As the entire series is encumbered with suppositions such as – *would be, could be, should be*, and the most commonly repeated word, *maybe*."

"Yeah, they were the good old days, Max. As a matter of fact, I kind of wish we could strike up a big fat doobie... right about now," he cheekily grinned.

Max chuckled, "That would be bloody awesome... and it would certainly give a new meaning to being – *sky high!*"

Jessica cracked up laughing at Max's comment and at the very thought of them stoned off their faces.

"But mate, in all seriousness, and to try to answer your previous question. Yes, I'm actually beginning to believe that this is a worldwide conspiracy! And it possibly involves many secretive alphabet agencies, who probably only discovered the true shape of our Earth as recently as the 1950s or 60s. And the knowledge was kept privy to only a few."

"Because the fact is until then, they couldn't even reach the required altitude to confirm the true shape of the Earth. And I reckon that when they finally worked out that we aren't living on a spinning ball, they just kept it top-secret. Reason being, that they know that the majority of people can't handle the truth."

"But don't you think they would have told us by now, Max?"

"Nah, I don't, Sam. Because the spinning ball-Earth fallacy has been instilled into society for over 500-years, so you just keep propagating the lie, because disclosing the truth would be a huge admission. It could even cause a world-wide revolution with street protests if *'the powers that be'* just came out and admitted, *'Oops. Sorry, everyone. We had it all wrong. The Earth is actually flat!'*

"That's bloody frightening, Max!"

"It sure is, bud. And you know, people would start to question everything if they found out that they were hoodwinked about the very place where they live."

"I gotta say, Max, that stranger things have happened. And they do say that the truth is stranger than fiction!"

Max replied, "They also say that the truth will set you free. But first, people just need to take a proper gander at the propaganda."

"True that," giving him a thumbs up.

"Sam, I'm beginning to believe that we're living during a rather unique time, where through the rise of technocracy, we've been programmed to perceive that our authorities and even scientists are our higher power. It's dictatorship at best. And in my opinion, most people are now far more fearful of their own governments than almighty God!"

"You're right, Max. They've controlled our way of life for far too long. And we appeal to their authority, thinking that they know better than us by enforcing laws that 'borderline' dictatorship governance – which, by the way, I never consented to!" Sam protested.

"And the word government etymologically translates to *mind control*," he added.

"That's insane, Sam! The word government means mind-control? How could I have missed that?" Jessica remarked.

"It's more than insanity, Jess. And quite often, the word-play is designed to keep us spellbound by using words to control and coerce us into submitting to their evil ways through spelling – or spells."

"Spot on, Sam. And you could even say it's mental enslavement by the establishment who control everything under the firmament. And they achieve it through entertainment for man's amusement. The end goal being mass bewilderment."

They smiled at his quip, witty words.

"And guys, I reckon the aim behind the grand deception is to keep us guessing as to our true purpose in life. It's mental enslavement at best; with the grand objective to hide the absolute truth that our Earth and all creatures on it were intelligently designed by an omnipotent creator. You know, kind of like this Earth was made for a reason; rather than humans randomly hurtling through space due to an unexplainable big explosion that created everything from nothing through mere happenstance."

"Exactly, Max," Jessica responded. "In my opinion, the theory of evolution and the ridiculous Big Bang theory were both devised to make us feel insignificant by influencing people to believe they are just another speck of dust in an ever-expanding galaxy. However, the theories are probably the most masterminded piece of bullshit that I've ever come across!" she said, fiddling with her earrings.

"100%! The theories were propagated with the aim to dumb down and distract humanity. But it's obvious that we're divine sentient beings – created by an omniscient intelligent designer."

Sam chimed in, "I agree. And wasn't it was the famous English astronomer, Sir Fred Hoyle, who said something along the lines of that the likelihood all life on Earth was spawned by a big explosion billions of years ago; is as improbable that an aircraft could be designed and assembled to precision after a tornado sweeps through an aeroplane graveyard? In other words, It's friggin impossible!"

"That's always a great analogy, Sami," said Max. "And I hope you know that the same applies to the heliocentric model. It's another impossibility. And the only reason people believe that they live on a sphere whipping around like a supersonic baseball through Space, is because a higher authority told them so!"

Max professed, "No one in their right mind would ever consider such a crazy notion about our Earth, based on their life experience. The Earth looks flat, and it feels motionless – because it simply is!" as he peeked out of the window for a quick glimpse of the view below.

"And as I said, it was only until the mid-1900's that anyone could even go high enough to confirm if the Earth is spherical or flat. But for hundreds of years prior – and without proof – everyone believed that they lived on a spinning ball, just because someone told them!"

"Yeah, I hear you, buddy. I hate it when you make sense," Sam smirked.

Max grinned, "Well, I do kick the occasional goal... you know."

"So, anyway; it's time to start questioning the science behind the heliocentric model and place it under intense scrutiny; rather than to blindly believe what has been presented to us as fact without prior investigation."

"Absolutely!" said Jessica. "Like everything, science should always be questioned and put under cross-examination. It's the very essence of the scientific process. It's all about seeking answers to nature through the zetetic method of inquiry with the sole intent and purpose of seeking the truth about the natural world. From memory, the method goes something like this: first, you make an observation that is followed by asking a question; then, you form a hypothesis or an explanation, where you further predict the observation based on the hypothesis; and then test it repeatedly before forming a conclusion. Oh, and I should also mention and emphasise that the results must be demonstrable and reproducible."

Sam had earlier briefed Jessica about Max's fascination with the Flat Earth theory. And unlike most people that would typically reject the notion without investigation, she contributed with keen interest throughout the conversation—having already conducted several hours of independent research on the topic; after watching the video 'The Flat Earth Litmus Test' on YouTube – sparking her inquisitive nature.

Jessica wasn't just your average waitress.

She'd recently completed her master's degree, graduating with honours at one of Melbourne's leading universities and working at the Pier Café as a part-time waitress, whilst seeking full-time employment as a structural engineer and was awaiting a reply for a position in Sydney. Where after meeting Sam, she was already beginning to reconsider her future.

"I hear what you're saying, Max. And having just completed a degree in structural engineering, we never explicitly studied the sphericity of the Earth. And we certainly didn't measure it as a group exercise!" remarked Jessica.

"And you could be right, Max. What if the powers that be are, in fact, hiding more land! How would we even know?" looking to Sam, eager for his consensus.

"I share the same sentiment, Jessica. And for some reason, I just can't shake the prospect from my mind. And who knows, what if that's where the true origins of the various cultures on earth originated from, and we've somehow lost this knowledge," Max proposed.

"It would be absolutely amazing, Max. And possibly the most remarkable discovery in modern times. But what still trips me out is why they wouldn't tell us if there was more land on Earth. I know we get lied to about many things, but this just seems a bit extreme. Don't you reckon?" asked Sam.

"That's a bloody good question! But I'm not sure why they would hide it! I haven't figured that part out yet," as Max unpacked his laptop to stream a video that he had earlier saved onto his hard drive, wirelessly syncing it to the onboard widescreen monitor that automatically raised out of the credenza – with the delicate push of a button.

"Although, the more I think about it, I'm starting to believe that they limit the liveable lands we have on Earth by presenting a globe. Which by default of its shape has a confined surface area, thereby promoting the principle of scarcity in a world controlled by consumerism. So I believe that if we can locate more land on Earth, then we will discover further resources that could be made available to humanity. And hey, let's not forget about the tourism opportunities, as I reckon most people would love to experience the adventure of visiting unknown lands, with its own ecosystem; especially with the possibility of observing mysterious creatures, beyond our wildest imagination."

Max joked, "Could you just imagine if there were giant-sized Kangaroos or Koalas?"

"Yep. There you go again, Max. You're freaking me out again; you crazy bugger," Sam laughed, throwing a few light jabs to Max's right upper arm.

"Oh, don't get me started, Sami!" playfully putting up his dukes and shadow boxing, as Jessica shook her head and giggled at their boyish antics.

Max loaded the video on the TV monitor.

"Hey, guys! Check out this footage taken from a high-altitude balloon that I found on YouTube. It shows that at an altitude of 120,000 feet, the horizon is not only flat – with no curvature whatsoever – but we can also see a localised Sun producing a hotspot directly above the clouds."

He elaborated, "It's like the Sun is close, just as it appears in real-life. Look; it's right there," pointing to the television screen to highlight the Sun's localised hotspot, which was shining peculiarly close to the roof of the clouds.

"Holy shit, Max. What's our current altitude at the moment?" Sam enquired.

Max picked up his smartphone loading up the Gulfstream's Android application, which synced a myriad of data from the aeroplane's onboard flight system. Including the ability to view any of the ten 4K high-definition cameras installed onto the plane's exterior – that presented views from various vantage points – directly onto the large LCD screen.

"You gotta love technology these days, don't you?" he boasted.

The data loaded within seconds. "Well, according to this app, we're currently flying at 43,420 feet, which is almost maximum altitude for this aircraft. So effectively, the footage that we are viewing on-screen right now was taken from three times our current altitude. And as you can clearly see, even from that height, there is no curvature whatsoever!"

"And, hey... look, guys; the water in the glass is still level," as Max pointed to the glass tumbler on the credenza.

Like many people, Sam had always thought he could see the Earth's curvature during the countless domestic and international flights he had taken during his life – but he reluctantly confessed.

"Max, I always thought I could see the curvature of the Earth by simply looking outside an aeroplane window. But from up here, it looks as flat as a pancake!" leaning forward to look out of the sizeable oval-shaped window.

Jessica chimed in, "Did someone say pancakes?" rubbing her belly.

"You're like a bottomless bit, Jess! I don't even know where you put it, babe!" teased Sam.

"Hey, there's always room for pancakes... and ice cream," she smiled, wishing they could miraculously appear right before her eyes.

After hours of discussion outlining his audacious plan to find more land on Earth, Sam and Max dozed off in their luxurious leather recliner seats; as Jessica, famished, was served a club sandwich by the accommodating flight attendant, Sonya. She then curled up on the sofa to watch a chick-flick, and halfway through the movie returned to her seat for a nap.

Captain Andy entered the cabin to find all of his passengers snoozing. He lightly tapped Max on the shoulder, gently waking him to announce they would be landing for their scheduled stopover in Dubai. Where the crew would have time for some rest and recreation whilst the aircraft was refuelled and replenished.

"Why don't you join me in the flight deck, Max? We're currently about two hundred clicks from Dubai."

Max rubbed his eyes, stretched like a cat, and then eased out of his seat; groggily walking to the flight deck to chat with the pilots, as the plane began to descend for landing—meanwhile Sam cuddled closer to Jessica, who was now snuggled up tight beside him and fast asleep.

"If we stand on the sands of the sea-shore and watch a ship approach us, we shall find that she will apparently "rise" – to the extent, of her own height, nothing more. If we stand upon an eminence, the same law operates still; and it is but the law of perspective, which causes objects, as they approach us, to appear to increase in size until we see them, close to us, the size they are in fact. That there is no other "rise" than the one spoken of is plain from the fact that, no matter how high we ascend above the level of the sea, the horizon rises on and still on as we rise, so that it is always on a level with the eye, though it be two-hundred miles away, as seen by Mr. J. Glaisher, of England, from Mr. Coxwell's balloon. So that a ship five miles away may be imagined to be "coming up" the imaginary downward curve of the earth's surface, but if we merely ascend a hill such as Federal Hill, Baltimore, we may see twenty-five miles away, on a level with the eye – that is, twenty miles level distance beyond the ship that we vainly imagined to be "rounding the curve," and "coming up!" This is a plain proof that the earth is not a globe."

WILLIAM CARPENTER

18

A pristine pearl-white SUV with dark tinted windows awaited the trio at Dubai international airport that Max organised to escort them to visit the tallest tower in the world, the Burj Khalifa. And in particular, the Sky Lounge, located on Level 148, offering visitors a birds-eye view of the world.

Following a frantic drive through heavier traffic than Jessica had ever experienced in her life – they arrived at the entrance of the tower thirty minutes later.

"Welcome, Mr Carter. We've been expecting you. It's a fine honour to have you and your guests in our acquaintance," said the guest ambassador, Ahmad—ushering the group through the majestic ground floor lobby to the elevators. Jessica and Sam were in awe, admiring the opulent minimalistic Giorgio Armani designed interior when Max chuckled after hearing Jessica quietly exclaim, "OMFG! Do you friggin believe this place?"

"Yeah, it's pretty bloody spectacular... hey, Jessica," replied Sam, looking around observing the lobby in astonishment as they walked along the wide corridor, flanked with floor-to-ceiling digital paintings showcasing some of the best attractions in Dubai. It was like nothing they had ever seen before.

Renowned as one of the fastest in the world, the elevators of the Burj Khalifa can reach the Sky Lounge in approximately one minute, cruising at 10-metres per second – whilst offering passengers an interactive digital display – as it ascends toward the heavens to the 148th floor.

Sam casually conversed with Ahmad in fluent Arabic, and even though he'd taught Max many Arabic words during their friendship, the only word that Max recognised – was *hubbibi*.

The elevator doors opened, exposing the contemporary styled Sky Lounge, where the view that trumped the neighbouring high-rise buildings suddenly gave Max a case of vertigo.

Ahmad signalled his staff to serve refreshments of sparkling mineral water, fresh dates, and Arabic coffee.

"Thank you, Ahmad," sipping the strong coffee – savouring the aromatic flavour.

"You are most welcome, Sir Max."

"Oh my God! These views are just to die for. I have to take some photos to share on my social media page," said an excited Jessica reaching into her handbag for her smartphone, and commenced snapping photos.

Sam pressed his nose against the floor-to-ceiling glass window, gazing toward the artificially made Palm Jumeirah islands. His hands immediately began to sweat from the sensation of standing just over half a kilometre above sea level. The view before him extended as far as his eyes could see.

Max pointed to the distant horizon and curiously asked, "What is that, Ahmad? Is that a sandstorm?"

"Yes, Sir Max. This is a sandstorm that is occurring right now in the distance beyond, and it's quite normal. We have many of them throughout the year, often sweeping sands across our city and darkening the sky."

"That's amazing. And may I just ask you, Ahmad, how far would you say it is?" Max asked inquisitively.

"That storm is at least 200-kilometres away from our destination, Sir. And I can assure you all that there is nothing to worry about. It appears to be heading in the opposite direction. And allow me to further reassure you by saying that this building is not only the tallest in the world – but also the strongest. We have nothing to worry about! Nothing at all!" Ahmad proudly proclaimed.

"Oh... please don't get me wrong, Ahmad. I'm not concerned, it's just amazing how far I can see right now. And shouldn't the sandstorm be over the curvature of the earth?" Max quizzed as he motioned a curve with his hand.

"Sir, in my country, there are many people, including Sheiks, that believe that Earth is flat – and to say otherwise is considered as heresy. This is why you can see so far right now. All this beauty you see before your eyes... is by the design of Allah. Or God. As you may call him," he declared.

"Yes, I agree, Ahmad. I also believe... I mean, I also know the earth is flat and that we are not spinning around on a ball," as Max made a circle motion with his finger.

"This is good to hear, Sir. It appears to me that humanity is finally awaking from its deep slumber."

"Please walk with me, Sir Max. Allow me to show you something that may interest you," guiding them into a room to present an oversized clock on the wall that depicted a map of a Flat Earth resembling the azimuthal equidistant projection of the Earth.

The map akin to the United Nations logo and other world organisations, including the International Maritime and International Civil Aviation Organizations; and similar to the clock and the water feature located at Darling Park in Sydney where Max had recently visited with Sam on a "getaway party trip" to sunny Sydney while Zoe was away. The park's design strangely resembling the "flower of life" and the Fibonacci sequence, with its beautifully manicured gardens. The interior of the building a marvel to the eyes of any Flat Earth enthusiast, with the ceiling graced with a depiction of the stars aligned as zodiacal creatures.

Jessica and Sam politely excused themselves from the discussion, slipping away to the observation deck to grab a few moments of privacy. But first, they stopped to select a plate of exquisite finger-food from the elaborate set banquet, while Max continued to converse with Ahmad about Flat Earth – sharing his belief that there could be more land or even continents to be discovered before the ends of the Earth.

"Max, this is very, very possible, Sir. We have many ancient myths and stories about mysterious lands located at both the North and South pole. It is written in our history books that there were once giants on this Earth. And maybe they originated from these lands beyond."

"Giants?" Max quizzed.

"Yes, Sir Max. It sounds bizarre, but I implore you to investigate. There are many giant footprints and megaliths that remain on this Earth until this very day."

"Okay, I most certainly will, Ahmad. Thank you very much for sharing the information with me. I will research the topic when I return home to Australia."

"You are very welcome, Max. Anyway, please let me know if I can assist you any further. I must leave you for a short while," said Ahmad after receiving a message in his earpiece, where he said, "Enjoy your visit, Sir Max," shaking his hand before walking to the elevator. Briefly stopping to instruct his staff in Arabic along the way – by double-clapping his hands to hurry them along.

Walking to the outdoor observation deck of the skyscraper, Sam noticed an information display. "Hey Jessica, have a look at this! It says here that you can witness the Sun setting twice in one day from this tower. It states that you can observe the Sun disappear over the horizon from, say, level 20. And if you then travel up to the 140th level, you will see the Sunset again. Therefore, witnessing two Sunsets in just one day," as he read the script on the digital display.

"It also describes that during the period of Ramadan, the residents at the lower levels of the building can break their fast sooner than the residents at the top levels; who have to wait for a further two minutes to break their fast."

"I've heard that too, Sam. And I recall an astrophysicist explain that it's due to the Sun disappearing behind the Earth's curvature. But I'm not sure why anyone would even make such a stupendous claim that can be easily debunked. Because that fact is, the phenomenon can be explained due to visual perspective, and it also makes sense on a Flat Earth, too," replied Jessica.

She clarified, "You see, if someone is standing at say ground level, then their ability to see distant objects is limited due to many factors, including angular resolution. Because our eyes can only see so far based on our visual perspective relative to our height, but even if one simply stood on the rooftop of a house or climbed a tree – then they would see much further. The point being, as we progressively gain altitude, we can see further distances with respect to the height gained."

"Seems pretty logical and straightforward to me, Jessica."

"Yeah... it is, Sam. And we don't need to be an astrophysicist or rocket scientist to figure it out. It's just common sense. But some white coats often forget to use it, as they get lost in theoretical science whilst disregarding applied natural science! I've seen it occur at the university I attended, several times over."

"That's very true, Jess. Unfortunately, common sense doesn't seem to be so common anymore. And the way I'm starting to see it is that science is never settled. We have much to learn about where we live. Climate change, fossil fuels, medical breakthroughs, and the works!" stepping closer to embrace her; as they enjoyed the glorious view of the bustling city and distant landscape below.

"Exactly, Sam. It's also my opinion that science isn't settled. And you're right; we still have much to discover," replied Jessica.

They snuggled close, embracing each other even tighter, both pondering about their future together, as they watched the world go by.

19

After examining the Flat Earth clock on the wall, Max joined Sam and Jessica on the glass-wrapped observation deck of the Burj Khalifa—the deck renowned as the highest in the world.

"Looks pretty bloody flat to me!" Max remarked, appreciating the vantage point.

Sam chuckled, "Yeah... I can't argue with that, Max. It sure bloody does!"

Jessica inquired, "Hey Max, I was just wondering, how do the seasons function on a flat Earth?".

"I can't answer that question definitively, Jessica – because there's still much to learn. However, Flat Earther's believe the Sun is local to us, rather than the absurd belief that it's 140 million kilometres away. Anyway, check this out!"

He reached into his pocket and grabbed his smartphone, loading the "Flat Earth Sun, Moon & Zodiac Clock" app that creatively depicted a 24-hour clock juxtaposed over an azimuthal equidistant map of the Earth whilst also exhibiting the position of the sun and the moon in real-time.

Max pointed to the screen, "As I was saying, the Sun is close in proximity, and it circles the Earth every day. Creating daylight, then darkening the skies as it leaves our location, whilst the Sun continuously circuits our Earth providing precious light and warmth to all creatures. Almost like an hour-hand circling over the face of a 24-hour analogue clock," as Max circled the boundaries of the map with his pointer finger.

"It's just as it appears, as everyone can observe the Sun moving across the sky, rather than the irrational belief that daylight is created by the Earth rotating twice-faster than the speed of sound toward the face of the Sun."

Max emphasized, "I implore everyone to stop and think about that at some point in their lives. You know, to ask themselves; does the Sun move across the sky during the day, or are they spinning?"

"That's interesting," Jessica curiously replied. "Because now that I think about it: I would say it's obvious that the Sun moves."

She reaffirmed, "Yep. Definitely. No doubt about it!"

"Yeah, it certainly is obvious, Jessica. You could even say it's life-changing when the penny finally drops. And to deny what one sees with their own eyes – is borderline foolish."

"Absolutely, Max," said Sam as he snapped a photo of Jessica with his phone, then turned the camera to take a selfie with the three of them in the frame.

Max explained, "Anyway, so as the Sun circuits the Earth, it gets closer to the Tropic of Cancer, creating longer days and summer for the Northern Hemisphere. And then it traverses southward over the equator to create summer for the Southern Hemisphere when it reaches the Tropic of Capricorn. And the Sun forms an analemma during that period when tracked over a 365-day solar cycle. It's quite simple when you think about it."

"Hey, by the way, Sam – did you know that the Sun's analemma is where the infinity symbol was derived? Because the Sun's motion is infinite and forms the figure eight during its path, and probably why so many Asian cultures feel lucky about the number eight."

Sam glanced at the infinity symbol tattoo on his forearm, never before considering the tattoo's significance he acquired after a wild night partying at Kings Cross in Sydney – back in 2004.

"Really? I didn't know that, Max," he replied as Jessica gently clasped his forearm, admiring the tattoo.

Max elaborated, "It's as if the Sun's path around the north-polar centre expands and then contracts annually. Creating warmer, longer days in summer, allowing the Sun to nurture crops, trees, plants, and every living creature across this plane. Energising everything in its path!"

"I must confess that I can't explain it all, as it's well beyond my comprehension, at this stage of my research. However, alternative science is offering new explanations. And from what I've learned to date, we have a toroidal magnetic field encompassing our Earth that creates some type of electrochemical reaction, consequently creating an electromagnetic or dielectric force. For example: we know that magnets influence saltwater under experiment; but freshwater isn't affected. Anyway, it's as if there's a natural cycle within this aethereal toroidal field. You know, our Earth may even behave like some type of battery discharging positive energy. The Sun naturally ionising and energising the Earth as a perpetual cathode; the Moon somehow behaving as an anode. Ongoing research could even unlock a new insight into the theory of gravity, or free energy! But who really knows?"

Sam concurred, "That's true, Max. We've still got a lot to learn. And now that I think about it, it's more than obvious that the Sun and Moon both move across our sky! Because, when I view the Moon through my telescope, it appears that it's moving. So, the more I thought about it – with my new awareness – I reckon that it's kind of nonsensical to propose that the Earth spins!"

"Exactly, buddy... and it never occurred to me before researching this topic. But whenever I look up to a clear night sky, you are right; it is more than obvious that the celestial objects circuit the Earth. You know, like a masterminded timepiece—eternal celestial mechanics engineered to represent a giant skyclock to keep our life in tune – if you will. Perpetually signifying our days, months, and years. It's a systematic realm that works like clockwork!"

"No shit, Max!" Jessica remarked. "Because, did you know that the Bible also says that the Sun circuits the Earth? You see, it states that the biblical character Joshua stopped the Sun and Moon in its track for three days. So, the more I think about it, how the heck did the Earth stop spinning without causing havoc to all creatures on Earth?"

She explained, "Because, when you think about it with an open mind, everything on Earth should have been flicked off into Space by the sheer natural forces of both centrifugal and centripetal force caused by the sudden loss of velocity. You'd have to ask yourself: did our Earth just stop spinning and wobbling through Space – and then, did the Earth just magically start spinning again?" she hypothesized.

"Is that so, Jessica?" Sam responded, intrigued by her comment. "As I've been researching ancient civilizations for almost two decades, and many other cultures also claim a similar occurrence – almost precisely as you described. Where they also asserted that the Sun suddenly stopped in its track for three days! But I must confess that I haven't picked up a Bible for a very long time. I've been meaning to give it another read someday. That is... if I can even find it!"

"I'll get you one, Sam," she swiftly offered. "I don't attend church anymore, and I don't subscribe to any particular religion, but I truly believe in the word of God. And I've trusted his word to guide me – all of my life. One of my favourite quotes is, '*Let God be true, and every man a liar*'."

"Easy does it, Jessica! We're not all liars!" Sam kidded, somewhat surprised that Jessica was quoting passages from the Bible verbatim.

She clarified, "I'm so sorry, Sam. I honestly didn't mean it like that."

"What I meant to say is that I trust in God. And I try not to stray far from his word. In fact, it says in Genesis there is a Firmament that covers our Earth, created to separate the waters above us from the waters below."

"And it kind of made me question the Rayleigh effect, which is how they explain why the sky is blue. So I started to consider that, hey – maybe the sky looks blue during daylight, just like water appears to be blue in the oceans, seas and lakes during the day."

"Water up. Water down. It's simple!" she confidently suggested.

It had been many years since Sam stepped foot into a church, and although he was now leaning toward an agnostic faith; having been an atheist for a moment in his life – after like many people blaming God for war, famine, and everything else 'bad' in this world. He was now open to the possibility of a creator, even though he preferred to use the modern-day axiom – "intelligent design".

Although Sam didn't partake in practising any particular religion, he had unenthusiastically studied the Bible during his education at an elite secondary college, and was aware of the Firmament. And in particular, he had extensive knowledge of the final chapter in the Bible – the Book of Revelation. Whereat, the time of reading, he thought the Bible was just a fairy tale for grown-ups, but was now beginning to reconsider his opinion.

Jessica continued, "It's quite odd the more I think about it."

Whilst brushing a few strands of hair away from her face, Sam asked, "Why's that, Jess?"

"Well, you see, the science behind the heliocentric model suggests that we live in a pressurised environment surrounded by an infinite vacuum of Space. But the further I consider it, you can't have atmospheric pressure without the necessary antecedent of a solid physical barrier to seal an environment. Because according to the second law of thermodynamics, the gaseous pressure on Earth would be sucked into the vacuum of space. Which scientists presume the pressure gradient is something like: ten to the negative seventeen Torr; even at the lower regions of Space."

She elaborated, "And it can't be reasoned by gravity. As gravity is not a physical force and therefore cannot create a tangible physical barrier at the Kármán line. And they even say this pressurised contained atmosphere spins in lockstep with the rotation of the Earth. Purportedly, 1,037 miles per hour at the equator," as Max and Sam listened in awe at her extensive knowledge.

She justified, "To me, a dome, or a firmament, as the Bible refers to it, that shields us... well, it just makes sense. It seems as if this place was built for us. To protect us and to nurture us – with all the goodness we need."

She pointed skyward, "So it appears to me that we may live under the 'Thunderdome'!"

Sam turned toward Jessica after briefly taking the opportunity to view the distant horizon through a digital telescope that practically resembled a modern-day gaming console.

"Wow, Jessica! You're kind of tripping me out right now! But you know what, I have to agree with you: as our world does seem kind of perfect," blown away by her broad, intelligent, scientific, philosophical and theosophical wisdom of the world. Left somewhat short of words, and now more than ever grateful to have spontaneously build up the courage to randomly ask for her phone number – recognising that she was a one-in-a-million.

She said, "I'd hate to go all Biblical on you guys – you know, like a preacher; but from what I've learned to date, is that there are many passages that suggest the Earth is geocentric and flat with a dome-type structure encompassing us. And the more I think about it, the notion of a spherical Earth wouldn't have even been considered as a possibility when the first Gospels were chiselled in blue sapphire stone – said to be a symbolic reminder of the blue sky above."

Max nodded in agreement, "I hear you, Jessica. It's quite remarkable how the ancients would've even known about the possibility of a firmament thousands of years ago. Someone even shared a meme with me that suggested that there are over two hundred biblical passages that refer to a flat, enclosed, immovable Earth."

"Really, Max! That's amazing. I didn't realise there were that many," she replied.

"You know what I think?" Jessica rhetorically asked.

"What, Jessica?" replied Sam and Max – almost in unison.

"I think the truth will finally set us free," she replied.

"That's for sure, Jess."

"Too right," said Max in an elegant British accent.

Max enthusiastically clapped his hands and rubbed them together.

"Anyway, Let's get out of here. London is calling," where they proceeded to the elevator, warmly farewelling Ahmad along the way and thanking him for his kind hospitality.

"*I confess that I cannot imagine how any human being, in his proper senses, can believe that the Sun is stationary when, with his own eyes, he sees it revolving around the heavens, nor how he can believe that the earth, on which he stands, is whirling with the speed of lightning around the Sun, when he feels not the slightest motion.*"

DAVID WARDLAW SCOTT

20

The Gulfstream's 7,500 nautical mile range, fast refuelling capabilities, and her refined, luxurious, spacious interior configuration fit for either business, relaxation, or entertainment; were some of her best features.

Now back in the air flying high above the clouds, 'chasing the Sun' towards London, as they flew the final leg of their long journey; where Max was ecstatic to be soon again reunited with Zoe.

Max had numerous discussions about Flat Earth with Captain Andy. And although the conversation initially sparked a somewhat fiery debate, Andy eventually realised that the concept was not as ludicrous as it first appeared. Especially having witnessed a localised Sun and Moon simultaneously situated above the clouds at the opposite ends of the horizon. And after much deliberation – and confirming the position of the Sun using a Sun and Moon calculator – he ascertained viewing them both at the same time would be impossible on the heliocentric model.

Andy spent several years flying military aircraft, including F18-Hornets, in the No. 77 Squadron for the Royal Australian Airforce. However, despite being an expert in flight dynamics, he never considered the shape of the Earth during his entire career. Where, like most pilots, he just took it for granted that the Earth he was flying over was a sphere.

However, when Max asked Andy if pilots compensated for the curvature of the Earth during long-distance flights, Andy had a sudden epiphany that he'd never made an adjustment or correction for the assumed arc radius of the spherical planet. Either during flight simulation training or throughout the thousands of accumulated hours flying supersonic fighter jets in the armed forces.

And nor did he compensate for the Earth's curvature during his newly found career as a licensed commercial pilot. After some initial resistance on the subject, he acknowledged to Max that flying over a spherical surface would physically require constant vertical course correction by the pilot or the autopilot system to account for the sphericity of the Earth.

Upon further investigation, Andy's calculations affirmed that a pilot who is cruising at 800-kilometres per hour would have to pitch the aircraft's nose downward at a rate of approximately 850 metres every minute – or almost 20 metres per second to account for the terrestrial radius of the earth. Otherwise, an aeroplane maintaining a constant cruising altitude for one hour – without adjusting for an arc radius – would be climbing into the upper atmosphere, effectively flying up to the stratosphere, where the aircraft would be hypothetically travelling towards Space within several hours of flight.

But many pilots were now realising – after being introduced to the concept of a flat Earth – that they were flying thousands of miles, from continent to continent, without making corrections to account for the theoretical curvature of the Earth.

And in fact, it was to the contrary.

Because pilots are trained and instructed to maintain the orientation of an aircraft to fly perfectly level – once they reach their predesignated altitude – by using the altimeter, artificial horizon indicator, and attitude meter, which in turn are controlled by the aeroplanes gyroscope. Fundamentally guiding the aircraft in maintaining a relative position to a level horizon over a Flat Earth.

And some pilots were beginning to admit the glaringly obvious fact the Earth is flat, although somewhat reluctantly. Especially with the possibility that they may lose their jobs, or much worse – end up in a straitjacket for even suggesting such a crazy notion!

Furthermore, contrary to pilots accounting for curvature, pilots are trained to pitch the aircraft's nose slightly upward rather than downward to compensate for wind resistance flowing over and under the wings. Therefore, improving the aircraft's angle of attack, resulting in a smoother flight and significant fuel savings.

Andy also realised that the horizon is not only flat as far as the eye can see – even when flying at maximum cruising altitude, but the horizon always remains at eye level regardless of the elevation. Contrary to what one would expect to observe, as they ascend over a spherical surface, as the higher one climbs, it would fundamentally suggest that the horizon line should drop accordingly.

He also began observing long distances from the flight deck by using his military-issued high-powered binoculars. Instantly realising that the Earth curvature math was just not holding up to his observations. Because on a clear day with minimal haze and atmospheric distortion, he could frequently see many large cities from nearly 1,000 kilometres away.

Max and Sam joined the pilots in the flight deck.

"Hey guys, did you know that gyroscopes single-handedly debunk the globe Earth fairy-tale," said Andy. "As the aircraft's gyroscope proves that an aeroplane's orientation does not deviate once it's achieved altitude, and proof positive that an aeroplane travels over a level plane because, again, the gimbal on a spinning gyro never deviates."

Andy pointed to the onboard mechanical gyroscope. "You see, a gyroscope is designed to maintain rigidity in space. We zero it off at the airport. Then spin-it-up to find relative sea-level: or cage the device; and once we do that – there is no independent outside force, or inside acting force, that can affect it."

"That's fascinating, Andy. And if I've got this right: are you saying that the gyro will physically determine and indicate which way is up and down? Is that correct?" Sam queried.

"Yes. That's an affirmative, Sam," replied Andy. "And we'd have absolutely no chance of flying at night or within heavy cloud cover without it."

"We rely on it more than any other instrument, apart from the fuel gauge... of course. And the gyro never shows an axial tilt or deviation during flight, as one would expect if we were flying over a spherical surface."

Andy tapped the attitude indicator on the dashboard. "You

see, Sam, it's synced to this gauge right here, which accurately represents and indicates an artificial horizon. You know, the more I think about it: we'd be lost without it! Especially when we are banking left or right. Because you're spot-on, Sam, the artificial horizon accurately indicates and guides a pilot to which way is up – and which way is down."

"And to top it off, the gyroscope's gimbal never tilts when we fly into a new hemisphere. You see, if we were flying over a sphere, and let's say we began our journey at the equator, then by the time we got to the North Pole: it would mean the gyro would have a ninety-degree differential than its original position at the equator. However, that doesn't occur!"

He concluded, "A gyroscope cannot lie. It's as simple as that!"

"That's fascinating, Andy. So, therefore, can I assume that even gravity can't influence the gyroscope?"

"Yep, you've got it, Sam. The hocus-pocus of Gravity has no direct effect on any gyroscope. In fact, that's what I also believed, but the more I researched the primary function of the gyroscope, the more I realised that Max is not as crazy as I thought," he chuckled.

Max laughed then replied, "I hope you know... that I'm beyond crazy," mimicking a crazy face by widening his eyes and poking out his tongue.

"Hey, fellas – I've been telling James all about Flat Earth."

"James, why don't you tell the guys what you think about the subject."

"Well, for me, as a pilot – the biggest clue that gave it all away was landing an aircraft."

James clarified, "Because, if we had to land this plane on a runway that was moving with the rotation of the Earth, whilst we are flying in a different frame of reference to the Earth; then pilots would have to factor for many variables, including the orientation of the runway. And even worse, the current latitude on a spherical Earth, as the spin of the Earth supposedly differs considerably at various latitudes."

"For example, they say it's 1,666 kilometres per hour at the equator, and approximately 1,000 clicks per hour in Australia; and zero, at both the North and South Poles. So, you could just imagine how difficult that would be... right? It would be like trying to jump onto a moving walkway or a treadmill!"

"And not to mention that travelling westward – on a ball spinning eastward at 1,600 kilometres an hour, means you should reach your destination sooner. There is no way a plane can travel over 700 kilometres per hour, against a surface spinning at over twice that speed in the opposite direction, without compensating for it!"

"Hmm... fascinating, James. So, are you saying that doesn't happen?" asked Sam, to reconfirm what he just heard directly from the co-pilot.

"Yes, that's correct," he affirmed. "Pilots have far too much to consider while we prepare for landing. And a spinning Earth isn't one of them!"

"That makes perfect sense, James! Hey, I love the view from your office, by the way," as Sam soaked in the glorious panorama from the flight deck.

"Yeah... I have to admit that it's not too shabby at all," James chuckled. Now appreciating more than ever that his new career co-piloting a prestigious Gulfstream would never have happened – if his parents didn't randomly gift him with a 2-hour flying lesson in a Cessna over Melbourne. That sparked his interest to fly high above the clouds.

Sam smirked, "Not too shabby in the very slightest," nodding in agreement whilst observing the flight console, trying to make sense out of the intrinsic instruments – most of the data displayed on elaborately presented LCD screens.

Andy asked, "Max, have you seen that flight training document from NASA that affirms that pilots are trained to fly over a flat – non-rotating Earth?"

"Are you for real, Andy? No... I haven't seen it, by the way. Where did you find it, if you don't mind me asking?" the pitch in his voice elevating in excitement.

"Well, I went over some of my old flight training manuals, and I found a document from NASA that defines flight dynamics. The funny thing is that I now carry it with me to show other pilots," reaching into his leather folio to retrieve the document.

"Because it says right here that..."

"A linear aircraft model for a rigid aircraft of constant mass flying over a flat, nonrotating Earth is derived and defined. The derivation makes no assumptions of reference trajectory or vehicle symmetry. The linear system equations are derived and evaluated along a general trajectory and include both aircraft dynamics and observation variables."

Andy further explained, "It goes on-and-on – but the gist of it is that pilots aren't trained to fly around a spinning ball, and there are many other documents that support it. Some even from the Federal Aviation Administration."

"Awesome find, Andy. Because if a pilot was constantly adjusting the aircraft to follow the curve of the Earth... then, I'm pretty sure they would know it! Isn't that right?" Max postulated.

"Exactly, Max. You got it, pal! And the problem is compounded exponentially the faster a plane is travelling. So, therefore, a military jet cruising at over Mach 3 – like the Lockheed SR-71 Blackbird, with a top speed of over 3,500 kilometres per hour – well then, the pilot would have to factor for the curvature of the ground below, even more so."

"But, it's nonsense. No pilot has ever compensated for curvature; even though some I've debated with have claimed that the aircraft's auto-pilot and the magical force of gravity were doing it for them!"

"You're blowing my mind, Andy. In my opinion, that's proof positive right there!"

"Bloody oath it is, Max."

"And another document I have here that summarises flight dynamics coincidently mentions the words 'Flat Earth' in its concluding remarks, which also assumes a flat, non-rotating Earth."

"As well as that, we never experience a deflection based on the Coriolis effect, as one would expect if the Earth is spinning at a variable speed at the various latitudes – as James earlier explained."

James interjected, "Precisely, and we certainly don't fly sideways at the equator; or upside down in Australia. The very concept is rather ludicrous!" he smiled.

"Wow. That's mind-blowing to hear directly from a pilots mouth," remarked Sam. "Why hasn't anyone even thought of that before? It's ridiculous to believe that we are flying sideways on a ball right now! Because everything on the plane is still up – including us! And Max, your experiment with the glass of water proves it!"

"I think it does too, Sam. And you know what, mate? I'm just bloody excited that you agree."

"Yeah, I do agree, Max. I know I've been rather hard on you about it, but this spherical Earth is beginning to sound like crap the more I question it!"

"That's good to hear, Sam. And don't worry about it. It's all good."

"You know, I won't quite say that the Earth is flat at this stage, but for me, the ball-Earth concept is beginning to lose credibility – and rather fast!" he admitted, as much as he didn't want to.

Max ecstatically high-fived Sam, feeling elated that his friend was finally beginning to see the light—momentarily thinking back to the day when he first began to question the true nature of the world around him. A moment that most Flat Earthers could easily recollect.

James brought up to discuss the many other anomalies that he'd discovered during his research into the topic, briefly describing how the aircraft's aeronautical functions, including flight instruments, assume Euclidean planar principles – which for all intents and purposes, are designed to operate over a flat surface.

He also explained how air currents that flow within the jet stream also assist aircraft to gain speed and fuel efficiency. And the many emergency flights that were required to deviate to the nearest hospital made far more sense based on the azimuthal equi-distant map or what many were beginning to refer to as *the Flat Earth map.*

"Hey, Andy, did you know that the word horizon is derived from horizontal, which means flat and level? It's why they call it *horizon* and not *curvizon*," Max joked.

Andy laughed, "Well, she looks pretty flat to me," gesturing to the level horizon before them.

"Also, it's called an *aeroplane* for a reason – it's not an *aero-curve*," Max cheekily smirked, thinking that Flat Earther's had all the best jokes.

Andy chuckled, "Good one, Max," reluctantly laughing at his corny joke.

Max was on a roll: "And you'll never hear this from a pilot. *'Attention all passengers. This is your Captain speaking. Please fasten your seatbelts. We're about to fly upside down to Australia'!*" as he mimicked speaking on a microphone.

But Andy had enough of Max's corny jokes.

Shaking his head whilst smiling, he kicked them out from the cabin to prepare for the descent to their final destination.

London's, Heathrow International Airport.

21

Captain Andy descended the plane smoothly through the dark clouds hovering over London for landing.

"Minutes later, the aircraft's wheels safely touched the tarmac at Heathrow Airport just after 10 am, where two vehicles awaited to transport the passengers.

"I'll catch you later tonight, guys. I'm heading off to a meeting. Make yourselves comfortable at the apartment. It's all on my tab. Don't be shy."

"Oh, I almost forgot to tell you. If you're up for it – we're meeting up for Zoe's farewell dinner. Make sure you wear your finest threads, as I hear it's quite snazzy. I'll text you the details."

"Thank you so much, Max. You are too kind. It's been a trip of a lifetime so far, and I can't wait to meet Zoe. She sounds amazing," said Jessica, hugging him warmly.

Sam and Jessica arrived at the luxury apartment located on the Embankment in Chelsea, which offered a spectacular view of the River Thames being drizzled upon by light rain. After checking in and without wasting any time, they showered, changed their attire, and went sightseeing for the day – both keen to see some of London's famous architecture and attractions.

Max had the entire afternoon to his leisure. As Zoe would not be available until 6 pm, where they were to meet with her friends and colleagues for cocktails at her farewell party – at a ritzy new bar in the heart of London.

Although Max's primary reason to visit London was for Zoe, he had an ulterior motive; and arranged a meeting with one of the leading professors at Cambridge University – and a colleague of his close friend Edward – to witness a Foucault pendulum operating firsthand.

Designed and constructed by Léon Foucault in 1851, the Foucault pendulum was touted as the first practical device to demonstrate Earth's rotation – and thus "proved" the Copernican heliocentric model to the weary masses. During the era where many could hardly even write their names, let alone comprehend the complexities of the Copernicus cosmological model of the Universe.

Max reached out to shake his hand. "It's an absolute pleasure to meet you, Professor Crowe. Thank you for taking the time to meet me today."

"Likewise, Max. Welcome to the prestigious Cambridge University. Edward has told me all about you and the very reason for your visit today."

"May I just begin by saying that I find the topic of discussion rather intriguing!"

"It sure is intriguing, Professor."

"By the way, Edward sends his best regards. He's told me all about his days studying with you at Cambridge. He wants to know: can you still guzzle a pint of Guinness in under seven seconds?"

"Ah, yes. Those were the good old days, Max. It feels like a lifetime ago. But no, I think it's more like seventeen seconds, these days," laughing while guiding his guest through the elaborate halls graced with paintings of some of the brightest minds to attend the University since founded in 1209.

"Allow me to present the contraption, Max. This is the Foucault pendulum," he pointed, as they entered the large exhibition area showcasing the device.

"What a fascinating mechanism, Professor Crowe. I've seen the pendulum demonstrated online – but I've never had the privilege to see one operate firsthand."

"Please... just call me Richard. Allow me to demonstrate."

"By the way, can I just make an admission before we begin, Max?"

"Yes, of course. Please do, Prof... I mean, Richard. Go for it!"

"Well, you know – I've been a professor at this University for over twenty years. And during that time, I have educated countless students, with many even graduating to be professors at leading universities around the world," as a group of young female students admiringly giggled at Professor Crowe's charming looks – as they walked past holding their study books.

"Yes, I've heard a lot about you, Richard. Thank you for taking the time to meet with me today. Edward highly recommended that I see you whilst I'm in London."

"Well, I'm rather glad that he did, Max."

"You see... until Edward called to explain the reason for your visit, I'd never actually put critical thought into the device or questioned it using the scientific method, for that matter. I almost feel like I've been duped," as he released the pendulum to swing it in motion.

"Don't be so hard on yourself, Richard. Edward also feels like he was kind of duped too," as they quietly watched the pendulum sway.

"The thing is, Max, I soon concluded that if the Coriolis effect is responsible for the pendulum's bob to shift orientation gradually – or to arc, whilst swaying back and forth: then the Coriolis force should influence other apparatus; including aircraft, for example."

"Certainly, Richard. That was also my conclusion – after watching numerous demonstrations online. And shouldn't wrecking balls around the world be hazardously swinging right now if the Coriolis effect was fact?" he joked.

The professor chuckled, then elaborated, "Anyway, Max, since looking into the device sceptically, and after extensive investigation: I discovered that the contraption essentially has a built-in electromagnetic component and even a motor, to keep the bob swinging."

"And a quick online search will confirm that Coriolis is only a fictitious force; there's nothing real about it at all! It's smoke and mirrors at best! However, I didn't realise that was the case until Edward called me, and we had a lengthy two-hour discussion about the apparatus. And that's when I became aware that the gadget was just pure tom-foolery!"

Max respectfully listened to the professor.

"You see, they say because the Foucault pendulum is in a second reference frame to Earth – that is, detached from Earth's surface – it demonstrates an apparent drift and deviation over a duration of time, and it's due to the Earth rotating underneath the pendulum."

He elaborated, "It's a rather ingenious device, Max; however, I started to ask myself that if that was the case, then why aren't aeroplanes, helicopters, hot-air balloons, or artillery bullets affected by the Coriolis effect? Which, by de facto, would also be in a second reference frame to Earth?"

"Indeed. I share the same sentiment, Richard. And I concur with your conclusion," replied Max, attempting to sound intelligent and sophisticated.

"Max, in science – we call the experiment: affirming the consequent. And it's a logical fallacy in which the premise is assumed to be true without warrant and where the experimental outcome is taken for granted."

The professor explained, "It means that just because a certain phenomenon exists – in this case, the pendulum swings and arc's over a period of time – that its effect correlates to the rotation of the Earth, and this assertion is a fallacy. Especially if one hasn't hypothesised all possibilities from the onset. And, of course, the end result can only lead to experimental failure, or even worse... confirmation bias. Or worse again... intentional deception. And quite often, scientific experiments are skewed to support one's beliefs. Scientists have been caught out on this many times before."

"Yes, I've found that people do like to cling to their beliefs. Almost religiously, one could say," replied Max.

"They certainly do, Max. And did you know that the pendulum produces anomalous behaviour during eclipses, described as the Allais Effect?" asked Richard, shaking his head. Disappointed that he'd failed to see the anomaly, considering the evidence was almost smack-bang in front of his face.

"No. I didn't know that, Richard. That's rather fascinating. And, the more I think of it, it appears to me that we may live in an electromagnetic universe."

"It surely does appear that way; the evidence is becoming abundant. And through comprehensive inquiry, I've concluded that there is not one single experiment that can detect the Earth's motion – that is, without bias. It's as if it's non-existent. Just as the physicist Henri Poincaré and many others have proclaimed."

"Zero motion and zero curvature. That's what I've discovered, Richard. I've conducted many hours of study into the topic, with the original intent to debunk Flat Earth. However, the only motion and movement I have been able to detect is the growing Flat Earth movement," joking with his newly acquainted friend.

"The movement does seem to be gaining popularity and momentum, Max. And from what I've seen to date, it is growing exponentially," slowly nodding his head in deep thought, whilst guiding Max to the hallway as the pendulum continued to swing.

22

Max was preparing to leave the University, having spent most of the early hours of the afternoon with Richard, when they stumbled across Professor Titus. A hard-core professor, well known within the campus for his stubborn, authoritative demeanour.

"Professor Titus, I'd like to introduce you to Max Carter. Max is visiting us from Australia today, and I've just demonstrated the Foucault Pendulum."

"Good afternoon, Mr Carter. It's a pleasure to meet you. What did you think of the apparatus?" shaking Max's hand.

"It's a pleasure to meet you too, Professor Titus. Well, in all honesty, as impressive as it is, I'm not quite sure we can assert that it proves the rotation of the Earth."

"Excuse me! What are you implying, Mr Carter?" crossing his arms, somewhat displaced and patently triggered by the accusation.

"Well, Professor – I've conducted many hours of research on the Foucault pendulum, including the Coriolis effect: and it seems to me that although Leon Foucault discovered some great inventions – like the gyroscope. I'm not at all convinced that there is a direct correlation through cause and relation between a pendulum swinging and the rotation of the Earth."

"Mr Carter! This University is one of the oldest and finest in the world, and we certainly don't conduct magic tricks around here! And let me just tell you, young man, that Foucault discovered this amazing contraption in 1851 and has since conclusively demonstrated the Coriolis effect, irrespective of your eccentric commentary," the Professor replied, who was peeved by Max's audacity to question established science.

"I do apologise, Professor. Please don't be offended by my critique. As I said, it's a very impressive device. However, I just don't believe it proves Earth's rotation. As I hope you know, I've learned that even it uses an electromagnetic device to assist its motion and needs to be carefully configured according to its latitude. Therefore, the crux of it is that the pendulum's motion is influenced by other forces and not the cause of the alleged rotation."

"That's preposterous!" he angrily charged back.

"Foucault's pendulum definitively proves the rotation, and it has proven so beyond a shadow of a doubt for almost two centuries. I hope your research wasn't from a collection of YouTube videos and memes, Mr Carter!" the professor ridiculed.

"I respectfully disagree with you, Professor. You see, more modern-day experiments including the Michelson-Gale and Michelson-Morley experiments suggest the Earth is not in motion; and quite to the contrary – is motionless, just as it appears."

The professor begrudgingly listened.

"Because, their experiments failed to detect any of the four opposing velocities of Earth's motion and suggested that it is the aether and the celestial objects in the sky – or the celestial sphere – that evidently orbit the Earth instead."

Max turned and gestured toward the pendulum. "Regardless of what that antiquated device suggests."

"And the astronomer, George Airy, also failed to detect the rotation of the Earth? Hence why they called the experiment, Airy's Failure! It gets worse, Professor, as the Sagnac experiment completely obliterated Einstein's theory of relativity and also proved the existence of the aether."

Max reiterated, "Every single experiment that set out to substantiate the heliocentric model subsequently proved the opposite: that the Earth is stationary!"

"Hmm," the Professor murmured, his awkwardness evident to all present.

"And, Professor Titus, may I remind you that all of these experiments were conducted well before YouTube was founded. And prior to the birth of the internet, for that matter. So please don't patronise me with your condescending, snide remarks!" Max confidently smiled.

The professor rebutted, "Who are these people you speak of? We don't use unsubstantiated claims around here, Mr Carter!"

"That's very convenient, Professor! But I hope you know that countless physicists conceded their findings were correct. And that is, that the Earth is motionless with an aetherial sky orbiting us. As opposed to the Earth spinning and ballistically corkscrewing through the Universe! And even your high-prized Einstein said, *'I have come to believe that the motion of the Earth cannot be detected by any optical experiment'.*"

"Oh, I see what we have here! It appears to me that we have a conspiracy theorist and a science contrarian amongst us."

Titus continued, "Let me just say, Mr Carter, we disapprove of your kind around here. I didn't realise that you Australian's were so paranoid! If you are so confident that you can prove that the Earth does not rotate on its axis, why don't you partake in our astrophysics course? I would love to see how long you would last!"

"I would not dare to waste my time, nor money!" Max replied.

"By the way, Professor... I don't care if you call me a conspiracy theorist. Because the fact remains that you have failed to provide sufficient evidence to verify that the Foucault pendulum demonstrably proves Earth's rotation."

"And may I just add – that concerns me, Professor. Furthermore, it seems that you have an issue with me questioning science!"

"Yes, I do have an issue with you refuting established science, Mr Carter! We've proven the shape of the Earth – and it was millennia ago. The science is settled. Our Earth is spherical. And it rotates on its axis, regardless of your archaic beliefs!"

"Whatever you say, Professor," signalling quotation marks with his fingers after the word professor.

Professor Titus was not impressed, and the redness of his grumpy face suggested he was ready to explode; but by this stage – Max didn't care, as he stridently ranted on.

"You know what, Mr Titus? Most people may speculate that the discussion about the shape of the Earth is solved and settled. But I beg to differ! And there are now hundreds of millions of people around the world, who are also questioning science. And we're growing in numbers exponentially beyond your wildest dreams – or should I say... your worst bloody nightmare!"

"That's just bollox!" the Professor angrily replied.

"Call it what you want, Professor. But let me remind you again that there's not one single experiment that empirically proves that we live on a spinning ball. And you're just going to have to deal with it!" Max replied, staring at him firmly eye-to-eye.

"Mr Carter! We've had some of the smartest minds of all time who have attended this University. And I find it highly disrespectful that you are questioning the likes of Issac Newton and our beloved and recently departed Professor Stephen Hawking," the professor now rattled by his encounter with Max.

"That's quite a pitiful response, Professor, if I may say so!"

"Because, although you have condemned me for questioning science, you have failed to provide substantiated proof that the Earth is spinning! All I hear from you is presuppositions. And your appeal to consensus and authority by standing on the shoulders of theorists – will never prove that the Earth is a spinning ball!"

"Maybe you didn't hear me, Mr Carter! We do have all the answers, but you, Sir, are just too stubborn to accept them... for some strange reason!"

He pointed his finger toward Max's chest and said, "Here's my advice to you the next time you visit, please be sure to wear your tin-foil hat, Mr Carter!" his face now reddened with anger.

Max was just about ready to knock his block off but resisted, and instead took a deep breath and replied with cool, calm logic.

Well. Kind of.

"You seem rather triggered, Professor. Is something wrong?" he teased; where Max could tell by his demeanour that he should have retired many years ago, but probably preferred to year-after-year torment the young indoctrinated students at the university.

Professor Titus was beyond angry; his voice was shaky, and Max knew the ad-hominem attack was coming.

"We have a grand-old saying that we use around here when people like you question established science. Up yours, Mr Carter!" said the grumpy old professor whilst storming away.

"Right back at you, Professor 'Tight-Arse'!" as Max gestured by placing the cup of his palm over his forearm – indicating where his grandfather would hang his umbrella – as the sound of his voice echoed throughout the hallway.

Composing himself, he said, "Thank you for your time today, Richard. It was great to spend the afternoon with you. And may I sincerely apologise for my heated conversation with Professor Titus? It was most unprofessional of me. I feel quite embarrassed about it, I must say!"

"It's quite alright, Max. Don't worry about him. He's just a grumpy-old stubborn prick! And to be quite frank about it, I loved seeing you get in his face! It was an absolute gem to watch. It was my pleasure," he chuckled.

"And Max, there are many people just like him within this institution. So, it's good to see them get rattled in their cage once in a while. You just keep doing what you're doing," amazed at how ballsy Max presented himself to one of the most highly esteemed professors at Cambridge University.

"Thanks, Richard. I appreciate your kind words," shaking his hand, once again apologising for his outburst.

"Oh, I almost forgot. Edward tells me that you're planning a mission to find more land on Earth. Let me just say, Max, that although you Aussies struggle to beat us in cricket lately, you sure do have some big-balls!" he chuckled.

Max laughed, "Hey, I'm not sure about that, but I'll tell you what... I feel that something has inspired me to help change this world for the better. And I just want to help people realise the truth about where they live! The more I think about it; I'm sure my parents would have appreciated it too."

"That's very philosophical of you, Max. I've also lost my parents. And I wish they could see me now. I feel kind of lost without them."

"I completely understand, Richard," Max compassionately replied, as he looked away attempting not to shed a tear – wishing he could share his success with his parents and that he'd spent more time with them. Rather than devoting most of his days crunching code relentlessly on his computer – for years on end.

Toughening himself up, "To be honest, Richard. I don't care if the Earth is flat or if it's a spinning ball. But for some reason, I feel compelled that it's my duty to prove it either way."

"Again, I love your philosophical approach to the topic, Max. I believe science and philosophy – kind of go hand-in-hand. And never in my life have I felt so enlightened after discovering the possibility that the Earth may be flat and motionless, just as my natural senses suggest—and as the good book states."

"Don't tell anyone around here, Max, but just like you, I'm strongly leaning towards the idea that we don't live on a spinning ball," Richard confessed.

"It's an enlightening feeling to find the truth, Richard. That's why I'm so committed to spreading the message."

"Yes, indeed... it sure is. Anyway, thanks for visiting, Max. It's been an absolute pleasure meeting you. But I must leave, as I have a lecture to attend at 3 o'clock, and I can't keep my students waiting!"

Shaking his hand, "Yeah, I better get out of here too, Richard. As I have a function to attend in London at 6 pm," leaving with an invitation for the professor to visit him 'down-under' in Australia as they went their separate ways.

23

The black taxi battled the bustling London traffic – attempting to cross one of the busiest cities in the world, during the busiest time of the week, on a Friday afternoon.

Max's driver endeavoured to take a shortcut and was stopped by an attractive female traffic controller holding up a road sign, safeguarding random roadworks that were inconveniently blocking half of the street.

"Oh, bugger! They always choose the worst time of day to work on these damn roads. Sorry, Sir – it looks like there's going to be a slight delay," said the courteous taxi driver.

"That's quite okay. I'll get out right here. I believe I'm only a few blocks away from my destination."

"No problem, Sir. That'll be £142.75. Will you be paying by cash or by card?"

"By card... thanks, mate. Make it an even £200, will you?" as Max tapped his credit card on the electronic reader.

Jumping out of the cab, Max rushed down Rennie Street, realising he was running late to meet Zoe at her farewell cocktail party, when his phone rang.

"Hey, honey. Are you far?" asked Zoe.

"I'm just around the corner, sweetie. I'll be there in a jiffy," hanging up on the call and walking briskly under the drizzle, when his phone rang again – Max immediately recognising the United States dial code.

Answering the call. "Hello – this is Max."

"Hey, Max. It's Jeremy from Aurora Flight Sciences in Virginia."

"G'day, Jeremy. Hope all is well, mate."

"I'm doing great, Max. Thanks for asking."

"My apologies, Jeremy, but I really can't talk right now. I'm in London at the moment, and I'm running late for an appointment."

"I'll only be a minute, Max. I just thought I'd drop you a quick call to advise that your application is on track. We should have an answer for you next week; or the week after, at the very latest. But, it's all looking good so far."

"That's great news, Jeremy. Thanks for the call. I'll buzz you back over the next few days. Is next Tuesday or Wednesday okay with you?"

"Sure thing, Max. You take care of yourself," as Max punched the air in excitement – after hanging up on the call.

Arriving late at the Lyaness Bar – a new fancy venue that overlooked the River Thames – he quickly tidied himself up in the men's room by flipping up the nozzle of the hand dryer to dry his hair, and after making himself presentable, Max proceeded to the main lounge.

Dashing towards him with open arms the moment she saw him, they embraced as Zoe grabbed his face, kissing him passionately for what seemed like an eternity.

"Max, you're late!" she pulled away, blushing by the cheer of her colleagues who were applauding—happy to witness the charismatic couple once again reunited.

"Sorry, I'm late, Zoe. I had last-minute business to take care of. But... I'm here now, so let's grab a cocktail," guiding her over to the long, glamorous bar.

He gazed into her eyes and said, "You look gorgeous, my darling," embracing her waist. Astounded by the fact that she looked younger – every time he saw her.

"I've missed you so much, my honey bear. But what happened to you? Where's your tie? And your dinner jacket?" she asked.

"Well, it's a rather funny story, Zoe. You see, I had a meeting at Cambridge University today with a really smart professors, and the day just went so fast – that I didn't get a chance to change my attire."

"What the heck were you doing at Cambridge, Max? Actually... just forget I asked. I don't even want to know!" raising her hand as if to display a stop sign.

"That works better for me too, Sweetie," he cheekily quipped, showing his most innocent smile.

"Let's dance, Babe," and without a further word, Max gently grasped her arm leading her toward the empty dance floor; where they began to groovily jive away to the sound of the Bee Gee's, *"More Than a Woman"*—where the DJ cranked up the sound after seeing the gorgeous couple take centre stage.

She laughed with vigour as they rocked away in sync – Zoe instantly reminded of his crazy spontaneous antics.

Zoe often wondered why she left Max to pursue her ambitious career in the first place. Now more than convinced that the corporate world was overrated; and often fuelled by narcissistic, psychopathic egos.

But more importantly, being in her mid-thirties, Zoe also realised that her internal body clock was quickly ticking away and was now ready to give up her corporate ambitions to settle down with Max.

Zoe was tipsy, having consumed more champagne than usual, and after a long night partying with her colleagues and with her beloved Max by her side, she was ready to go home.

The ride in the Uber was a rather embarrassing moment for the driver, as the reunited couple snuggled and kissed all the way back to her apartment.

Where Max was just hoping to finally get a glimpse of those little red-knickers.

24

Weeks after returning to Melbourne from his weekend get-away to London with Max and Jessica, Sam was beginning to see the world around him from a new perspective.

Despite his initial resistance to the possibility of a Flat Earth just months prior, it was becoming apparent to Sam that he was not standing upside down and flying through Space on an oblate spheroid—as he once blindly believed.

Where it was now more than evident to him that the Sun passes overhead just as it appears; rather than our Earth spinning in an eastwardly direction to create day and night. And following extensive research looking for answers, Sam could not find any reproducible experiments or tangible evidence that demonstrably proves that water can bond to the exterior of a pressurised ball – that's zipping through an infinite vacuum of Space.

Although he was still finding it challenging to comprehend the motives behind the grand deception, Sam was shocked to see that even a past President of the United States, Barack Obama, mentioned Flat Earth during several climate change speeches. Denouncing Flat Earth as a crazy conspiracy theory, raising laughter from the crowd when in 2016, he said: "*We don't have time for a meeting with the Flat Earth Society.*"

The comment intrigued Sam.

As a matter of fact, Obama referenced the '*Flat Earth Society*' during multiple public speeches, as did numerous politicians; and after researching the FES website, Sam was immediately suspicious of their misinformation and disinformation tactics.

The reason being was the Flat Earth Society were asserting the preposterous notion that our Earth is a flat disc flying through Space, and the upward acceleration of the "flying disc" accounted for the gravitational constant of 9.8 m/s^2.

After considering such utter nonsense, Sam thought, "What is this crap?" Because he had never heard a Flat Earther who believed or even mentioned such a wildly ridiculous claim. Swiftly realising the FES was just a propaganda based group using misinformation and disinformation techniques; established to discredit the Flat Earth movement as a form of damage control. Whereby, it's blatantly obvious to anyone that trusts their natural senses that they are not accelerating upwards, as per the preposterous claim made by the Flat Earth Society.

He surfed the internet relentlessly for hours on end, corroborating claims from both globe Earth defenders and Flat Earthers. Where Sam then stumbled across a video of Wernher Von Braun, a German born American aerospace engineer who later became a space architect for NASA. Spearheading the Apollo moon missions after John F. Kennedy announced in 1961, the ambitious goal for the United States of America to land a man on the Moon by the end of the decade.

Following World War II, Wernher was smuggled into America in 1945 under a clandestine operation coined as "Operation Paperclip" that spanned the 1940s and 50s – where 1,600 Nazi engineers, chemists, technicians; together with over 100 rocket scientists covertly migrated to the United States and beyond. Many associated with developing Wernher von Braun's brainchild: the V-2 ballistic missile. Where most became American citizens; often given new identities to conceal their horrendous past.

However, it was the numerals of a Biblical Psalm engraved onto the headstone of Wernher Von Braun's gravesite that now caught Sam's attention.

Locating the Bible that Jessica had gifted him, he looked up the verse, and the exact Psalm was right before his eyes:

'The heavens declare the glory of God; and the firmament sheweth his handywork' ~ Psalms 19:1.

Again, his conspiratorial and sceptical mind went into over-drive as he wondered why the head of NASA would refer to the "firmament" on his gravestone? Because this is the guy that was supposed to have been responsible for getting people into Space!

Sam couldn't help but to constantly wonder about the mo-tives to hide the shape of the Earth. Now suspiciously pondering whether the Space programs were implemented to hide the true nature of our reality. A fixed enclosed system built by a creator '*just for us*', as Jessica had mentioned weeks earlier.

Stubborn from the very get-go about the concept of a Flat Earth, the possibility that a Creator could be watching over us was Sam's biggest resistance. But he now pondered that if our Earth is in a favoured position in the Universe, then it widely implies that everything was designed and created for a purpose. And, by default, creation requires a creator. Since nothing with such grand precision could be created by cause of a cosmic accident billion of years ago. So, he was now beginning to realise that he may have been wrong about the possibility of a grand Creator too.

However, Sam had to admit that when he heard that Flat Earthers were also questioning the theory of gravity and suggest-ing that the theory is not what we have been told: he thought that these people had lost their friggin minds!

With that in mind, just to recap the list of conspiracies: Flat Earthers were not only saying that the Earth is flat and motionless. But they were also suggesting that Governments and international Space agencies were collaborating to fabricate a false reality of our Earth as part of the deception. And now, strangely enough, claim-ing that the theory of gravity is bogus!

It was getting absolutely bizarre!

But truth be told, Sam always had a problem with the scientific explanation for gravity, even as a child. And still recalls his teacher demonstrating gravity by spinning a bucket of water in a circular motion in front of the classroom. Now blatantly apparent to him that it was, in fact, the combined effects of surface tension and centrifugal and centripetal force that contained the water in the bucket, and not the force of gravity!

Sam was beginning to understand that the theory of gravity was often whimsically used to explain several phenomena. Frequently exploited as the "go-to" reason people refer to in the aim of justifying that they live on a spinning ball hurtling through Space.

He found that sometimes gravity is a force that pulls, and sometimes it pushes. Sometimes, it makes objects stick within a geo-synchronous orbit. And other times, it allows things to magically float, like clouds, dust particles, and mist that floats wardly on a wintery night – shunning the powerful force of gravity.

However, most people could not attempt to explain why things fall, let alone explain the complex fundamentals behind the theory of gravity. And in an attempt to prove gravity, many people often simply pick up and drop their keys, with some angrily and unwisely dropping their smartphones on a table and saying, "There you go!" as they check their phone for damage.

If pressed on the matter, on which type of gravity, whether Newtonian or Einsteinian: most people express a look of total bewilderment.

Because, the theory of gravity is exhaustively exploited to rationalise many physical phenomena, not only used to justify natural phenomena here on Earth, but to also theorise the laws of attraction of the celestial objects orbiting above.

In its most basic definition: the theory of gravity – as defined by Newtonian physics – is used to substantiate why things fall downward toward the Earth's magnetic core at 9.8 m/s^2 by way of mass attracted to mass—furthermore utilised to explain how the Moon is synchronously locked into orbit with our Earth, whilst also suggesting that the Moon's gravity influences worldwide tidal motions on a daily basis. But as a keen fishing enthusiast, Sam soon interestingly realised that the tides didn't correlate to the Moon's orbit. Where it is frequently noted that two high tides per day are consistently measured in many places around the world. But the Moon only passes once per day.

Additionally, Newtonian gravity is used to substantiate the reason why our Earth is synchronously gripped in a perfect "goldilocks" like orbit around the Sun, as the Sun careers through the

Universe at millions of kilometres per hour—spinning perpetually for the last 4.5 billion years. Whilst miraculously containing Earth's gaseous atmosphere from escaping into outer Space; ultimately defying Newton's second law of thermodynamics.

Then, there's the gravity that attracts millions of tonnes of water to Earth's surface in the form of expansive oceans, and enables container ships to magically cling to the underside of the Earth while traversing these oceans. Also permitting aeroplanes to fly upside-down, unbeknown to the passengers; shunning their God-given natural senses. But Andy already explained to Sam that a plane flying upside-down – justified by gravity – is absurd.

And the same universal explanation for gravity is also used to justify why people supposedly standing upside down, or down under, in the Southern Hemisphere – whether in Australia, Argentina or Africa – somehow don't feel the antipodal effect.

Where again, the theory of gravity irrationally substantiates the conundrum using a mathematical equation that most people pretend to understand in an attempt to appear sophisticated – or to just "go with the flow". In a day and age, where "double-thinking" and questioning authority, especially science, is practically considered a thought crime.

But it gets worse, given that the theory of gravity is also said to cancel out or counteract notable physical forces, such as centrifugal force and centripetal force.

And at a more complex level, it also applied to explain and rationalise how our Universe was fashioned in all its manifestations; with advanced gravitational theories presupposing the origins of the Universe and all of its galaxies via the Big Bang Theory.

In Sam's opinion, the author of 'The Atlantean Conspiracy', Eric Dubay, questions it best:

> *"Now, even if gravity did exist, why would it cause both planets to orbit the Sun, and people to stick to Earth? Gravity should either cause people to float in suspended circular orbits around the earth, or it should*

cause the earth to be pulled into the Sun. What sort of magic is 'gravity', that it can super glue people's feet to a ball-Earth, while causing Earth itself to revolve ellipses around the Sun? The two different effects are very different, yet the same cause is attributed to both."

It was becoming apparent to Sam that the Copernican model required the theory of gravity by default. Ingeniously devised to desperately rationalise how a human can live on a sphere that spins without knowing it.

The point being, without the concept of gravity, no one would have accepted the notion that they live on a spinning ball. And probably the very reason why it was masterminded in the first place. Vital in justifying the heliocentric "sun-worshipping" model by using mathematical garb to bewilder the human mind, rather than disclose the true objective nature of reality.

And what about Isaac Newton and Albert Einstein – what was in it for them? Well, they were just obeying ancient Kabbalistic teachings as per the writings of their mystical master, Hermes Trismegistus. With his "as above, so below" philosophical teachings.

So, it's no wonder why they thought that just because planets appear spherical – that our Earth must be spherical too! The very notion: as ridiculous as suggesting that just because a light globe on a ceiling is spherical, the floor must be spherical too!

But most importantly Sam realised, that if there is no observable radius to our Earth, then the formula for gravity needs to be reconsidered. Where the formula necessitates for Earth to have a measurable radius, and therefore, it would have a direct consequence to the "experiment" conducted by Henry Cavendish in the 1800s to measure the assumed gravitational constant. By default, his backyard experiment was flawed and based on false assumptions; presupposing and relying on the Earth to have measurable curvature (or arc radius) as defined by Eratosthenes' observations. However, just like others, who had been looking for many years, Sam was yet to find axiomatic proof of any curvature to the Earth – whatsoever!

He wondered, can antiquated experiments that rely on false positives to verify a bias presupposition genuinely be accepted as definitive reasoning to why objects fall?

And, is the downward force which we refer to as gravity – even a force? Or, could gravity, in its simplest explanation, be referred to as weight – as per its Latin origins: gravitas?

Or is it a 'way of order'? And the 'way' must return everything to a final resting point, where it will seek equilibrium. In the same manner and natural effect that an inflated balloon submerged underwater, when released, will rise to seek equilibrium at waters level through the natural law of buoyancy – as defined by Archimedes' principle; the physically observed laws of density and buoyancy.

So, what makes things fall and accelerate downward – if it's not the pulling force of gravity that we've all been taught to believe?

Well, simply because it must! It's the way down! Abiding by and respecting the natural laws of density, buoyancy, and equilibrium—together with electromagnetic and electrostatic forces.

And one could argue with the solid conviction, that the lift of an object enacts the downward motion. The "down" is just the way the object moves to seek stillness once again, where it will then rest unconditionally, or at equilibrium; unless enacted by another force.

It seemed to Sam that people were bamboozled into accepting the theory of gravity as fact through faith rather than empirical evidence. And he felt that the theory of gravity was the "wrapping paper" for the globe Earth lie; since it wraps all of the answers to the Cosmos and beyond into a singular theory that magically explains everything.

He then remembered one of his favourite songs by one of his favourite rappers, as he rapped the lyrics, *"Snap back to reality, oh' there goes gravity,"* as Eminem famously rhymed.

After extensive investigation on the topic and much deliberation, in Sam's opinion, gravity was officially sacked for not pulling its weight!

"*Most people in England have either read, or heard, that Sir Isaac Newton's theory of gravitation was originated by his seeing an apple fall to the earth from a tree in his garden. Persons gifted with ordinary common sense would say that the apple fell down to the earth because, bulk for bulk, it was heavier than the surrounding air; but if, instead of the apple, a fluffy feather had been detached from the tree, a breeze would probably have sent the feather floating away, and the feather would not reach the earth until the surrounding air became so still that, by virtue of its own density, the feather would fall to the ground.*"

LADY BLOUNT, "CLARION'S SCIENCE VERSUS GOD'S TRUTH"

25

Max was restless. Once again struggling to get a good night's sleep.

The constant niggling in his mind that there could be hidden land on Earth now consumed his thoughts almost day and night. And waiting for approval for the Odysseus Pseudo-Satellite was building a level of anxiety that he'd never experienced before.

Softly kissing her forehead, he gently slipped out of bed so he wouldn't disturb Zoe from her deep sleep, who was still trying to acclimatize to Melbourne's time zone after such a long period away from home.

Max was back at his computer.

The dim glow of light from his monitor and the moonlight shining through the floor-to-ceiling windows, softly lit the room; where he tapped away on the keyboard looking for new topics to research, deciding to search Google for long-distant photography.

Unbeknown to him at the time, he was about to present new arsenal for the Flat Earth community with further ammunition to prove the Earth was flat. And it was via a single photo that he found on the 'Beyond Horizons' website.

The photo, snapped by a professional photographer on a clear day, thanks to exceptional weather conditions and the skill of the photographer, Marc Bret: clearly showed the mountain ranges of Pic de Finestrelles to Pic Gaspard in France (the French word Pic, meaning peak), and at over 440 kilometres, or 273 miles, holds the current Guinness World Record for a long-distant landscape photo.

Max inputted the data – including the distance and elevation of the mountains – into an Earth curvature calculator. And after considering all factors, he realised there should've been approximately 8 kilometres of hidden curvature, with the mountain peaks expected to be obscured by the downward curvature of the ter-rain over that vast distance.

However, if it was one thing that Max had learned to date: was discernment. And to never trust just one source for his research.

Opening another tab in his already overly clustered browser – in an attempt to verify the calculations, Max received varied results from another website. Swiftly realising that their calculator was flawed and suspiciously manipulated by using a 'standard' refractive index within the formula. However, everyone knows that there is nothing standard about our anisotropic atmosphere, where the atmos can be influenced by various environmental factors: including temperature gradients; humidity; dust; haze; the topography of the terrain—together with many other variables.

Even so, and not surprisingly, the Earth was once again mysteriously missing the expected curvature over that distance. And attempting to verify the math using multiple Earth curvature calculators, founded on the principle of Pythagoras theorem for spherical trigonometry, and based on the premise that our Earth has an equatorial circumference of approximately 40,075 kilometres, with an assumed radius of 6,300 kilometres: presented Max with similar results.

Max surmised and concluded by using common sense and logic: No curve. No ball. It couldn't be simpler than that!

He couldn't help but wonder if humanity would have ever delved so deep into nonsensical pseudoscientific theories if – over the centuries – women had more say in the field of natural science. The point being, not many women would put up with such obvious malarkey. Where it is evident that eccentric masculine egos have dominated science and astrophysics for many centuries, and at a level where an entrusted humanity would ever in the wildest dreams expect to be deceived at such a grand scale.

However, if Hypatia of Alexandria taught women anything during the early days of astronomy, after she was publicly skinned alive with sharpened seashells for simply offering her hypothesis, was that the subject was to be dominated by "wise" old men with long-grey beards.

Although Max was somewhat of a closet Flat Earth researcher – still unwilling to publicly admit he was a Flat Earther, he shared the long-distant photos and subsequent website on a social media group dedicated to the Flat Earth community.

And within several minutes, was pleased that others were not only sharing the long-distant photos; but a member of the group contacted Max to inform him that he would be using the evidence during a Flat Earth lecture to be presented in England the following day. And just hours after presenting his finding to the group of people discussing Earth science, there was even a YouTube video exposing the discrepancies of the missing curvature that quickly raised thousands of views.

Max was blown away by his discovery and was eager to tell Sam.

Sam's phone vibrated. It was a text message from Max.

"Hey, bud. Are you still up?"

Sam replied within moments. "Sure am, pal."

"You hungry?"

"Always. LOL."

"Want to grab a pizza?" adding a pizza emoji to his message.

"Count me in!"

"Cool. I'll pick you up in twenty or so. I'll text you when I'm outside."

"Awesome, Max! See you soon."

Hopping into his car minutes later, Max drove along Beach Road to Sam's house, and upon arrival, sent a text message to let him know he had arrived.

"Yo... Samurai!" shaking his hand after he climbed into the car.

"Hey there, Maximus. How ya doing, big buddy?" adjusting the position of the passenger seat.

"I'm great, Sam, but for some reason, I just couldn't get to sleep. It's only ten o'clock, and Zoe has already passed out for the night," as he quickly accelerated down the street.

"Ah, the poor girl. How's she settling in?"

"Zoe's great, and she's wrapped to be back home. So am I – for that matter."

Enjoying a casual discussion whilst driving to grab a bite to eat, Max suddenly noticed a car he thought was suspiciously following them.

"Don't make any sudden moves right now, Sam. But can you see the vehicle behind us?"

Cautiously leaning forward in his attempt to look into the passenger side mirror inconspicuously, Sam replied, "Yeah... I can, Max. What's up?"

"Well... I'm pretty sure that I saw the same car earlier this evening. It was parked outside my apartment building. Seems like someone is following us."

"No way, Max! Are you sure?"

"I know what I see, buddy! I'm going to take a left turn down the next side street. Let's see if they can catch up!"

"Good idea, Max. Go for it!"

Max pulled a hard-left down Chapel Street in an attempt to lose the suspicious black SUV.

"I told you, Sam. Someone is friggin following us!" now engaging the gearbox of the car into manual mode.

Sam shouted, "Punch it, Max! Get rid of the bastard!" realising that he was suggesting to his crazy friend – to be even crazier.

But, before Sam could even finish his words, Max was using the paddle shifts located behind the steering wheel and manually gearing at high revs through the backstreets of St. Kilda. His trusted BMW 7-Series tightly gripped the corners with its advanced all-wheel-drive traction control system, powered by a twin-turbo-charged V12 engine.

With the van's headlights fading from view, Max continued to skillfully manoeuvre the car around several corners, losing the black SUV many blocks prior but continued "pedal-to-the-metal" along the tree-lined streets.

The vehicle revving loudly until finding a secluded place to park; Max killing both the engine and lights with a push of a button.

Still tightly gripping the door handle, Sam shouted, "What the heck was that about, Max?" slightly slumping into the leather seat.

"I'll be buggered if I know, Sam!" his hands lightly trembling on the steering wheel.

"You gotta give this 'Flat Earth' shit up, Max! I'm not sure what you are getting yourself into with this 'finding new land' thing, but it seems like a dangerous idea to me!"

"It's all good, Sam! Maybe it was just a coincidence."

"Well, it was kind of freaky! Wouldn't you agree?"

"Yeah, yeah... whatever, Sam!" as he pushed the engine start button to continue the drive to the pizzeria, whilst repeatedly gazing into the rear-view mirrors; but without further incident arrived at the destination several minutes later, after parking the car down a secluded side street.

They ordered a large gourmet pizza, ravioli, and a Mediterranean salad to share, eating in silence as they occasionally looked around the restaurant; still thinking about who the heck could have been following them.

"Max, as I said, I'm kind of concerned about this 'finding more land' plan. Have you told anyone else about it?"

"Um, yeah, I've told a few people so far, Sam. I've also enquired about buying a UAV style drone from America. But, hey, don't worry about it. I was probably, you know... just being paranoid," said Max, trying to defuse the incident.

"Hmm... I bloody hope so, Max. Anyway, it's getting late. Let's get out of here!"

They exited the restaurant, cautiously looking around for a sign of the black SUV. But the coast was all clear, and with an overwhelming sense of relief, they looked at each other and burst into laughter.

26

Rising early the following morning, Max prepared breakfast for Zoe, where he attempted to replicate Elena's breakfast special of poached eggs and smashed avocado on toast.

They sat side-by-side at the kitchen island catching up on the gossip from Zoe's time in London, where he was more than ecstatic to have her home again and his life back to some normality.

"I'm just going to get a bit of work done, Sweetie," gently kissing her forehead to connect with her pineal gland – before heading to his office.

Zoe lazed on the sofa flicking through the channels searching for a movie to watch; casually dressed in her comfy tracksuit pants, hooded windcheater and Ugg boots – just like a classic Aussie bogan. However, after not finding anything worthwhile to watch, she joined Elena in the kitchen for another coffee.

Max was secretly elated that the Odysseus pseudo-satellite was just six weeks from delivery; after his credentials flawlessly passed scrutinous checklists following cross-examination from ASIO and Interpol agencies – cleared as "non-suspicious".

And Max knew that if his mission to find more land on Earth was to be successful, he needed to build a team of experts to join him, as he obviously couldn't complete the mission on his own.

But more importantly, he needed to make the mission as safe as possible for the accompanying crew, where no person in their right mind would depart to an unknown destination without a failsafe plan, or even more so, without solid, tangible proof of more land. And Max was confident that the Odysseus would provide him with a method to prove it unequivocally.

However, nothing worried him more than announcing to Zoe that he wanted to venture beyond unknown horizons to find unexplored land. Because anyone who knew Zoe's feisty nature – well, they very well understood that she was going to crack it!

Opening his password-protected word-processing document, he continued to compile a list of skill sets required, essential to make a crewed mission a success. And to date, his short-list comprised of a pilot, navigator, flight crew, security personnel, doctor, nurse, botanist, cooks, a theologian, and a biologist; amongst many others. The list was becoming extensive. Even after trimming down the numbers, it would take approximately thirty brave crew-members to accomplish a manned expedition.

Closing the file, Max was once again researching Flat Earth. Relentlessly trying to absorb as much information on the subject as possible.

He noted that Flat Earth researchers were conducting independent experiments from various locations across the pond; including long-distant laser tests across flat-level water, and long distant observations with high-powered digital zoom cameras – many exceeding 100-kilometres. With the researchers sharing their experiments on dedicated websites, video channels, and via various social media platforms.

Two independent researchers, who in their efforts to "Test the Globe", went to the extent of debunking a weather reporter; who the latter ludicrously asserted that a long-distant photo sent in by a viewer, Joshua Nowicki, which clearly showed Chicago from across Lake Michigan (spanning a distance of approximately 100 kilometres – or 60 miles) was a superior mirage created by an inversion layer in the atmosphere. Where the reporter claimed: *a reaction between cold and warm air bent the city skyline from over the horizon back toward the viewer*.

During a broadcast on the evening news, the weather reporter also said, *"What you are seeing here, is a mirage. We typically would not be able to see this from the Lake Michigan shore…"*.

However, the researchers went out of their way to test the claim by zooming into Chicago on a clear day with a powerful camera and documented – via still photography and videography – that they were able to view the city from various vantage points as they travelled across the lake in a boat. And thus proved it was not a mirage that enabled the city to be seen from that distance, as alleged by the weather reporter.

Whereas, Max had already ascertained that (irrespective of its container) water will always remain level at rest: including across the largest lakes on Earth – such as Lake Michigan. As water can be scientifically and demonstrably proven to be level at rest via the laws of hydrostatics and fluid dynamics. The law empirically states – through not only common sense, observation, and experiment, but also via the scientific method – that the surface of water always remains level at rest in a stable equilibrium. And that includes the water contained within the grandest lakes across the world.

Although Max had conducted optical experiments using binoculars and a telescope across the bay, he decided to independently test long-distances across Melbourne and found that the "go-to-device" was the Nikon Coolpix P1000 digital camera. With many within the Flat Earth community referring to the camera as "The Globe Buster", due to its ability to zoom into distances that should be hidden by the elusive curve of the Earth.

And Max now wanted one.

Shutting down his computer, Max joined Zoe and Elena who were chatting and giggling whilst enjoying a cup of coffee in the kitchen.

"Sorry to interrupt you, ladies. But hey, Zoe, do you feel like heading into the city to do some shopping?"

"Did you just say 'shopping', Max? You don't have to ask me twice," Zoe joked – jumping up from her chair with enthusiasm and hugging Elena.

"I'll be ready in twenty minutes, Sweetie-Pie," even though Max knew she would be more like an hour or so.

Arriving in the city just before noon, they rode a crowded tram along Collins Street. Max rather enjoyed catching public transport on occasion, enabling him to engage with life's daily grind and also reminding him of his days as a younger man; running amok with his mates, riding trains, trams, and buses – until the late hours of the night. Often missing the last train home to the south-eastern suburbs from the city, which ultimately meant a long walk home.

Exiting the tram, they proceeded to walk along the crowded footpath. "Hey, where are we going, Max? The good shops are that way!" pouting her lips whilst pointing toward the boutique fashion stores located at the top-end of Collins Street.

He laughed at her antics. "Just going to find a camera store, Honey," now using the map on his smartphone to guide him. "There's one right around the corner," he said, as they casually chatted whilst walking toward the store – firmly clutching each other's hand.

The song *"Down Under"* by the Australian band Men at Work was ironically playing when they walked into the camera store as Zoe looked at Max and giggled.

The salesman from the camera store was fascinated by Max's requirements, as Max didn't hesitate to clarify the reason for his visit: explaining that many people were using the P1000 camera to see well beyond the alleged curvature of the Earth. Informing the salesman that people in New York were claiming they could view the Statue of Liberty from over 100 kilometres away on a clear day – which he stated should be hidden behind approximately 700 metres of physical curvature.

"Sir, what are you trying to verify?"

Max kidded with him, "I'm actually trying to prove the Earth is flat," where Zoe blushed by his brazen honesty.

The salesman queried, "Wow! Are you a Flat Earther? I've heard of you guys online. I also saw something about it on morning TV not too long ago."

Max was stunned. It was the first time he'd been referred to in public as a "Flat Earther", and he was surprised that the young man had even heard of the term. He thought, "Better than being called a 'Flat-Head'," or any of the other derogatory terms often used by the globe defenders during the many heated online debates and discussions that Max had participated in over the years.

He briefly pondered about the rise of the Flat Earth community and wondered if the message was finally gaining traction across Australia. The answer was an astounding "yes". Because, although the subject was still taboo for discussion around most dinner tables, Max was meeting more and more people that had been exposed to the premise that our Earth may be flat. And many of them were already Flat Earth converts.

Max replied, "Well, yes... I must admit that I am beginning to think the Earth is flat. Because it looks flat and feels as if we are motionless. And I certainly don't think I'm standing upside down right now. So, yeah, I guess you could say that I'm a Flat Earther," he self-assuredly smiled.

"Cool. You're the first one that I've met," he replied, while unlocking the glass display cabinet handing Max the camera.

"Wow... it's pretty heavy! What's the zoom capability on this thing?" Max queried.

"Actually, Sir, that's possibly one of its best features as it has a super impressive 125x optical zoom. It's a top-rated camera for various applications and is perfect for both recreational and professional use. It's a great choice – and very easy to operate. We sell quite a few of them."

"Sold! Say no more – I'll take two!"

"Consider it done, Sir."

"Come to think of it... can you kit me up with the extra options?"

"Sure thing! I'll get that sorted for you right away," replied the friendly, helpful salesman, who began to walk toward the storeroom to check for stock.

"Oh, actually... could you kindly gift wrap one of them?" Max politely asked. "You see, I'm going to give one to a friend."

"Too easy. No problem at all. I'll be right back. In the meantime, why don't you help yourselves to a coffee or a refreshment?"

"Thank you. We will do," grabbing a bottle of spring water from the refrigerator to share with Zoe as they browsed around.

The salesman returned with Max's purchase in two separate carry bags.

After briefing the salesperson with a quick synopsis on the Flat Earth theory for a few minutes, he collected his parcels, thanked him for his outstanding service, and excitedly began to exit the store with his new toy.

"Oh, excuse me, Mr Carter. Just one last thing before you leave. Is there somewhere where I can access more information on Flat Earth? As I'm actually rather intrigued."

"Sure is. Jump online and begin the journey by watching the documentary *'Truth Does Not Fear Investigation'*. It's one of the best introductory videos on the subject. Just swallow the red pill, and enter the rabbit hole from there!"

"Okay. Thanks, Mr Carter. Most people pass off conspiracy theories with a hand-wave dismissal. But I'm in! I'll watch it later tonight with my girlfriend when we chill out and relax."

"Well, just be prepared to have your mind blown, young man – as this one is conspiracy fact," giving the salesman a cocky smile, cupping Zoe around her waist and exiting the store.

"Hungry, babe? Should we get some lunch?" he asked.

"I'm famished, Max! Let's do Japanese. Do you feel like Sashimi?"

"Yeah... sure do, babe. You got it!" he replied, hailing a passing cab which immediately pulled to the curb.

Max satisfyingly rubbed his belly following the scrumptious meal. "That was delicious. Shall we go shopping, Zoe?"

"I thought you'd never ask, Max," she beamed.

After spending the afternoon treating Zoe at some of Melbourne's leading fashion houses, Max couldn't wait to get home to tinker with his new camera.

"I'm friggin buggered, babe. Let's get out of here before peak-hour hits. I'll book us a ride," fumbling for his phone – his hands loaded with shopping bags, with one of the bags containing a personal gift that Zoe chose for Elena and her family.

27

Max unpacked the camera and browsed the user manual inside and out as soon as he arrived home. And although the shoreline to the beach was less than two hundred metres from his apartment, there was just one thing preventing him from setting up the camera for long-distant optical experiments—which was to charge the battery overnight.

Zoe called out, "Max... dinner's ready!"

Elena had earlier prepared and baked Moussaka – Max's favourite; so after placing down his new camera to charge, he sat to an elegantly prepared table setting, pouring a glass of red wine for Zoe, where they enjoyed a romantic candlelit dinner.

A big feed often meant a good snooze. So in a food-coma, Max snuggled up with Zoe on the couch to watch a movie. And what was meant to be a short catnap resulted being a solid three-hour sleep. Where they later stumbled to bed with stiff backs to continue their sleep on their far more comfortable king-size bed.

Waking early the next morning, in the hope to use his new camera – Max looked out the window and thought, "Typical bloody Melbourne weather!" as it was grey, miserable, and the rain was bucketing down.

Nonetheless, Max spent the morning familiarising himself with the basic features and functions of his newly acquired toy by watching online tutorials. Together with various videos of people zooming into boats, lighthouses, container ships, the Sun, and the Moon; and even distant planets – with their high-zoom cameras.

Later that afternoon, he called Sam inviting him to conduct long-distant observations across Port Philip Bay for the following day, as the weather and humidity were predicted to be ideal.

"Sounds great, Max. What time did you have in mind?"

"Well, if the weather holds up to expectations – any time around noon. We'll also grab some lunch," where they discussed Aussie Rules Football for several minutes before hanging up on the call.

*****

Max handed Sam a gift-wrapped parcel. "Here, buddy. This is for you!"

Tearing open the gift wrapping. "What the heck! Thanks, Max. I've been thinking of getting one of these babies," giving him a friendly man hug.

"You're more than welcome, Sam. I hope you enjoy it."

"Thanks again, Max. You're a champion!" he ecastaically replied, admiring the camera.

"Let's set mine up right over there," Max pointed, as he unfolded the sturdy tripod on the path just metres away from the shoreline and approximately two metres above sea level – facing the camera towards the horizon.

After zooming in with his new super-zoom camera. "Booyah! I've got one. Check this out, Sam!"

Max pointed toward the skyline, "There's a ship just beyond the horizon that can't be seen with our naked eye. But when I zoom in with the camera, I can bring the entire boat back into view – hull and all!"

"Wow, Max. What a spinout! This camera is friggin mind-blowing. It looks like the container ship is floating above the water. Is that some type of mirage?" Sam curiously asked.

"Yeah, it is! The effect is called Fata Morgana. And it's an optical illusion or phenomenon that creates an invisible or transparent narrow band just above the horizon, caused by light rays bending when they interfere with the layers of different temperatures in the atmosphere. So with the right conditions, we'll see various effects including all types of mirages. You'll also sometimes see the same illusion occurring over a hot tarmac road during the summer; where it appears that there is water on the road in the distance – when, in fact, there isn't."

Sam smiled, "Fata Morgana, hey!" briefly reminiscing about his first girlfriend, Morgana, as he picked up a nearby pebble, skimming it across the calm water.

They spent the next hour zooming into container ships and recreational boats that had disappeared over the horizon; also viewing distant mountains including the You Yangs mountain ranges: an Australian Aboriginal heritage site located 70 kilometres away from their destination and only 320 metres maximum elevation. Furthmore, observing Mount Macedon from over 100 kilometres away, with almost the entirety of the 600-metre-high mountain in full view: where both should have been obscured behind several hundred metres of terrestrial curvature.

The distances observed with the new camera far exceeding their initial observations during their outing on the Zenith Star.

"Hey, Max – I've got an idea! Let's grab the camera and drive around the bay stopping at various vantage points to see how far we can observe. And if I can see Melbourne from Rye Beach; and Rye beach from Melbourne. Well, then I might even finally admit that the Earth is flat," Sam confessed; motioning a straight line over the distant horizon with his hand.

"Great idea – let's do it!" packing up his camera, where they then headed toward Max's car.

Positioned just above sea level, they spent the afternoon observing expansive views from various locations throughout Port Phillip Bay; and using both their unaided eyes and the new digital cameras, they observed: sixty-four kilometres from Rye Beach to Melbourne CBD; over seventy kilometres from Melbourne to Geelong; and to conclude their experiments for the day, also observed Portarlington from Chelsea Beach from 36 kilometres away. Which at its maximum elevation of only 10.5 metres in height – should have been hidden behind approximately 60 metres of physical curvature.

Their observations completely obliterating the purported Earth curvature math, which implies the Earth should curve at an approximate rate of eight inches per mile squared.

But the elusive curve of the Earth was again – nowhere to be found.

Using his car phone, Max called a golf club situated on the northern tip of King Island – which at its closest point is located 100 kilometres from the Victorian mainland – to ask if they could see Melbourne. A lady with a beautiful French accent answered then explained that although she hadn't seen it personally, she said that her boss had seen the mainland of Victoria from the island on many occasions.

Driving home later that afternoon, Sam confessed, "Well, Max, I never thought I'd ever say these words out loud, but I reckon the Earth might be flat!"

"Yep. It sure is, pal," replied Max. "And it's friggin beautiful at that!" trying not to make a big deal of Sam's confession—as much as he really wanted to do so!

"*Sometimes people hold a core belief that is very strong. When they are presented with evidence that works against that belief, the new evidence cannot be accepted. It would create a feeling that is extremely uncomfortable, called cognitive dissonance. And because it is so important to protect the core belief, they will rationalize, ignore and even deny anything that doesn't fit in with the core belief.*"

FRANTZ FANON

28

Max carefully slid up the zipper on his faded denim jeans, then slipped on a tight white t-shirt, black leather jacket, and his Ray-Ban Sunglasses. Zoe, still snuggled up in bed checking him out, wittily remarked, "Who the heck are you trying to be today? John Travolta?" never letting an opportunity pass to roast Max; as they mutually enjoyed doing so.

He pointed to her and started singing, *"You're the one that I want... ooh, ooh, ooh – honey!"* while grooving away; Zoe could not help but to crack up laughing at his spontaneous shenanigans.

Knowing she was right, he jived into the walk-in closet and put on a dark overcoat to disguise his hideous outfit. But that wasn't going to work either! The more inconspicuous he attempted to dress, the more ridiculous he looked: finally deciding to wear his favourite tailored suit to blend in with the morning rush hour by dressing business-like for the day.

It had been a while since he last suited up. After selling his company just eighteen months prior, Max preferred to dress casually whilst he relished his time from early retirement in the workforce.

Pecking Zoe on the lips, he said, "I'll be back in a few hours, honey," then headed toward the elevator, where the lift doors automatically slid open.

"No worries, babe. By the way, don't forget we have a lunch date with my parents today. Make sure your back in time!"

"Oh, shit! I almost forgot! Yeah... okay, honey – see you soon," as he stepped into the elevator pressing the button for the lobby.

"Good morning, Max. You're looking sharp today!" said Henry upon seeing him approach the door.

"Thanks, Henry. I haven't worn this suit in a long time, so I just thought I'd see if it still fits me."

"Well, I have to say – that you look mighty dapper, Sir. I hope you enjoy your day," opening the doors to the glorious sunshine and bright blue sky.

"Right back at you, Henry!" slipping past as Max headed toward Port Melbourne Station, where he boarded an early train to the city.

Arriving in the city shortly after nine o'clock, Max's attire now seemed a great choice, as the morning rush hour meant that he was now lost amongst the other suits in the crowd.

Exiting the station, he crossed the road and swung down the first alleyway, looking behind him to see if anyone was following.

He continued along the alleyway, then abruptly stopped and crouched down whilst pretending to tie up his shoelace. Once again taking the opportunity to look around to see if anyone was suspiciously following him.

After withdrawing cash from an automatic teller machine, he folded the notes and placed them into the breast pocket of his suit.

Entering the empty cafe, he proceeded to the last table, sliding into the bench seat and pushing aside a copy of yesterday's newspaper – which looked as if it had been read a thousand times – as he waited for Roberto to arrive.

Roberto entered the café moments later and slid into the booth, seating himself adjacent to Max.

"Did you bring it?" Max whispered.

"Yeah, I did!" standing his briefcase under the table. "But, there's no need to act like James Bond, Max."

"I wasn't!"

"C'mon, man! When was the last time you wore a suit?"

"Well, I still do occasionally... you know!"

"Yeah, yeah... sure thing, Max! I haven't seen you wear a suit, for God knows how long!"

"Anyway, I've brought you something that I found in Japan. It's an ancient map of the world."

"Really, Robbie? Don't mess with me!"

"I'm serious, man! It's in the briefcase under the table," as Roberto shifted the briefcase towards him with his foot.

"Here, why don't you open the case and see for yourself!"

Discreetly looking around, even though there were no other customers in the diner, Max slid across the booth raising the briefcase onto the table. Simultaneously pressing the two silver latches to unlock the leather case.

"What do we have here?" he rhetorically asked, carefully pulling out the map from the protective tube and unrolling the document.

"Well, it's a photocopy of an ancient map drafted by a Japanese Monk. It is said that it was drawn over 1,000 years ago and has since been protected for many generations by the same family."

Roberto continued, "It shows more land on Earth. And by the looks of it, I reckon the ancients had a fair bit of knowledge about where they lived because how could they have an ancient map of the world that strangely resembles the world map on current United Nations logo?"

Max's brain was running wild; he now finally had a map in his hand that depicted more land on Earth.

"How the heck did you get it, Roberto?" he enthusiastically asked, whilst glancing over the geographical features of the map.

"Well, we were sightseeing from the highest lookout of Mount Fuji with a local Japanese family that my daughter Elyssa had met through a student exchange program."

"Oh, cute little, Elyssa. She has grown up so fast. I still remember her when she was just a baby."

"I know, Max. The river of time flows too fast."

"Anyhow, the hospitable family later invited us to their home, which they call a 'Minka', and we ate delicious Japanese food in one of the most exquisite Japanese gardens with perfectly manicured plants and Koi fish almost longer than my arm. It was gorgeous, Max. I wish you could have been there," Roberto explained, as Max patiently waited for his overly-excited friend to explain the origins of the map.

"Sorry, mate – let me get to the point."

"Well, after drinking many shots of Saké, I couldn't resist but to tell them about the concept of Flat Earth, where Miko explained that the ancient Japanese Monks, his ancestors, also believed that the Earth was flat."

"Really, Roberto? Are you saying that the Japanese also thought the Earth was flat?"

"Yes, Max. And the grandfather said he had something to share with me, and that's when he opened a well-preserved wooden trunk with a large lock, where he then unravelled some old manuscripts – with tattered up edges."

"I actually thought that he was going to show me ancient treasures, but I was wrong. And that's when he handed me an ancient map of the world, where his great-grandson Miko explained the map originated from the Shingon Buddhists – who drafted it almost one-thousand years ago."

"Friggin awesome. Great find, Roberto!" elatedly grinning from ear-to-ear.

Roberto elaborated, "Miko told us that it was found hidden in a Japanese Buddhist temple during the early 1900s. He didn't know much more about the map, but his family have safeguarded it for the last one-hundred years."

"That's mindblowing, Roberto!" still admiring the photocopy of the map.

"You know what, Max; I reckon you should look into ancient maps, because I believe you'll find more answers. You see, did you know that all maps preceding the 1500s were all based on a Flat Earth projection? Because before that, everyone knew the Earth was flat."

"Hmm... that's fascinating, Roberto."

Scratching his chin, Max asked, "So... what's that outer ring supposed to be?"

"Well, they say that's the Antarctic ice wall. They reckon it encompasses the entire Earth, like a big wall – if you like."

Max continued to stare at the map; mesmerized.

Roberto explained, "Because we all know that bodies of water must be contained. And the most elevated mass on Earth at an altitude of 2,500 metres is Antarctica. So, it makes perfect sense that we are surrounded by an impenetrable wall of ice: and the huge ice wall acts as a container. You know, it's like we live inside a really big-pond!"

"What? You mean like the ice-wall on the television series, 'Game of Thrones'?"

"Yeah, something like that, Max."

Roberto reiterated, "We live in a big pond with an ice wall surrounding us that contains all the water on Earth. Almost like what Auguste Piccard said after he ascended high into the stratosphere with his experimental high-altitude balloon in the 1930s, where to the surprise of many he claimed, *'It looked flat, with upturned edges!'*. The upturned edge was probably the ice wall. And don't they say Captain Cook circumnavigated Antarctica for something like three years. Recording tens of thousands of miles of impenetrable ice walls?"

Roberto softened his voice. "Max... and who bloody knows! Maybe there are other little ponds out there with hidden land or continents! It's probably the reason why politicians go to Antarctica soon after they are elected. I think one of the Pope's has visited too!"

"And we all know that ice floats; so maybe if you buy a big submarine, you could go under the ice-wall, and then 'pop-up' like a little penguin into one of the other ponds!" he chuckled.

"You little ripper, Roberto! Do you realise what you have done?"

"What have I done now?" shrugging his shoulders.

"You've freakin' solved it, mate!"

"I have?" he quizzed.

"Yeah, you have, bud. I'll explain later, as I really must go!"

"Likewise, Max. I'm already late for work!"

"Take care, Roberto. And say hello to the family for me," slipping five-crisp one-hundred-dollar notes into the breast pocket of his suit jacket.

"Thanks, Max. But you didn't have to do that!"

"Well, it's the least I could do for the risk you took, Robbie."

"It was too easy, Max. Anything for you, mate" as they shook hands and departed separate ways.

Max was ecstatic. As he now had a map to help guide him in a direction to find more land.

However, was the ancient map accurate? And could it be trusted as a reliable source?

Because any discrepancy would not only jeopardize the mission and his multi-million-dollar investment into the Odysseus: but the lives of the accompanying crew during a future manned expedition – which was to include some of his closest friends and colleagues.

* * * * *

Zoe called out, "Max... are you almost ready to go, honey-bear?"

They were heading out to a formal lunch function at a fine-dining restaurant with Zoe's parents, where she was excited to be seeing them again after having just returned from another trip around the world.

Zoe's father, a former Australian Ambassador, had groomed her for success from an early age. But with such a feisty character – even as a young girl – she resisted his ambitions. Where her father's dreamy hope that she would one day follow in his footsteps was at polar opposites to her aspirations; because Zoe grew up resisting any attempts from her family to mould her into a "pink-dressed prancing little princess".

"Max, we have to go – or we're going to be late! And whatever you do, please don't mention anything about Flat Earth!" as she applied her lipstick in front of the bathroom mirror.

"I'll try," he acknowledged, shrugging his shoulders while adjusting the knot of his tie.

"Max, I'm serious! My parents are snobs. If they hear any mention of conspiracy theories – they'll think we're crazy!"

"But... we are crazy, babe!"

"Max! Don't make me bite you again!"

"Oh, promises, promises!" he smirked, spanking her gorgeous little bottom as he passed by.

"Ouch, Max!" she shrieked.

He cheekily giggled, then said, "I'll be ready to go in five minutes, babe. Just going to make a quick call," as Max dashed to his office, quickly finishing up his call – then hurried back to the bedroom to grab his dinner jacket.

"People need to be aware that there is a range of models that could explain the observations. For instance, I can construct you a spherically symmetrical universe with Earth at its center, and you cannot disprove it based on observations. You can only exclude it on philosophical grounds. In my view there is absolutely nothing wrong in that. What I want to bring into the open is the fact that we are using philosophical criteria in choosing our models. A lot of cosmology tries to hide that.".

GEORGE F. R. ELLIS - PHYSICIST

29

"Isn't the Moon odd, Zoe?"

"Why do you say that, Max?" she queried, whilst gazing at the Moon and the multitude of stars through the sunroof on a gorgeous clear night.

They were at one of their favourite locations, Sky High, elevated over 600-metres above sea level in the Dandenong Mountains

It was where Max had taken Zoe on their first date – after they met through a mutual friend over three-years ago – and they often returned as a reminder of their first romantic night together.

He was an aspiring entrepreneur at the time who had almost lost hope in his ambition to make it big, often struggling even to pay the receptionists wage while growing his small but ambitious business. Frequently asking his family and friends for financial assistance to make ends meet – who were thankfully, always there to save his arse at the very last hour.

But the tides had turned, and Max was now rolling in cold-hard-cash. Even though he hated that saying, preferring to use the adage coined by the motivational speaker, Zig Ziglar, who said something along the lines of *'It's neither, cold nor hard. It's warm and soft, and it will go with anything you wear'*."

Following a romantic dinner at Sky High's restaurant, Max and Zoe chilled out in the car park that overlooked Melbourne's ever sprawling suburbs, as their hometown had over the years developed into a mega-city—now marvelled, as one of the most liveable cities in the world.

The Moon was in a waning phase, and as a keen amateur observer of the Moon for many years, Max began to question the mainstream explanation for the Moon's phases; observing several anomalies – especially when he would simultaneously see the Moon and the Sun in the sky, where the phase of the Moon did not correspond to the angular position of the Sun.

Max took a puff of a joint, blowing the smoke out of the Sunroof, where a large cloud of smoke lingered above the car. He then passed the joint to Zoe and elaborated.

"Well, honey, what I mean is if you watch the Moon's phases, you will notice that the phase – and the Moon's terminator line – remains constant throughout the night. Even though we are supposedly spinning at about 1,000 kilometres per hour in Australia, with the Sun, the Moon, and the Earth – spinning and orbiting each other as we rocket aimlessly at preposterously wild speeds through an endless black void."

"And the strange thing is that everyone on Earth observes the same phase of the moon – regardless of the viewers angular position. So effectively, a person viewing the moon from Australia will see the same moon phase as, for example, someone in Europe. You see, if our Earth is constantly revolving away from the Sun in an eastwardly direction – then, in my opinion – I think a constant moon phase lasting several hours would be an impossibility! Wouldn't you agree, Zoe?"

"I must admit... that no one's ever asked me that on a date before," she cheekily smirked.

"Ha-ha. Good one, sweetie. You got me," he chuckled.

"But, I see what you're saying, Max. I've never really put much thought into it, but I think you're right," taking a small puff and passing it back to him.

"And Zoe, the Moon is in such perfect sync to our planet, and with such precision, that everyone on Earth only ever sees the same face of the Moon. No one has ever seen the far side of the Moon from Earth."

"Why is that, Max? How do you figure? So, is the Moon flat too?"

"I'm not sure, Zoe. It appears to be spherical, but in my belief, no one has ever been to the moon to verify it."

"Anyway, astronomers say it's because as our Earth rotates, the Moon also rotates at about 10-miles per hour, and whilst it orbits around the Earth, it counteracts our ability to see the far side of the moon."

"Wow... that's trippy, Max! Seems a bit coincidental to me."

After a few moments of silence – mesmerised by the twinkling stars in the night sky and the glistening lights across the city, Max asked, "Zoe, did you know that the ancients believed that the Moon somehow creates its own light and that it's not a reflection of sunlight?"

"No, I didn't know that, Max."

"So, I'm beginning to believe that the moon charges itself from the Sun, then loses its plasma charge or illumination over a twenty-eight-day cycle. You know, kind of like a battery losing its charge over 14 days, then being charged again over the next 14 days of the month. With some type of plasma charging effect."

"Do you really believe that, Max?"

"Yeah, it sounds crazy... but I really do, Zoe."

"And you know, I think our ability to see a full moon during the day also totally debunks the heliocentric model. Because it's impossible that a light source from 140-million kilometres away could light up the front face of the moon – if the moon is only 400,000 kilometres away. Since you simply can't illuminate the front of an object from behind it!"

"Okay! That makes sense, Max. And the moon looks nearby to me! There's no way it's that far. I can even see some of the craters with my own eyes."

"Precisely, Zoe. And that large crater on the left-hand side is called, Aristarchus; which is supposedly only 40-kilometres wide. And I reckon even with the best vision; I highly doubt that anyone could see something that size, from over 400,000 kilometres away."

"Yeah, of course! I'd also say it's impossible," Zoe replied, reaching out to hold his hand.

"And, honey, while you were away, I had the chance to witness a Selenelion eclipse, where the Sun and moon were both visible above the horizon at the same time. Which also completely debunks the mainstream version of eclipses. As a matter of fact, the Royal Society confirms over fifty occurrences of a Selenelion eclipse during the last few hundred years."

"I've also been thinking about the Moon, Max. I'm starting to doubt that they landed on the Moon fifty years ago. The physics just doesn't add up!"

"Really, babe? What made you change your mind?"

"Well, I started to think about the physics behind the Apollo missions, and I began to realise the impossibility that they were able to leave Earth's atmosphere while the Earth is being pulled through the Universe at preposterous speeds."

"Good point, Zoe," he said, smiling at her.

"Picture this, Max: there is a car cruising down the highway, at say 100-kilometres per hour, and a fly is buzzing around in the car enjoying a free ride. And we know that the fly can freely move around inside the car because it would be contained within an enclosed atmosphere."

Max listened attentively.

"So, what would happen if you opened the window, and the fly was sucked outside? Can the fly get back into the car whilst the car is in motion at 100-kilometres per hour?"

"Yeah, I see what you mean, Zoe."

"It gets even better, my dear Maximilian," as she continued to explain, "Because the science suggests that when they went to the Moon, they had to leave Earth's atmosphere to get there. Just like the little fly leaving the atmosphere of the moving car. Now let's pretend that a balloon – which we'll say is the moon – was tied to the car's towbar, and somehow the fly was a lucky little bugger and managed to land on the balloon."

She rhetorically asked, "So my question is, how could it get back to the car? As it would have to fly faster than the car to get back in!"

"I'm buggered if I know, Zoe! But I like where you're going with this."

"And Max, the same physics would apply with a rocket leaving Earth's atmosphere; especially if we keep in mind that our Earth is supposedly travelling around the Sun at tens-of-thousands of kilometres per hour, and that the Sun is flying through the Universe at millions of kilometres per hour."

"That's a brilliant point, Zoe! The craft would be left behind and lost in space. It would never be able to catch up to our Earth again! You're right: basic physics, actually debunks the moon landings!"

"Exactly, Max! And not to mention, how in the name of science did they even slow down when they reached the Moon; seeing that they were travelling 40,000 kilometres per hour to get there! Did they have magical rocket brakes?" she joked.

Max chuckled, "Nice one, Zoe. And how did they change their space-nappies during the three-day journey on the way there? It must have been pretty smelly in that space capsule!" Both laughing; then wincing at the very thought on how three-men could tolerate being in an enclosed pressurised spacecraft with dirty, poopy diapers.

"Max, I reckon that if men did in fact land on the Moon fifty years ago, then we would have cameras on the Moon looking back at our Earth, twenty-four-seven by now. You know, they could undoubtedly charge a subscription fee for the service because I'm quite certain that millions of people would happily pay a monthly fee just to watch the Earth spin – or even zoom back to Earth and view their current location. Especially given the camera technology we have available, in this day-and-age."

"However, according to one of the astronauts from NASA, they've apparently destroyed the technology to return to the Moon. So, I'm starting to believe that they staged the Moon landings, just to show us a fake photo of Earth."

"Spot on, Zoe. I love the way your brain works, my darling. And they've even stated that they've lost all the telemetry data and the original videotapes too. Thousands of reels of footage and data have mysteriously disappeared!"

"Yeah, sounds like BS to me, Max. I'd say it's just to muddy the fact that they didn't even go in the first place. They would be busted 'big-time'... if we just had the opportunity to forensically scrutinise the footage!"

"Oh my God, Zoe! What great timing."

Max pointed toward a distant light that was traversing the skyline. "Look over there! Check out that light that's moving across the sky. That's supposed to be the International Space Station."

"No way, Max! It's the first time I've seen it. And what do you mean by, *'supposed to be'*?"

"You see, sweetie, they say the ISS is currently orbiting us at an altitude of 440-kilometres above the Earth and travelling at over 27,000-kilometres per hour. But if you look carefully, it looks like it's just a light in the sky. It's possibly a high-tech drone beyond our knowledge, given how slow it's currently moving across the sky."

"Because I don't believe that it's travelling over twenty times the speed of sound. I just can't fathom that humans are capable of travelling that fast without feeling the effect! And if the ISS is over 400 kilometres away and just larger than a commercial aircraft, how can we even see it? As it would be similar to trying to see an ant from fifty metres away."

"It's hard to say, Max. But the more I look at it right now, I do agree. And I've seen some pretty dodgy footage from both NASA and the ISS while I was away."

"You have, Zoe?"

"Yes, I have... Mr Max Carter!" she cheekily replied, squinting her eyes. "Don't you worry! I've been doing my homework. But, I still have many unanswered questions about Flat Earth. Like, what about the north star Polaris, Max? As it can be seen from London – that is, when we had a clear night – but I've never seen it from Australia."

"That's actually a great question, Zoe. I'll try and explain it."

"Just imagine if you were standing in the middle of a huge department store and you looked up to the ceiling and there was a light directly above you. Let's call that light, Polaris."

"Yeah, okay," wondering where he was going with his explanation.

"So, then imagine if you walked to the furthest part of the store and looked up. The same light would no longer be above you – as you would have to look over yonder to see it. And if you could just visualise a department store one-hundred times the size of the biggest store on Earth, then I highly doubt you would see the light at all. As visual depth perception, perspective, and the angular resolution of our eyes would limit your ability to view it."

"Hmm... I highly doubt it too, Max. That makes perfect sense – I see what you mean. I'm beginning to realise that life is all about perspective. We have a mental and optical perspective, and until we grasp the latter; we fail to see the world as intended."

Max thought about her profound comment before replying, "You're right, babe. Life is all about perspective."

"It certainly is, Max."

"And Zoe, if you think about the sheer distance of Polaris – how in the bloody hell could anyone even see it with their naked eyes? As they say, it's around 433 light-years away; and one light year equates to almost eight trillion kilometres! I'm not going to do the math, but I'd say it's impossible. Even with distance parallax; as they also say, Polaris has a massive radius of something like – 35 million kilometres!"

"I'm buggered if I know, Max. But it sounds like rubbish to me. I don't believe for one second that the human eye can see that far. And how the heck did they even measure it... for God's sake? Are they on friggin drugs!"

Zoe continued, "And you know, they tell us that we travel billions of kilometres through the Universe every year; but all the stars and constellations have remained in the same place for thousands of years. Even the Greeks, Egyptians, and the Mayans recorded the same constellations that we see in the night sky, noting Polaris as the north star, which has since never moved its position."

"Precisely, Zoe. And the stars simply look like twinkling lights to me. Just like the city lights are twinkling down there. And they look pretty darn close. Not trillions-and-trillions of miles away –

as modern astronomy leads us to believe."

"Yep, I think the stars are close too, Max. It almost feels like we can reach out and touch them right now."

He reached out to hold her hand. "It sure does, babe. And the weird thing is that although we can see the stars and the planets move throughout the night sky in perfect orbits, we've all been bamboozled to believe that our Earth spins and that the stars are fixed. It's a bit like someone standing next to a river, seeing it flow, then forming the conclusion that the river is motionless and that they are somehow moving. It's nonsensical. Humans have been ignoring their senses – for far too long."

Nodding her head in agreement, Zoe turned to face him. "Max. I have something to tell you! I've gotta get this off my chest."

"What is it, Zoe?" his face now filled with concern.

"Well, you see... I didn't just take that job in London for the opportunity alone. You were kind of scaring me with all your talk of Flat Earth, and I just felt like I had to get away from it all. I was confused and a little concerned that you were going crazy."

"Really, Zoe? Why didn't you tell me? And why does everyone keep calling me crazy lately?"

"Well, I tried to tell you, Max. But you just didn't listen. You were too wrapped up in your own little bubble."

"I'm so sorry, Zoe. But, you are right; this whole Flat Earth thing is consuming me. I'm going to shut it down! No more! I'm done with it! It's over!"

"No, Max! I'm glad that you shared it with me. Because, the more I thought about it, well, I'm also starting to believe that the Earth is actually flat."

"Marry me, Zoe!" he said, gazing into her green eyes.

"Oh, stop it, Max!" she giggled.

Clearing his throat. "I'm trying to be serious here! Will you marry me, Zoe? Will you be my wife?"

"Yes... I will. I will, Max," leaning over to kiss and embrace him.

Max reached into his pocket and pulled out a sparkling square-cut diamond ring that he had previously purchased, because he'd planned to propose to her before she suddenly left for London, many months prior.

But he was grateful. For his patience had shown him just how much he really loved her – and knew that she felt the same.

He placed the ring on her finger, where they locked into a long passionate kiss.

Max then ecstatically yelled out of his window to the occupants of the nearby parked cars, "She said yes!" as they flashed their high beams and tooted their horns in reply; because Sky High was known to Melbournians as a popular spot for popping the big question.

"If we move away from an elevated object on or over a plain or a prairie, the height of the object will apparently diminish as we do so. Now, that which is sufficient to produce this effect on a small scale is sufficient on a large one; and travelling away from an elevated object, no matter how far will cause the appearance in question – the lowering of the object. Our modern theoretical astronomers, however, in the case of the apparent lowering of the North Star as we travel southward, assert that it is evidence that the earth is globular! But as it is clear that an appearance which is fully, accounted for on the basis of known facts cannot be permitted to figure as evidence in favor of that which is only a supposition, it follows that we rightfully order it to stand down, and make way for a proof that the earth is not a globe."

WILLIAM CARPENTER – 1885

30

Establishing the direction to send the Odysseus pseudo-satellite was proving far more challenging than Max envisaged. And with a hefty US$12-million price tag, he wasn't about to risk his investment without conducting stringent due diligence.

Max was recently approved for the delivery of the Odysseus, but it was his secret for now. Not even disclosing his acquisition to Zoe or his most trusted friends.

He'd already begun to acquire various equipment to build a mission control centre. Accumulating apparatus, including amongst other items: a spectrograph, oscilloscope, spectrum analyser, and a wavemeter. Which he believed would enable him to establish the aircraft's distance from its home base, including the ability to differentiate landmass from any ice mass.

But the million-dollar-question on where to send the Odysseus – which he'd nicknamed "Epica" – remained unanswered; even though there were only two apparent choices.

That is – whether to explore the restricted North Pole at the centre of the earth. Or should he send the Odysseus over the equally restricted Antarctica? Which is somehow protected by numerous countries under the guise of the Antarctic Treaty—established in 1959 by twelve nations as original signatories.

At this stage, both in his opinion – were a wild-guess at best.

It seemed that he was not the only modern-day man to postulate the existence of hidden land beyond the horizon. Because millions of Flat Earthers were also now questioning whether there was more land and civilisations yet to be discovered before the widely ridiculed "edge of the Earth".

Strangely enough, his inquiry into ancient cosmological beliefs immediately signified synergy and consistency relating to the cosmology of our universe by most ancient cultures: all believing that the Earth was flat – and that we are favourably positioned at the centre of the Universe.

And as a prolific researcher of ancient megalithic structures across the world, Max believed that our forgotten ancestors had advanced knowledge that we have yet to comprehend. Evident by the ancient structures that remain on Earth – primarily unscathed – that may hold secrets to our past. In many cases, the complexity of the architecture and construction techniques implemented are beyond our comprehension and ability to replicate; even with modern-day machinery.

Many of these mind-boggling megaliths mysteriously positioned across energetic ley-lines and often built to consistently and repeatedly align with the constellations in the sky for many millennia; including the Great Pyramids of Giza in Egypt, Angkor Wat in Cambodia, Mayan pyramids in Peru, together with many other pyramids positioned across the world. And in more modern times, even the nefarious Georgia Guidestones – with its dystopian guidelines or prophecies inscribed in multiple languages onto upright-standing granite slabs; is also precisely and continuously aligned to Polaris via a small keyhole that focuses on the North Star – every day of the year.

Knowing the ancients were able to build structures that accurately aligned with the celestial bodies thousands of years ago, still standing firmly and aligning with the same stars to this very day, Max was convinced that the ancients were far more advanced than given credit. So he wondered if their ancient maps could also lay clues to our past, including the map gifted to him by Roberto.

Zoe was on the couch in her silk-dressing gown – looking kind of sexy after dolling herself up for the night; however, she sat alone flicking through the television channels trying to find something decent to watch. And she couldn't help but suspiciously wonder – even if it was just momentarily – whether Max was having an online affair. Or was he just addicted to watching porn! Where it seemed that he was far more attracted to his bloody computer!

And let's not forget about the abundance of large packages she'd often witnessed couriered to the apartment, where he would hastily send the couriers away to the lock-up garage in the building's basement—swiftly explaining that they were just components for his new computer server. But the deliveries were for the Odysseus, as Max was yet to tell Zoe about his ambitious project.

He rolled a joint, stepping out onto the balcony to unwind – when he suddenly recalled the peculiar star-forts located around the world. Now pondering if there could be similar star-forts in the new world. Or what if there were buildings that resembled what people were now touting as "Tartarian" style architecture.

Max was no different to his ancestors who once sailed the seven seas in the hope to discover more land, which gave rise to numerous historical voyages from well-known conquerors and explorers during their valiant expeditions. Like, Alexander the Great, Magellan, Columbus, and Captain Cook; who sailed the world searching for more land on Earth. Often with nefarious motives, and more often than not, at the unpleasant suffering of the original inhabitants.

It has been suggested that Queen Isabella of Spain was so impressed with Columbus's theory that there could be more land beyond the horizon – including valuable resources and minerals; that she funded his expeditions in return for the bounty that he discovered. Some have even imaginatively hypothesised that Columbus promised to deliver the secret "elixir of life" to Queen Isabella – from the faraway mystical fountain that grants the drinker immortality and eternal youth. However, he quite obviously failed to deliver on the promise.

Most ancient cultures described the world as a flat, motionless plane; including Egyptian, Greek, Maya, Inca, Aztec, Norse, Hindu, Vedic, Chinese, Indian, Babylonian, Persian, Japanese – and even one of the oldest, most remote civilizations on Earth: the Australian Aboriginals. Who commonly described a flat immovable Earth, with a dome-like structure covering the sky; created by an omniscient creator to protect all life on Earth.

Hungry for information and to expand his knowledge about the ancients, Max delved into the history books, always believing that "knowledge-is-power". And that people should arm themselves with it, at any chance they could.

He soon acknowledged that prior to the discovery of modern America by Columbus, the Apache's always knew the Earth was flat and motionless. Never in their wildest dreams would they have considered it to be a spinning ball, careering through Space.

Similarly, before Captain Cook sailed into Botany Bay on HMS Endeavour, the Aboriginals also believed the Earth was flat; and through Dreamtime talked about rivers of water in the sky, with a serpent living in the rivers above. The Australian Aboriginal conception suggested that our Mother Earth is covered by a dome stretching out beyond the horizons; held up by two brothers at each end of the expansive Earth.

In Egyptian mythology, Nut was the goddess of the sky. Often depicted with her body immersed with stars as she held up the heavens above, protecting Earth's inhabitants with her outstretched arms and legs acting as pillars arching over Earth. Similar to holding the Yoga position, "Downward Facing Dog".

In Greek mythology, Ouranos was the God of the sky. Gaia was the personification of the Earth, and the Greeks imagined the sky as a solid dome of brass called "stereoma" decorated with wandering stars. Its edges rested upon Earth's outermost limits, with Atlas condemned by Zeus to hold up the sky on his shoulders. The body of water encircling the Earth referred to as the "Okeanos", distinctly translating into the English word, oceans.

The Ancient Greek's held a vast understanding of the Earth where they lived upon, and when the philosopher Pythagoras initially presented his model of a spherical Earth to the masses, it was considered heresy and shunned by the majority. Where it took two millennia for the heliocentric Sun-worshiping model to gain even a scintilla of traction, and only after being reverse-engineered from the Ptolemaic, geocentric model of the Universe. The apparent and obvious fact that the Sun orbits the Earth was inverted as the polar opposite and ingeniously rationalised through a mathe-

matical construct labelled as calculus by the inventor, Issac Newton. Again, only after the theory of gravity bamboozled humanity
into believing that it was possible to live upside down – or even
sideways, for that matter - on an axially tilted planet.

Further proof of the ancient Greek's solid belief and understanding of a geocentric system is the Antikythera mechanism,
which was recovered from a shipwreck off the coast of the Greek
Island Antikythera in 1901 by a group of Italian pearl divers—believed to be designed and constructed by Greek astronomers, circa
150BC to 250BC. The device, considered by modern-day archae-
ologists as one of the oldest analogue computers ever developed;
was configured to replicate the Metonic geocentric calendar, and
accurately predicted astrological events – including the motion of
the Sun, the Moon, and all her phases. Furthermore, predicting
solar and lunar eclipses and the procession of the luminaries with
precision. Ancient Greek's referring to these luminaries in the sky
as Planate, or wandering stars. And the Antikythera device could
predict their motions with extraordinary accuracy.

The astrolabe – an astronomical device also invented during
the Hellenistic period, was designed and modelled to represent a
handheld representation of the geocentric universe. And amongst
many of its functions, the astrolabe accurately identified the heavenly bodies and determined the position of the Sun, Moon, stars,
tides and seasons with extreme precision.

The Maya believed the Earth was flat with four-corners, imaginatively thought to be on the back of a giant crocodile that rested
in a pool of water. With the sky and heavens multi-layered and re-
tained by God's supporting the weight of the Earth at each corner.
Others believed that the sky was reinforced by four giant trees that
reached the heavens – with the "Tree of Life" or Hyperborea located at the centre of the world. The Mayans envisaging the celestial
bodies as a representation of a sky-clock, with their calendar accurately indicating the day, month, seasons, the astronomical year
(some say, even the ability to predict the future), and had supreme
knowledge and wisdom of the Sun, Moon and Stars including Zo-
dicial representations of the star-aligned creatures orbiting above.

The modern-day misconception about a Mayan apocalyptic event that would wipe out all humans on Earth on the 21st of December 2012 was just a glamorised Hollywood myth. But in reality, the literal definition for the word apocalypse, when translated from its Greek origins, refers to an "awakening" and revealing secret knowledge to mankind by a "lifting of the veil". Ironically, similar to the great awakening that a large section of society is currently experiencing!

The Chinese also held the similar belief of flat, square, and motionless Earth – with the heavens above round; and had unparalleled knowledge of the constellations. Rumour has it that the Ying and Yang symbol signifies the Sun and Moon in the sky – depicting day and night. Others say that the Ying represents the Sun moving across the sky creating daylight; the Yang being the motionless dark Earth at night.

Sunlight; being radiant, warm, and life-giving – offering sustenance via solar energy to all creatures and organisms on Earth. The moonlight; cold, putrefying, and septic in nature. And when measured with a laser thermometer under a controlled experiment, the reflected light is noticeably cooler than the moon's shade by a few degrees—confirming that moonlight is not reflecting the warm radiance of the Sun.

Numerous religions and their accompanying texts, including the Bible, the Quran, and the Torah, postulated that God placed water on Earth and water in the sky; and separated those waters with a firmament—otherwise frequently referred to within the Flat Earth community as – "*The Dome*".

And Max couldn't help but wonder about the dome.

How high was it?

How far did it span?

And was it actually even real?

Although Max was brought up as a Greek Orthodox Christian, it had been a long time since he had stepped foot into a church – or even picked up the Bible, for that matter. So after constantly hearing reference to the firmament, even by Sam and Jessica, he dusted off his Bible and versed himself on the first page to confirm what the Bible stated.

It describes in Genesis that during the week of creation, God created the Sun and the Moon as separate lights in the sky and that he placed the stars in the firmament, a word that most had never considered in this context prior to hearing about Flat Earth. The passage contained within the very first verses in the King James Version of Genesis states:

> *"Let there be a firmament in the midst of the waters,*
> *and let it divide the waters from the waters."*

The Hebrews also believed the sky was a solid dome, and they called the vault of heaven "Raqiya". With the Sun, Moon and stars fixed to the solid dome or the firmament. They also believed the Earth to be stationary and immovable; basing their entire cosmology and cosmogony around a geocentric model of the Universe, with our Earth favourably positioned at the centre of everything.

Quite remarkably, the verses in the Torah were almost identical to other cultures; where Max found the following Biblical passages from the KJV rather intriguing.

> *Chronicles 16:30: "He has fixed the earth firm, immovable."*
> *Psalm 93:1: "Thou hast fixed the earth immovable and firm ..."*
> *Psalm 19:1, "The heavens (shamayim) tell out the glory of God, the vault of heaven [raqiya] reveals his handiwork."*

The Qur'an states that the Sun and Moon, run on their fixed courses in a circle calculated with measured out stages for reckoning.

> *Qur'an 2:22: He who made for you the earth a bed [spread out] and the sky a ceiling and sent down from the sky, rain and brought forth thereby fruits as provi-*

sion for you. So do not attribute to Allah equals while you know [that there is nothing similar to Him].

Qur'an 20:53: He who has, made for you the earth like a carpet spread out; has enabled you to go about therein by roads (and channels); and has sent down water from the sky. With it have we produced diverse pairs of plants each separate from the others.

It was becoming rather evident to Max that ancient civilisations had a firm understanding of the cosmos, many years before the Copernican heliocentric model was first proposed in the 1500s to masquerade objective reality. And he was astonished to find that all ancient cultures believed in the same form, structure, and design of the world around them.

The cosmological overlap of a domed covered Earth mentioned by all ancient civilisations seemed implausible to Max unless there was some truth behind it. For, how could they all come to the same conclusion on the perceived reality of the world where they live, despite no method of communication between them?

Being: a Flat Earth – with a protective dome. Possibly inadvertently revealing the true definition of the word "Domain".

Max now had more than a strong hunch that our ancient ancestors knew more about this world than we've been led to believe. In particular, after Roberto presented him with an ancient map of the world; where Max's intrigue led down a path to meticulously deciphering a diversity of world maps. Including the Mercator projection, the Gall-Peterson projection, and the Gauss–Krüger maps. Suddenly realising that world maps based on a spherical Earth strangely all have anomalies; with our most widely used map – the Mercator Projection – the most distorted.

Countless ancient cartographers and explorers depicted land that is currently not portrayed in modern-day maps. And Max couldn't help but wonder whether blockbuster movies that portrayed advanced civilizations living a utopian lifestyle in some far-away land; were, through some kind of mockery, showing us the truth in plain sight.

Going back in time, Urbano Monte's 'Map of the World Book', published in Milan in 1587, also showed more land. And in 1597, maps by the cartographer Gennaro Picicaro somehow showed more land in the south pole and depicted expansive territories named Circulus Antarcticus. Said to be beyond Terra Incognita. Strangely his drawings even illustrating unique exotic animals in fine detail.

These ancient maps not only showed more land on Earth, but they also indicated place names, settlements, rivers, mountains, and valleys in great detail – including the mysterious and intriguing ancient Tartarian empire.

In the 1500s, the Mercator map exhibited additional land at the North Pole, and many ancient cultures similarly and oddly enough speculated the same: Mount Meru, a magnetic mountain located at the centre of the North Pole – or the centre of the Earth. And Max wondered if this could be the real meaning behind magnetic north and where all compasses point!

And the further Max researched ancient maps and the globe model, he realised that a spherical Earth could only possibly contain a certain amount of landmass, by default of its limited surface area. And he could not help but speculate if that could be the reason why Earth's inhabitants are educated from an early age on the notion that they live on a spinning ball—possibly suppressing the truth that there is more land to be discovered across this expansive Earth that we live upon.

The synergistic beliefs between all cultures and religions provided Max with a glimpse of hope.

Optimistically believing, that if the world awakened to the true nature of reality. That being, the united understanding that an all mighty creator designed and constructed this world for a reason. Where, although it would only be a single step – he thought it could be a major steppingstone to unite humanity.

Perhaps bridging the gap to build a better, more understanding world; if everyone realised that there could be only one creator, rather than bickering about who's God, is the right God. And who knows, it could once-and-for-all potentially unite humankind to engage in a collective intelligence to permanently solve persistent issues that plague this world.

Max often thought that anything to the contrary could potentially lead humanity to its own demise.

Life was starting to make more sense to Max – in a weird kind of way.

And Max's inquisitive nature had to know the answers to the questions that were on everyone's lips.

Is there an edge to this Earth?

Is there a firmament?

Or is there more land on Earth?

And he had an ambitious plan to find out!

But he quickly snapped back to reality after Zoe called out to him in her sexiest voice, "Max, let's go to bed."

He did not have to be asked twice.

For nothing is secret, that shall not be made manifest; neither anything hid, that shall not be known and come abroad.

LUKE 8:

31

The Antarctic southerly winds chilled her face as Zoe tightened the cashmere scarf around her neck, where she briefly questioned whether Melbourne was indeed comparably colder than London.

After climbing into the driver's seat, she shifted the automatic transmission of the van into reverse gear.

The beeping sound echoed in the underground car park as she called Max on his phone to hurry him along.

Zoe had hired a van earlier in the day and loaded over fifty care packages into the back that she planned to hand out to the homeless during one of the coldest nights in Melbourne, as an unexpected bitter southerly wind swept through the city on a chillier than average mid-September night.

Jessica and Sam were waiting at home, but bizarrely, Max was running unusually late—as being tardy was not his style.

He answered the phone after the first ring. "Max, get up! I know you hardly slept last night. But we've got to go, sweetie pie!"

"Sorry, Zoe. I'll be down in a jiffy, babe. Just give me a few minutes," hanging up on the call – clumsily slipping on mismatching socks, throwing on a hoody top, sliding on his tracksuit pants, and tying up his sneakers.

He was beyond tired from the prolific research. His mind, kind of frazzled.

Opening the door minutes later, he said, "Sorry I'm late, hon," still rubbing the sleep from his eyes after his short nap.

He attempted to explain himself. "I only had four hours of sleep last night. My sleep pattern is so out of whack lately."

She exhaled loudly, "Yeah, I've noticed! Anyway, get your cute little butt in here," she giggled.

"Get in! Close the friggin' door... it's cold!" she insisted.

"Hurry it up, Max! Jessica and Sam are waiting for us!" while giving the pedal a light push to rev the engine.

"Yeah, yeah, okay!" he chuckled, while climbing into the passenger seat of the van, "Go for it! Hit it, babe!"

After pressing the remote control, the roller-door in the underground car park opened and set a green light as Zoe chucked it into gear, hitting the road to Sam's house. Giving Max 'that look' for keeping her waiting that nearly every man has received since the dawn of ages.

"You're a strange little cookie... aren't you, midnight Max? You know that I love you dearly, but when are you finally going to get your shit together?"

"Yeah. I just might... one of these days, babe," he cheekily smirked, being the only response he thought of; still wishing he could just continue sleeping on his warm, comfortable couch.

Arriving at Sam's several minutes later, Max slid open the side door, and shouted, "Get in, guys!"

"Brrr! Bloody hell it's cold tonight!" exclaimed Sam, rubbing his hands together and sliding into the rear bench seat with Jessica as he closed the door.

"Holy shit – it's freezin' out there!" Jessica shivered, huddling close to Sam.

"It sure is! Sorry, we are late, guys. I slept in. My bad!"

"No worries, Max. It's all good." Happy to have spent more time cuddling with Jess in front of a warm fireplace that kept them toasty as they waited for their arrival.

Sam asked, "Aren't we supposed to be heading into summer?"

"Supposed to be, Sam. But, far out – it's friggin freezin' out there tonight, isn't it?"

Sam quipped, "Maybe it's because Melbourne is close to the ice wall?"

"Yeah, it could be, Sam," laughed Max. "It sure bloody feels like it, right now!"

They randomly cruised the streets of Melbourne, stopping at various locations serving cups of hot chocolate from their flasks. Whilst handing out Zoe's care packages that included important necessities such as a woollen blanket, bottled water, snacks, toiletries, and even vitamin supplements, among other handy supplies.

Each package was thoughtfully prepared to provide a spark of hope to each recipient. Zoe also including a handwritten message inside a sealed envelope – together with a fifty-dollar note. Offering words of wisdom, hope, and advice to each beneficiary of her meticulously prepared packages.

After handing out the last care pack to an elderly gentleman that captivated their hearts with his intriguing life story, Max asked Zoe to stop the van as he leaned out of the window and called out, "Is that you, Jerry?"

Jerry responded, "Max - I can't believe it! It's been such a long time!" as he stammered toward the van, carrying a worn-out navy-green knapsack over his shoulder.

"What the heck are you doing out here?" Max queried, somewhat shocked to see his old work colleague walking the side streets of Melbourne at eleven o'clock on such a cold, miserable night.

"She left me, Max!" he whined. "After working my arse off at our beloved Computer Tech and devoting twenty-one years of my life to the company, it all ended up being a total waste of time! Because I found out she was friggin sleeping with another man. And it was my manager – of all people! And it just so happens that the prick has a mansion in swanky Toorak! Apparently, it was an inheritance from his grandparents!"

"The lying, cheating bitch!" Jerry angrily cursed. "It took me years to figure it out. Because I genuinely trusted her."

"Shit! I'm really sorry to hear that, Jerry."

"Yeah... shit, alright! Because she took friggin took me for everything, Max! And I'm now living life on the streets like a pauper! And you know, I haven't friggin had a hot meal with a knife and fork, since who bloody knows!" leaning his head down and kicking a nearby cigarette stub.

Max reached into his pocket and said, "Here, mate – take this," stretching his hand out of the window.

"It's just a cool five-hundred for now. You helped me out during my early days. You taught me nearly everything I know about coding. So here, take it!" trying to hand him five freshly minted one-hundred-dollar notes.

Jerry took a step back. "Nah, Max! You don't need to do that, mate. I'm actually quite happy on the streets. I don't give a shit about anything anymore. I'm finally free. Best I've felt, in my whole entire life," declining his offer, trying to maintain his pride.

"Don't be stupid, Jerry. Friggin take it!" he insisted. "There's a motel just around the corner. Get yourself checked into a warm room tonight, and get a hot meal or two delivered to your room."

"Live it up a little. It's on me, mate," holding out the notes, still insisting for Jerry to take them.

"Thanks, Max. You know, room service right now sounds kind of cool!" reaching over to accept his generous offer.

"Please do it, Jerry! Look after yourself – for God's sake!"

Handing over his business card, Max offered, "And call me any-time you need anything. I may have an opportunity that might interest you," shaking his hand.

"I will do, Max. Thanks a million for your help. I hope you know that this means the world to me!"

"Anytime, pal. Let's catch up soon. Don't be a stranger."

"Let's do that, Max," giving a wave and a friendly smile to all as he walked away.

They eagerly awaited with bated breath to hear Max's story on how he knew a random stranger that was doing it hard by living his life on the streets of Melbourne.

"Who was that guy, Max?" Zoe inquired, her eyes welling up with tears by the chance reunion.

"Well, Zoe... Jerry is a veteran coder, and he started coding when C++ was first developed. He's an expert in the field. In fact, even better than me! And we worked together on some of the earliest computers. You know, computers that had those old floppy disk drives."

Max explained that crunching code was not an easy profession, and feeling for Jerry's predicament elaborated on the life of a coder.

He explained, "Yeah, one does enjoy the benefit of sitting in an office behind a computer avoiding the bullshit of day-to-day contact with the real world. But it has many downsides, including working to strict deadlines, which means spending extended periods away from home."

They began to appreciate that working in the field of information technology was not as glamorous as one would imagine. Realising from the encounter that it had paid a high toll on Jerry's life, as they watched him walk away receding from view around a corner.

*****

Waving goodbye to Sam and Jessica after dropping them off at Sam's house, Max and Zoe arrived home and went to bed later that night with the heartfelt satisfaction that they had done something helpful for their community – and promised each other to make it a constant event.

Yes, of course, they felt guilty for being in a luxurious home and in a warm, comfortable bed after witnessing the struggle of humanity firsthand.

But they were frozen-stiff from a cold night out on the streets of Melbourne and shivering beyond belief, where Max and Zoe snuggled together to warm each other up – falling into a deep sleep soon after.

32

Max was angry.

He furiously thought, "Yeah... I'll friggin find the edge of the Earth, alright – you bunch of 'ball loving' bastards!"

As by now, he'd not only been asked to find the "edge of the Earth"; but to jump off the supposed edge countless times and considered it a personal challenge to prove the naysayers wrong.

Max was drunk and his anxiety levels were at an all-time high, as there was nothing more that he wanted to do than to find unexplored land on Earth.

But before passing out for the night – for what could be his last night on Earth – he rolled a big-fat joint, as he had earlier scored a pound of the highest quality buds to bring on his journey; also sourcing a variety of high-grade cannabis seeds to harvest in the new world. You know – just in case!

They had earlier been to dinner with the crew at a fancy restaurant – where they ate and drank to their heart's content. Their final rendezvous together before embarking into the unknown world; Max's ambitious dream, for a very long time.

On the way home, Zoe, as the designated driver, giggled at Max as he sang with joy to the tune of Stray Cats on the radio, singing loudly, *"We're going to rock this town, rock it inside out!"* grooving and jiving in his seat, while clicking his fingers in tune to the song.

Arriving home, he left a trail of clothes behind him as he stripped off and drunkenly staggered out to the balcony wearing just his boxer shorts, smoking a joint to the very last puff. Max was soon off-his-face: his mind running wild with thought – outlandishly wondering how crazy it would be if certain celebrities had faked their deaths to escape this realm and moved to unknown lands. The thought triggered after he remembered a beer commercial about the very notion some years earlier.

Belly-laughing out loud, he vividly imagined the scenario of discovering a tropical island that featured an outdoor bar, with Elvis serenading music on his guitar; Ms Monroe strutting around in a pokey-dot bikini; Tupac busting beats; whilst Jackson slipped by doing the moonwalk.

"Heck of a party that would be!" he chuckled.

Drinking almost three-quarters of a bottle of quality scotch earlier that night, together with the smoke, soon made him drowsy. Where he then stumbled to his bed and was snoring loudly within minutes. Quite possibly the earliest he'd fallen asleep for months, while Zoe made final preparations for the adventure by folding and meticulously packing their clothes in Versace suitcases. She thought, "Well... if you're going to explore the world – then, you might as well do it in style!"

Waking up the next day with a mild hangover on the day of his long-awaited expedition was probably not one of his best ideas.

But after a solid eight-hour sleep, he bounced out of bed with vigour, had a hot shower and a hearty breakfast – that Elena had gladly prepared for him and Zoe; and was feeling on top of the world.

It was 4:20 am, Wednesday the 27th of March 2019, and they were ready to roll!

He promised Elena that they would return as she cried and pleaded for them to reconsider their journey because she had an awful feeling that something would go terribly wrong.

Little did she know that Max had left a vast amount of his fortune to Elena and her family upon the worst-case scenario, that they failed to return home from the expedition. A tragedy would inadvertently make her a millionaire.

But Max and Zoe were adamant about changing humanity by finding unexplored land, where they arrived at the airport hours later in celebrity style.

Local and international media crews awaited them and scrambled around Max's car as it pulled into the parking bay – hoping to get the money shot.

His security team arrived early to contain the kerfuffle from media representatives and to keep the situation under control.

A reporter pointed a microphone into Max's face, and inquired, "Mr Carter, do you genuinely believe that there is undiscovered land on Earth?"

He hardly had a chance to step foot out of his car but politely replied, "Well, we are not doing this – just for the fun of it!" closing the door behind him.

"You see, this expedition has been a dream of mine for many years. And I have invested a substantial sum of money just to make it this far!"

Another mainstream news reporter mockingly asked, "But, Mr Carter – what if there is a dome over the Earth? And what if you crash into it?" laughing at him.

Giving him daggers with his eyes, Max confidently replied, "Don't worry about it. I'm pretty sure that we won't hit the dome! We've studied this for many years. So, don't worry, we've got this!"

A rival reporter interjected, "But, Mr Carter – what if your plane runs out of fuel along the way?"

He sarcastically remarked, "Yeah, thanks for that! Who doesn't want to hear those words before they embark on a long-distant flight."

"Any further questions? Because, as you know... we've got a flight to catch!" as he proceeded to walk away, holding Zoe's hand.

Turning back, Max stopped to ask, "Oh... am I live on TV right now?"

"Yes, you are, Mr Carter. You're being broadcast live across the nation."

"Great. Well, I have some words of advice for any young children watching us right now. *Question everything. And if someone tells you not to question it. Then question it even more!*"

"Good luck!" the reporters called out.

"Oh, before you go, Max. Although I don't agree with your belief that the earth is flat. I wish you all the best on your journey. You will be remembered in history forever!"

Max smiled and waved to the small group who had gathered to watch them depart.

Some were holding large placards with encouraging words such as, "GO FOR IT, MAX!"

Other placards with bold black writing displaying, "THE EARTH IS FLAT!" portraying a hypothesised map of the flat Earth.

And there were even placards from the naysayers, with not so encouraging messages. As one of the hecklers held a sign that read, "DON'T FALL OF THE EDGE OF THE EARTH... YOU FREAKS!"

33

The Airbus A350, custom-fitted with ultra-long-haul fuel tanks took to the sky, where the determined men and women left every luxury behind in the hope of changing humanity forever.

The Captain warmly welcomed everyone onboard, as the crew that Max had coordinated excitedly discussed the opportunity to see the newly discovered land with their own eyes – after they witnessed irrefutable proof from the footage captured with Max's recently attained Odysseus satellite.

During the long flight, Pierre asked Max how he acquired his fortune.

Anyone that knew Max would acknowledge that he was innovative, highly motivated – and most importantly, he was persistent! So, after many years running his small business, developing specialist software to help corporations streamline their customer bases, he built a stable product that was the envy of internet marketing firms and companies worldwide. Widely promoted as the first off-the-shelf platform allowing marketing managers to self-manage their customers via a Customer Management System.

Max finally felt like he was onto a good thing, as the years of hard work and long hours crunching code – were finally beginning to pay off. And that's when he received the call that would change his life forever.

He explained to Pierre, and the few gathered around listening, that it was a typical day in the office when his receptionist gently knocked on his office door to inform him that a gentleman named Jordan Jones was on the phone.

Amber, his bubbly receptionist, said, "He's on line one, Max," still recalling her words, as it was their inside joke – because they only had one phone line.

At that precise moment, Max did not make the connection. However, Jordan Jones was a successful entrepreneur and an early pioneer of the internet since its inception. Now, a multi-billion-aire venture capitalist based in Silicon Valley, reaping revenues exceeding twenty million dollars per day after acquiring several high-profile brands.

Hungry for further acquisitions, Jones was eager to diversify his portfolio by procuring Max's internationally patented software.

A meeting was arranged, and after intense boardroom negoti-ations, a deal inked on paper, and Max retired with over 270 mil-lion dollars – in his pocket.

The celebratory parties ensued for weeks on end and are still talked about by his friends, to this very day.

Many hours later, the aeroplane's fuselage unexpectedly vio-lently shuddered. Instantly striking concern amongst the passen-gers and crew – who were now panicking and scrambling along the aisles and harnessing themselves into their seats.

"What the heck is going on, Captain!" the co-pilot nervously shouted.

All flight instruments suddenly indicated abnormal data, and it was nothing like the two experienced pilots had ever witnessed as they latched their seat harnesses tight.

Captain calmly asked, "Altitude meter?"

"It's gone, Captain!" the co-pilot replied.

"Attitude meter?"

"It's saying... it's saying that we are flying sideways, Captain!"

"The gyro?"

"It's fuckin spinning out of control! The compass needle is spinning too, Captain! What the fuck is going on?"

"Not sure! But we are losing thrust in both engines. Just calm the fuck down and strap yourself in for a wild ride, kiddo! This plane... is going down!"

The captain calmly announced into the microphone of his headset, "Attention all passengers. This is your captain speaking. We are experiencing major instrument failure. Please fasten your seatbelts tightly and follow the flight crew's instructions."

The pilots disengaged the auto-pilot function and were now manually flying the 200-tonne aircraft trying to maintain altitude. Now as lost as a sailor at sea, as all flight instruments continued to behave abnormally.

The co-pilot asked, "Can we salvage her, Captain?"

"I don't friggin know! Just keep your hands on the controls, and do exactly as I say!"

"Will do, Captain!" the seriousness in his face showing instant regret that he'd made the wrong decision by joining Max on his crazy mission.

The captain made a secondary announcement. This time, his voice – not so calm.

"Mayday! Mayday! Attention all passengers and crew. Brace yourselves, and prepare for an emergency crash landing!"

"I repeat! We are going down! Fasten your seatbelts securely, and engage emergency landing positions!"

Max almost crapped his pants, but he did not show a hint of fear. For he knew that if he were to let his guard down, then everyone else would lose faith too.

Rather than obey the Captain's safety instructions, Max checked all passengers to ensure that everyone was safely fastened into their seats, assisting Zoe to secure her 4-point harness seatbelt – that had been custom fitted to all seats.

The oxygen masks dropped as the passengers swiftly and without hesitation grasped to reach them – fitting the masks to their faces.

"Please... sit down, Max!" the pilot yelled, but before he could reach his seat, all systems restored, as if the compass had realigned to a new magnetic north. Additionally, the gyroscope and altimeter suddenly and thankfully restabilising.

The captain joyously announced, "Attention all passengers. We seem to have stabilised all systems and will inform you of any deviations. Please keep your seatbelts fastened until you receive further instructions from the flight crew."

The passengers and crew cheered ecstatically. In fact, most of them thought that their lives were over.

Max was still shivering inside but maintained a calm composure for the sake of everyone onboard, including Zoe, who he knew were dedicating their lives for MissionX; where many had left family members behind in the hope of finding a new world. Reminiscent to ancient sailors who sailed vast oceans and seas in the hope to discover new land.

Upon entering the atmosphere of the mysterious new world, they witnessed a picturesque landscape of beauty beyond their wildest imagination. With mammoth vivid-green trees sprawled across green plains and distant mountains almost peaking beyond the bluest and clearest sky that they had ever seen.

They continued flying as Max now cheered with excitement, then yelled, "We found it! Look down there!" gazing out the window from the right-hand side of the plane.

The crew rushed to their nearest window to get a glimpse of what Max was seeing.

It was a futuristic metropolis, the modern symmetrical architecture like nothing they had ever seen on Earth, with an organised flow of transportation pods swooping through the air in perfect harmony.

"Have you found anywhere to land, Captain?"

"Not yet, Max. We may have to put her down on the water."

"No way, Captain!"

"Yes, way, Max!"

"Don't worry. I've got this, mate. Just buckle yourself uptight. This might get a little bumpy!"

The captain looked at the co-pilot and said, "Let's put this old girl down!"

After dumping fuel to lighten the payload, the captain expertly glided the plane using the aircraft's fuselage to skim the belly of the craft along the water, until they came to a complete stop on the bay within a few hundred meters of land.

A small crowd of people assembled to witness the accident; emergency crews now racing toward the floating aircraft in some sort of advanced flying machines – that seemed to levitate above the water.

The security team didn't know what to expect, as Brendon – head of security – instructed the team to grab their assault rifles, where they clicked in their magazines, ready to engage in combat; just in case they faced hostility from the locals. But Max asked the security team to put down their weapons, as he noticed that the arriving mob looked non-hostile.

After the passengers were finally rescued from the plane – which was still floating in the bay; now thousands of locals gathered along the shoreline in awe—excited to get a glimpse of an alien vintage aircraft that had just entered their modern world.

* * * * *

It was another typical day in the tranquil utopian land of Kushna, where the harmony of the metropolis exuded positive energy that radiated amongst all living creatures. Crime, non-existent. Famine, not even a word in their vernacular, where resources were abundant and shared to all within a free economy.

Although almost transparent, the Moon – not much different in appearance to our own – stayed in a fixed position in the sky, with the Sun passing overhead providing twelve hours of daylight—disappearing, then reappearing, in some type of 'Pacman' style phenomena. Eclipsing the Moon once a day at noon, creating pitch-black darkness – where the locals would isolate indoors – leaving the city scarce of life for the hour.

Max met the elders of the community and spent weeks learning about their homeland and customs. Also being introduced to the Supreme Council of the Empire of Kushna: where he explained that the majority of humans on Earth believe they live on a spinning ball, and after summarising the heliocentric model – they laughed with vigour.

The Kushnians' wanted to know more about this "spinning ball theory", so Max did a stand-up comedy routine to a live forum which was streamed to hundreds of thousands of people, on what could be described as an advanced holographic television; and nothing like he had ever seen before. Immediately considering the enormous business potential of bringing the technology back to Earth.

But when Max mentioned the words "artificial intelligence", the audience fell silent.

"Are you saying that your society is replacing humans with robots and artificial intelligence?" asked the supreme leader. "Don't you realise your world has been through this before?"

In private, they presented Max with top-secret archives not privy to the civilians of Kushna. Explaining in detail that "Earth pond" had been wiped out tens of thousands of years prior after suffering a similar fate through the introduction of advanced artificially intelligent robots. Who became superior to mankind, eventually dominating and almost annihilating the entire human race.

After much deliberation, the Supreme Council put out an order to arrest and imprison the Earthlings. Mutually acknowledging that if they allowed them to return to Earth pond freely, it would be a significant threat to Kushna's existence. The elders of Kushna unanimously concurring during a secret meeting that Earthlings are a selfish race and that such an unfamiliar trait could jeopardise their future survival. In particular, if other inhabitants of Earth pond found out about them.

Because the Empire of Kushna never wanted to be discovered and kept themselves hidden for thousands of years by their intuition. And apart from the stealthy reconnaissance missions they would conduct over our Earth in their magnetic-hydrodynamic propulsion, or flying machines (misinterpreted as UFO's by people on Earth), they preferred to remain hidden from Earthling's.

After many years of being fascinated by UFO sightings and aliens, Max now realised that extra-terrestrials or aliens don't exist in '*outer-space*': but more like – the '*outer lands*'.

The Kushnians' believe that our world is tainted and they don't want anything to do with us, even though Max pleaded to convince them through countless debates that although we have war, greed, corruption, and famine; we are not bad people—but, his words fell on deaf ears.

Max and his accompanying crew were immediately arrested and taken to a dungeon to be locked away indefinitely.

He had been far too naïve on the matter, whereas never in his wildest imagination for even a moment did he consider the possibility that they could find themselves in such a grim situation.

* * * * *

"Faaark!!! What have I done!" Max screamed at the top of his lungs.

"Max! Max! Wake up!" said Zoe, rubbing his back attempting to comfort him.

"What's wrong, Zoe? What happened?" he asked, trying to get his bearings.

"You were having a nightmare, babe!"

"Oh, yeah, I guess I was," rubbing his eyes and gratefully sitting up on the side of the bed, flicking on the bedside lamp.

Wiping his brow with the back of his hand, he said, "Phew, that was bloody scary, Zoe!"

"What happened, Max?"

"Don't worry, Zoe. It's all good. I just had a horrible dream that we were locked up in a dungeon – on some faraway land!"

"Hmm... okay!" staring at him puzzlingly.

"Yeah, it's silly... I know. I'm cool, babe!" shaking his head and smiling. Thankful to be safe at home with Zoe and that it was all just a silly dream – as he got out of bed to take a hot shower.

34

"Max, I still don't understand why you are so obsessed with this topic!"

Sam elaborated, "You do know that I'm actually leaning towards the notion that the Earth is flat, but maybe I'm missing something, mate. As I can't quite grasp how it could possibly make a difference in my life!"

Max listened attentively, placing his smartphone on the table to give Sam his utmost attention.

Sam persisted, "That is, apart from it being just another conspiracy theory. Which, even if it were true, we can't do anything about!"

"You know, I've almost given up on this conspiracy stuff, Max. I'm just so happy to have met Jessica that I don't care about conspiracy theories anymore!"

They were outside on Max's balcony enjoying a cold beer while working up an appetite for an afternoon barbeque. The girls were inside drinking champagne and getting further acquainted with one another; as Zoe gave Jessica a guided tour of the apartment, as she excitedly showed off her new engagement ring; giving Jessica all the juicy details on how Max spontaneously proposed.

Sam was slightly annoyed with Max, as it seemed that he was bordering on a dangerous obsession with the shape of the Earth, rather than focusing on real-life issues. Because in his opinion, Sam didn't believe the subject was as important as other problems currently plaguing our world, such as the perpetual wars in the Middle East that created a mass exodus of refugees fleeing their bombarded cities as they attempt to seek safe harbour across borders.

Although Max respected Sam's resistance to the importance of the matter, he didn't relent; knowing that his reaction was just part of the path of discovery – and possibly the last stage of breaking free from the indoctrination.

The 19th-century German philosopher, Arthur Schopenhauer, suggested that all truth passes through three stages, stating, "*First, it is ridiculed. Second, it is violently opposed. And third, it is accepted as being self-evident*".

And Max had experienced – *all three stages!*

So, when Max realised the grand deception about the shape of the Earth, it meant that everything was now up for deliberation; including history, politics, cosmology, and even the existence of dinosaurs. Now firmly rejecting the fantasy that enormous dinosaurs stomped their feet upon our Earth, somewhat 66-million years ago.

"Mate... I'm also thrilled that you've met Jessica. She is quite amazing. And you know, she's pretty friggin smart – so I hope you can handle her," he teased.

Sam laughed, "Good one, ya boofhead," rubbing Max's hair which was longer than he would usually let it grow, generally preferring an easy to maintain shorter-styled cut.

"But, Sam; after our trip to London, it looks to me that Jessica is leaning towards the flat, geocentric model too!"

"I know, Max. What have you friggin done to her? And me... for that matter!"

"Hey, it happens to the best of us, Sam. I resisted the truth too, but I had to make a decision sooner or later. And for me, a Flat Earth makes a lot more sense."

"Okay, yeah, I gotta agree with you, pal; a spinning rock wrapped with trillions of litres of water flying through Space is just ridiculous – the further I considered it. And when I zoom into the Moon at night with my camera, I can barely hold the Moon on the viewfinder screen for more than a few seconds. So, I had to ask myself: am I spinning, or is the Moon moving? And when I thought about it – I reckon it's the Moon that is moving. There is no way I'm flying through the Universe at a million miles an hour right now!"

"Exactly, mate. It's undeniably obvious when the penny finally drops."

"And, Sam – with all due respect; I beg to differ, that knowing the real shape of the Earth won't change our lives. Because in my opinion, this topic of discussion is going to cause the largest conscious shift in modern society; and we all owe it to future generations to put this topic to bed... once and for all."

"You see, Flat Earth is not just about the shape of the Earth. It's more than that: because millions of people across the plane are suddenly beginning to think and question reality, rather than being consumed with pure utter nonsense and materialism. And you've gotta admit that we've all been subjected to overzealous governing on almost every aspect of our lives for far too long!"

"Just think about it, Sam; the powers that be control the people, the land, the food, the water, the skies, and beyond! So, you've gotta look at the big picture. Because, if the gatekeepers can deceive us about the very place where we live, then you could just imagine how far the deceit extends!"

"And when the world wakes up to the fact that our Earth is flat – then it's friggin, game on!"

"Far out... that's some scary shit, Max!"

"Yeah, it is kind of scary, mate! Could you just imagine the worldwide street protests that would occur if we all collectively agreed on this one single topic, in this overly divided world!"

"I get ya, Max. But the problem is, they've got most people in some kind of hypnotic state-of-mind. So, it's never going to happen! People just acquiesce – and they don't fight for their freedom like the good old days. Unfortunately, they just go with the flow."

Sam reasoned, "To be honest with you... I've been kind of confused lately, Max. The concept of a Flat Earth is doing my head in, and the motive isn't clear to me. The who, why, when, where, and how; is kind of important to me. I need to know it all before I can completely accept it as a fact!"

"I felt the same. It's confusing – and it takes a while to connect all the dots, as you have to shake off years of indoctrination. But sooner or later, we just have to admit – that we'll never know it all."

"Yeah, I guess we won't."

"I'm glad you agree, Sam. Even though some scientists believe they already have all the answers to life. And the mere mention of the word science in a news article these days, usually has people accepting it without a second thought!"

Frankly, Max was quite surprised that despite the fact Sam had seen the evidence through firsthand experiments and via countless hours of his own independent research. He still sat on the fence.

"Sam, it's evident that this world is going to buggery. Our freedoms and privacies are being systematically stripped away. And it seems to me that it's escalating, day by day! Soon enough, they'll be tracking everything we do!"

Max ranted on, "More laws, higher taxes, increased surveillance, governance, and perpetual wars. Before you know it, we'll probably have 'T800 Terminators' walking the streets and terminating people, just for not paying their speeding fines on time!"

"You friggin trip me out, Max. I love how your brain works, bud!"

"Right back at you, Sami," giving his friend a fist bump.

"But, do you want to know the real reason why this topic interests me, Sam?"

"Yeah, I do, Max!" taking a sip of his beer.

"Well, I believe that when humanity realises the Earth is flat, it will cause a huge conscious shift in societies behaviour. Because I reckon, when and if, the realisation occurs that we are all divine sovereign beings and here on Earth for a purpose – rather than space-monkeys living on a random rock flying through Space – then that's going to change the world!"

"Yeah, I guess it could! But, Max, I've been thinking of something: have you ever considered that maybe our Earth is just bigger than we are told, and that's why the earth curvature math is wrong – and the reason why we can see further than we should?"

"I have, Sam. But, the problem with that theory is: if our planet is larger, then it would need to rotate even faster than the alleged 1,666 kilometres per hour at the Equator to complete a daily revolution. So, therefore, in my opinion – I believe it's impossible!"

"Hmm... good point – you're right, Max. It's impossible – forget I even asked. My brain just can't absorb this, so I keep trying to find excuses to make the problem go away."

"I know what you mean, bud. Because I also sometimes wish that I could time-travel and return to the time before I heard about Flat Earth. But having said that, it's also changed my life for the better. The awakening was a huge moment for me. It even gave me goosebumps when the truth finally set in. It was a big moment in my life – and I'll never forget it. I gotta admit that maybe I even shed a tear!"

"There's nothing wrong with an occasional tear, Max."

"True, bud. And with the very thought that there could be more land to be discovered, I won't settle until it's proven... one way or another!"

"But, what about your luxurious lifestyle? Why would you want to leave it all behind just to find more land?"

"Well, Sam... what I've come to realise is that there's more to life than just money. You see, I want to help change this world, and the measly amount of money that I have can't do that."

"Yeah, right. Real measly. Sure thing, man!" Sam chuckled, looking around and admiring the view from the balcony of his grandiose modern apartment.

Max explained, "However, what I can do, is to assist the Flat Earth movement – and humanity, for that matter – by doing what a lot of people want to do. And that is, to explore beyond Antarctica. Because countless people are asking the question: is there more land across this infinite plane?"

"I hear you. But it's an insane idea, Max! You know that, right?"

"Yeah... I do. But, hey – someone's gotta do it. And you know that I love a good challenge!"

"I'd call it stubbornness!" Sam teased.

Max chuckled, "Yeah, probably! However, if we can find more land with additional resources, humanity could restore a level playing field. We've all been ripped off and for far too long. You know, we're still using expensive 'fossil fuels' that supposedly come from dinosaurs to run our vehicles, for God's sake! When we all know that there are other solutions. But, it's convenient for the few who are benefiting from the system."

Max continued, "And as a young kid growing up in the seventies, I always thought we would be flying into Space for a weekend holiday, and that we would all have flying cars by the year 2020; just like in 'The Jetsons' cartoon. But, we still have gas-guzzlers polluting the friggin atmosphere!"

"You still haven't answered my question, Max. Why would they lie about it?"

"Mate, I don't even know my motives, let alone the motives of others during the course of humanity... especially governments!"

It was a question that Max was repeatedly asked, since sharing the concept of Flat Earth with his friends – and he'd heard it about a thousand times, almost ad nauseam: *"Why would Governments and Space agencies lie about the shape of our Earth?"*

Although he didn't have a definitive answer to the question, where it would be impossible to definitively and conclusively know other people's motives, he always attempted to answer the question philosophically.

Max clarified, "But, what I do know is that when we falsely believe that we are living on a spinning water-ball flying through space, then it implies that we are here on this Earth by a cosmic catastrophe – as defined by the Big Bang theory."

Max pointed to the sky. "And they even push the false narrative, that there's more life out there somewhere, with some scientists even promoting the absurd notion that we were created by aliens! And they continuously indoctrinate people with pseudoscience, even preaching to humanity that their ancestors were chimpanzees – for God's sake! And let's be frank, that evolution still remains a theory to this very day. With no definitive proof. Because no one has ever observed a species changing kind. You know, as in witness an insect evolve into an animal – and they never will!"

"Max, as you know, I always questioned the theory of evolution, as it never really resonated with me. It goes against the grain of the magnificence that I see around me. I witness creation by design rather than by chance. Everything seems to be meticulously created for a reason. The perfection of this world could never be the cause of a random cosmic accident that formed all life from a single cell organism that somehow miraculously evolved after clinging onto a rock that crashed into this planet. Then unexplainably created every single specimen on Earth. It's nonsensical at every level. It's farcical!"

"Spot on, Sam. Evolution at a macro level is more of a philosophical construct rather than real science. It's a religion in itself. Just smoke and mirrors perpetrated by the powers that be in an attempt to stupefy humanity! And I reckon the grand objective of the ruling elites is to disenfranchise people from reality, with the ultimate goal to make people deny the possibility of a supreme creator... or God. Which by default, positions them as our 'higher-authority' and the ones to whom we must appeal to!"

"Max, I must admit that you have made me rethink everything that I once thought was proven as fact. However, I now realise that there's more to this world than I can ever imagine," Sam acknowledged.

"Hey, I went through the same process as you, bud. And it also made me realise that this world is not what we think it is."

Sam replied, "Yeah, I get you, man. It seems like they 'flat-out' lied about almost everything."

Laughing, "Yep. You got it, pal. 'Flat-out' alright."

"So, Sam, that's when I started to question life, and it got me thinking about God – almost on a daily basis; that I must admit, I had completely ignored for many years."

"Oh, that 'big-man in the sky' again, hey!" laughed Sam.

"Good one – but don't let Jessica hear you say that," he teased.

Max clarified, "Anyway, it was the concept that everything formed from 'nothingness' that sparked my interest. So, I began to question the Big Bang theory and the theory of evolution; and question it with an open mind. Because, if we didn't have a Big Bang that created everything from nothing – then effectively, the current theory of evolution holds no axiomatic truth to reality and is just more bullshit. And once we abandon it from the mix, you have to admit – it's more than likely that a higher power created this perfect world where we live upon."

"Yeah, it's kind of undeniable," replied Sam. "This world is abundant with perfection!" gazing toward the bay, admiring the crepuscular rays that were beaming through the fluffy grey clouds.

"And, Sam, if there really is a big man in the sky watching us from up above: then it makes a lot more sense on a Flat Earth. Because, where would you look up to God on a globe?"

Max then sporadically pointed around and asked, "Which way is Heaven on a spinning ball? That way... or that way?"

"Hmm... you're right; there is only one up – and only one down! And Max, it seems the masses fell for the theory of evolution hook-line-and-sinker – without thinking it through! And the worst thing is, they actually teach that shit at schools, and kids believe it – just because it's written in a science book! Besides, if they answer a question during an assessment that doesn't suit the narrative, they fail the curriculum!"

"Yep... just part of the early indoctrination, Sam. Schools don't teach children how to think; they teach them what to think! And it starts at preschool. Some parents even decorate their children's bedrooms with globes, decals of planets, and fake photos of the Earth. So, the brainwashing starts young! And the end goal is to fool the gullible public to believe they are just a speck of stardust flying through an infinite universe, born from a cosmic soup of atoms. Which just happened to align together in perfect harmony to create all life on Earth from a single cell organism, that for some reason decided to evolve."

Sam replied, "Well, it appears they are close to achieving the goal, Max. They even teach people that there are more stars in the

Universe than grains of sand on Earth. But who the heck has even counted them?"

"Precisely, Sam. As I previously mentioned, if they are going to lie about the shape of our Earth and all the bullshit fairy-tales in between, then there's no limit to what they will lie about next."

"Yeah, I get it, Max! You're right, bro," nodding in agreement.

35

Zoe and Jessica strutted out onto the balcony to join Max and Sam at the outdoor table setting, where Zoe poured a round of strawberry daiquiris as the sound of thunder rumbled the sky from a distant storm brewing over Melbourne's western suburbs.

She was looking gorgeous dressed in a form-fitted floral printed dress with blush high-heel shoes and with her long dark-brown hair tied back into a ponytail – resembled a young and glamourous Audrey Hepburn.

Max pecked Zoe on the lips then said, "Hey, ladies! Sam and I were talking about the theory of evolution again. I just want to ask, have you ever questioned with an open mind how the theory was founded?"

They collectively shrugged their shoulders.

"Well... we all know that Charles Darwin first proposed the theory, so let's start by questioning that crazy freak!""

"First, let me say – that I find it quite far-fetched to believe, that after Darwin travelled to the Galapagos Islands, he apparently theorised the concept of evolution by simply witnessing birds adapt to their environment over just a handful of years. And this remains the foundation for the theory, until this very day."

"Anyway, what really bugs me is that Darwin had several children – who were all strangely conceived with his first cousin – and rather than witness the evolution of his children by spending time with them, he chose to travel on a ship with strange men for months on end; just so that he could study the evolution of birds on some faraway islands!"

Sam rubbed his chin in thought. "Really, Max? What a friggin jerk! Could you imagine what any normal wife would say if you left them with several kids so that you could observe birds?"

"Exactly, Sam. She would probably say, "*Leave... you, asshole! I'll help you pack your bags! And I hope you die at sea – you freak!*"

Zoe looked at Max with a stern look and said, "You've got that right!" as they all laughed.

"But in all seriousness, anyone with a right mind would have to re-think the theory of evolution. And when one investigates the topic without bias, they will discover that a theory that suggests that all life on Earth evolved from a single cell organism after falling from the sky, and then miraculously coalesced and evolved into everything here on Earth is fallacious. You know, a theory that suggests that a banana evolved from a rock is not science, but rather, pure 'malakia' – I mean, malarkey!"

Sam laughed, "Yeah, it's malakia, alright!"

"Yep. Just pure mumbo-jumbo designed to make people believe the narrative that a primordial soup of dust created all life on Earth. And to perpetuate the grand deception that all life evolved from a big explosion of nothingness – billions upon billions of years ago. All, to solidify the biggest falsehood, that we live on a spinning ball that's dangerously dodging asteroids as we zoom through Space, with the upper atmosphere acting like a windshield made of gravity. Because, keeping people living in constant fear – is just part of the scam!"

"It's all BS, Max. It seems to me that they love pushing the notion of a cataclysmic doomsday scenario that may someday wipe out all life on Earth. Whether from a potential nuclear attack by a rogue enemy, an alien invasion from a far-away galaxy, solar flares causing gamma radiation, or an asteroid always 'just' missing our Earth. It's non-stop fear-mongering! And truth be told, if an asteroid was actually going to crash into Earth, I highly doubt they would even tell us; that is, until the very last moment!"

"Undeniably, bud! And besides, the deception is easy to achieve. They just keep adding extra layers to the lies. And with today's special effects that can literally mimic reality, mixed with high-paid actors in spacesuits under stringent non-disclosure agreements – and who are probably involved in secret societies – then it's easy! Not to mention the sort of trickery you can achieve with over $50 million a day!"

"What do you mean by... $50 million per day?" asked Sam.

"Well, that's NASA's budget... every single day! It amounted to over $19 billion in 2019, and they've been receiving billions of dollars from taxpayers for many decades!"

"Wow, that's a lot of folding stuff, Max!"

"Sure is, mate, and it all goes to waste by faking the possibility of Space travel. I've even seen videos that show 'bubbles of water' when they're supposed to be in outer Space, which kind of implies that the footage was filmed in NASA's Neutral Buoyancy Lab!"

Zoe chimed in, "Hey, it's more like hundreds of billions of dollars per year, once you collectively account for all international investment in Space. And NASA has received over a trillion dollars since their inception. You know, I'd love to audit their books, even for just one day. They are all dodgy. As shifty as you can get!"

"Really, Zoe?" replied Sam, "I didn't realise it was that much cash. And even just a portion of that could solve some of the world's problems. So why don't they invest that money here on Earth?"

Sam was noticeably angered by the revelation, and that's exactly what Max had been waiting for all this time: to see him get fired up!

Zoe shrugged her shoulders, "I'm buggered if I know, Sam!"

Sam pointed to the sky and said, "Why the heck are we wasting the money in Space, rather than solving problems that span the globe we live on?" after briefly doing the math as to what that money could buy if circulated on real-world issues.

"Precisely, Sam. I agree with every word you said – that is, apart from the word 'globe'," Max smirked.

"But you're right, and I've asked myself the very same question many times over. Why the heck are we looking up into Space when we have countless problems to solve down here on Earth? And the more I thought about it, the more it actually pissed me off! Especially when they still can't even show us a photo or live video of the Earth that isn't somehow doctored by a graphic design department. All they have to do is zoom-in to 'upside-down' Australia in real-time, whenever the International Space Station passes over our cities."

He elaborated, "Just show us real, close-up high-definition video footage of Australia from Space! Like kangaroos jumping around upside down. Or even an upside-down Sydney Harbour Bridge. Show us anything but ridiculous CGI and this whole subject can be put to bed!"

Jessica asked, "But what about all the companies that are involved in making parts for the spacecraft and satellites? Surely one of them would have blown the whistle by now. One of my cousins is an aerospace engineer, and he engineered a small piece for the toilet seat on the ISS. He's rather proud of his achievement. He constantly gloats about it at every Christmas gathering. Kind of annoyingly... I must say!"

"Who knows, Jessica. But, as a businessman, if I owned an engineering firm that was granted government contracts, or from whoever; well, as long as the invoices were regularly paid, then I really wouldn't care what they did with the part that I produced. And I'd most likely just keep quiet about it. Even if I knew it was a shonky scam. Wouldn't you?"

"Yeah, most likely, Max. I reckon most people would do the same. Just keep quiet rather than risk their livelihood. That makes perfect sense to me!"

"Spot on, Jessica. So, I truly don't know what direct benefit we get from Space programs; apart from that, it being just part of the grand illusion to keep people in the belief that outer space is habitable. And they talk about colonizing the Moon and Mars with futuristic cities, but we haven't even mastered that type of advanced living – right here on Earth."

Max shook his head in disgust. "The selfishness, let alone the foolishness is beyond comprehension!"

"I hear ya, buddy – but you know what still gets me, Max? I

just can't get over the fact that thousands – if not millions – of scientists could be lying to us about the shape of the Earth. It just doesn't seem plausible. Most of them are honest people who are searching for new and exciting discoveries. That's the only part of this theory that holds me back from completely accepting it. I just can't believe that they would lie about it!" still struggling to accept the motive behind the grand deception.

"I don't think that scientists are lying, Sam. In fact, I believe that most people on this Earth are inherently good, honest people – where these traits are somehow embedded into our DNA. And I suspect that the majority of scientists are the same. They are most likely good people trying to live their lives, feed their families, and pay the bills. You know, just like the rest of humanity. And it's also more than likely that they are too involved in their independent field of study, or, one could almost say, too compartmentalised to see the truth. And I highly doubt they would risk their careers, lifestyle, or credentials just to disclose the deception, as there's a lot of resistance to Flat Earth; if you haven't already noticed. And you know, in a way, I don't really blame 'em!"

"I gotta agree, that there sure is a lot of resistance, Max. I still remember the first day you told me about it. I thought that you'd finally lost your friggin mind!" teased Sam, as they collectively laughed.

"Not yet, mate... not yet!" Max chuckled. "But you have to admit that compartmentalisation occurs across many sectors of industry; it happens in the corporate world, within governments, and I would dare say that it sometimes happens in science."

"Hmm... yeah... you're right again, Max; because it certainly occurs at my work! The upper echelon are control freaks. I'm getting kind of sick of their bullshit, to be honest."

"Hey Sam, have you ever looked into how they built the atomic bomb that annihilated Japan during the second world war?"

"No... I haven't, Max. But for some reason, I'm pretty sure you're about to tell me," Sam baited, cheekily winking at the girls and taking a sip of his drink.

"Well, the Manhattan Project was one of the most compartmentalised and secretive projects to have ever been undertaken on Earth. I think it commenced in the 1930s and included over 130,000 individuals – many of them scientists. All, like programmed robots working toward a singular goal to build the most destructive bomb on Earth. Achieved, not only without disclosure to civilians, but even the majority of the scientists and engineers were unaware of what they were developing."

"It was all top secret! That is until they dropped the bombs over Hiroshima and Nagasaki – completely obliterating both cities."

"That's rather freaky, Max! I'm surprised that it wasn't somehow leaked, especially with that many scientists working on the project."

"It sure is freaky. So, if the puppet-masters can achieve that level of secrecy for the purpose of destruction, then anything is possible!"

"Oh, and may I also mention that the word science etymologically translates from the Latin and Italian word for knowledge or awareness. And anyone can have knowledge or know-how – not just scientists!"

Zoe interrupted, "Who's ready to eat? Max, why don't you crank up the barbeque? Jessica and I will finish preparing the salads," kissing him, then grabbing Jessica's hand and dashing away; who was eagerly listening to the entire conversation – but unusually, she remained conservatively quiet.

Sam pressed the igniter to strike up the barbeque. "Max, have you even told Zoe about your audacious plan to find undiscovered land?"

"Not yet," he replied, folding up the barbeque cover.

"Well, I hope you know that she's going to friggin hit the roof when you tell her about your crazy idea. You know that, right?"

"Yeah, yeah, I know, Sam. I'm not sure how to tell her, actually," taking a big sip of his drink.

"Good luck with that, champ!"

"Let's just leave it for now, Sam!" knowing deep in his mind that Zoe was going to crack it. No matter which way he sold it.

He hastily changed the topic of discussion.

"Anyway... We've got a big weekend coming up, Sam. I've just scored two tickets to the Collingwood versus Richmond preliminary final at the Melbourne Cricket Ground next Saturday. And I'm heading out bush on Sunday to meet Miguel; who's a former sniper that I met online. And you know, if we're lucky, we may even get a chance to shoot some rounds."

"You coming with me?" he asked.

"Bloody oath, Max. Count me in!" Sam eagerly replied, as they clinked their drinks.

"In the Middle Ages people believed that the earth was flat, for which they had at least the evidence of their senses: we believe it to be round, not because as many as one-percent of us could give the physical reasons for so quaint a belief, but because modern science has convinced us that nothing that is obvious is true, and that everything that is magical, improbable, extraordinary, gigantic, microscopic, heartless or outrageous is 'scientific'."

GEORGE BERNARD SHAW

36

An electrifying collective roar by the spirited ninety-five-thousand strong crowd echoed throughout the Melbourne Cricket Ground.

The game was just minutes from starting and hyped as one of the most anticipated preliminary finals in modern football, between the Collingwood Magpies and the Richmond Tigers – two of the most rival teams in the Australian Football League—ready to battle it out for the prestigious opportunity to compete in the AFL Grand Final.

Sam and Max cheered, "GO THE PIES!" from the top of their voices as their beloved football team ran onto the oval-shaped field.

The thunderous roar from the supporters and the jeering by the opposition reverberated around the stadium; as Collingwood tore through the large team banner as the team anthem blared through the speakers in tradition.

"Hey, Max – have you heard the claim made by some astrophysicist that an NFL football team in Cincinnati kicked a 40-metre field goal to win a game due to the deflection caused by the Coriolis effect?"

"Nah... I haven't, bud," Max replied, unwrapping a meat pie – loading the top with tomato sauce.

"Well, it was that quirky American astrophysicist, Neil deGrasse Tyson, and he claimed that the rotation of the Earth caused the football to weave through the goal by just a mere few centimetres. He did the numbers on it. But I reckon it's hogwash!"

"Oh, yes indeed... the good old Coriolis effect. Sounds like nonsense to me too, Sam!" taking a mouthful of his meat pie –

almost dripping tomato sauce on his clean white shirt, but luckily the drop landed just between his leather boots.

"Anyway, Max. I've done some extensive investigation into it. And if it were true, then Coriolis is one of the most selective forces on the heliocentric model. Second to gravity, when it comes to magic!"

"Good one, Sam", he chuckled, just minutes before the siren would signal the beginning of the game. The collective anticipation from the crowd created an eerie feeling that you could almost cut with a knife.

"Just think about this, Max," as Sam then rattled off some sports trivia. "The longest kick by an AFL footballer is 105 metres, with no account for Coriolis. The longest ski jump is 246 metres, with again, no account for Coriolis. And the longest golf shot is 366 metres, with no account for friggin Coriolis!"

"Max, nobody, and I mean nobody, in the entire history of sports – even going back to the days of the ancient Olympic games – has ever accounted for the Coriolis effect; otherwise, they would have all needed an advanced degree in physics."

Max laughed, "Yeah, just more baloney, Sam."

But the laugh didn't last long, as Max shook his head and said, "I still can't believe I was stooged by all that spinning ball shit!"

Sam gently nudged Max with his elbow in jest, "Mate… and if the Coriolis effect actually existed, then spectators watching javelin events would be in constant fear for their lives!"

Laughing at his joke while slapping his knee, "That's a bloody classic, Sam. I've got to remember that one."

"That reminds me, do you remember that high-altitude Red Bull jump some years back?" asked Max.

"Yeah, I do! That's the crazy dude that jumped from a high-altitude balloon from the 'edge of space'. Wasn't it like from over 120,000 feet – or something like that?" Sam asked, as the crowd went wild after one of their lead players kicked a 50-metre goal from the boundary line, just moments after the beginning of the game.

"Spot on, mate! And the Red Bull jump also debunks the claim regarding the NFL field goal. Because Felix Baumgartner ascended into the upper atmosphere for three hours, but only landed 80-kilometres from the launch site. So, why didn't he land in the Pacific Ocean if he ascended over our Earth for hours on end? Because technically, he should have landed about 3,000 kilometres away from the launch site if the Earth spins at about 1,000 kilometres per hour in New Mexico."

"Hmm... good point, Max. Because, if the Earth was spinning – as they say, it does – then the Coriolis effect would've certainly sent him off course. No doubt about it! And doesn't space technically begin at an altitude of 100 kilometres – otherwise known as the Kármán Line? So, why did they call it 'the edge of Space'?"

"And you're right, Max: I also can't believe I was duped by all the freakin' bullshit!"

"Don't worry about it, Sam – we all were! And they showed us a curved Earth at that altitude, but the reality is that we wouldn't even see the Earth's curvature from 120,000 feet – and scientists now admit it. So, they obviously used a camera with a wide-angle fisheye lens to catfish us with falsified footage! And don't forget that during a presentation, Neil deGrasse Tyson said that you wouldn't see Earth's curvature based on Baumgartner's altitude. Paraphrasing, he said that at an altitude of 120,000 feet, '*That Stuff is Flat*' while also motioning a level surface with his hand!"

"Ah... shit, Max! Our best player just got carried off the field with an injury. Let's hope we don't get the collywobbles again!"

"It wouldn't be nothing new. But nah... don't worry, Sam. We've got the big American fella on our side, and it looks like he's in great form. He'll kick a few goals for us... for sure!"

"I friggin hope so, mate. We can't lose this one. Not again!"

"Hey Max, what about the ridiculous claim that when toilets get flushed in the Northern Hemisphere, the water spins in the opposite direction to toilets flushed in the Southern Hemisphere? What do you think of that? Some 'Flat Earth debunker' claimed that it proves the Earth is spinning. But what do you think?"

"It's preposterous – that's what I think! Just another absurd myth!" as Max had done the research on the claim and knew that it had been extensively debunked, together with the allegation that cyclones spin in opposite directions depending on whether in the northern or southern hemispheres, is the cause of the said Coriolis effect.

Max elaborated, "First, they make us look to the sky for proof of where we live: then they mockingly make us look in a friggin toilet bowl. All whilst we ignore the apparent stillness of the ground that we stand on. But in essence, Sam, water drains down a toilet bowl or a sink, in accordance with two factors; the shape of the basin – and the direction in which the water is introduced into the container. It has nothing to do with the rotation of the Earth!"

Sam concurred, and they put the subject aside as they continued to enjoy the rest of the game, cheering for their team as the siren sounded for the beginning of the final quarter. And with just twenty minutes remaining in the game – after leading from start to finish – Collingwood had a comfortable buffer over their opponents.

Max and Sam were elated; because it now meant that their beloved football team, were heading towards another Grand-Final.

The siren sounded the end of the game where the rowdy Collingwood supporters cheered with delight, singing their team anthem at the top of their voices. Max and Sam soon after exiting the stadium to avoid getting trapped amongst the horde of spectators.

"Hey Sam, I'm going to meet that sniper guy tomorrow morning. Are you still coming along?"

"What sort of a bloody question is that? Of course, I am!"

"Brilliant. Let's leave at around eight o'clock tomorrow. Should we bring the girls along?"

"Nah, they'll probably just get bored."

"Yep, you're right, big buddy; what the heck was I thinking?" laughing as they victoriously headed toward the nearest bar to celebrate the triumph with a few celebratory drinks.

37

Max set the cruise control of his vehicle to the posted speed limit of 110 kilometres per hour but was soon after pulled over by a Highway Patrol car after being caught by radar, overtaking another vehicle at almost 40 kilometres per hour above the limit.

The flashing lights of the police vehicle parked behind him gave him an overwhelming sense of discomfort while he waited for justice to arrive in the form of another speeding fine.

After checking his driver's license details using the onboard computer in the police vehicle, the officer reapproached the driver side of the car and handing Max the fine; she firmly said, "I'll be lenient on you this time. But, hey, take it easy on the road, will ya? We've had countless accidents around here lately. So please... be careful!" she insisted.

"No worries... I sure will, officer," he replied, thankful that he didn't just lose his license for another six months—placing the speeding fine into the centre console amongst the others.

They watched the police vehicle depart to continue patrolling the roads and looking at Max; Sam said, "Jeez... she was pretty hot, hey!" raising his eyebrows. "You know, they do say that there's nothing better than a good-looking woman in uniform!"

"That's true... except when they ask you for money!" Max joked, punching the throttle with his foot to continue driving along the two-lane highway whilst briefly trying to mentally calculate the remaining demerit points on his driver's license.

They were driving toward the Victorian Highlands to visit a colleague that Max met online.

His name was Miguel – an American ex-pat who migrated to Australia from far-west Texas and was once a sniper for the United States Marine Corps—where Max took the trip to visit him to discuss the Coriolis force and its effect on snipers firing their weapons over extensive distances.

Max was also eager to invite Miguel on a manned expedition upon confirmed sighting of land from the Odysseus, and he thought it would be a breeze convincing him. But little did he realise the resistance he was about to face even though Miguel staunchly believed that the Earth was flat.

Sam slid on his sunglasses, "Far out... that Sun is bright today, isn't it? How far do they say it is again, Max?" he asked, as they drove to Miguel's secluded property located 250-kilometres north-east of Melbourne.

Max gently accelerated to overtake a semi-trailer then carefully hugged the car back into the left lane, replying, "Well, according to the heliocentric model, the Sun is said to be between 91.4 million miles away – or around 140 million kilometres away from the Earth at Perihelion, which means 'close to the Sun' in Greek. And they reckon it's about 94.5 million miles at Aphelion, which means 'further from the Sun'. And, by the way, 'helio' is the Greek word for the Sun."

"Really? I didn't know that, Max. That's interesting. And thanks for the Greek lesson. You know, it's all a little bit Greek to me right now!" he giggled.

Smiling, Max said, "Yeah, it sure is. And one of the first people to 'accurately' propose our distance to the Sun was a Jesuit priest and astronomer named Maximilian Hell. Freakish name, isn't it?" he chuckled.

"No friggin way, Max," Sam laughed. "Who would ever name their kid 'Max Hell'? He must have copped a pretty hard time at school! What do you reckon?"

"Yeah... it would've been hell, alright!" Max snickered.

"Anyway, Sam, look it up yourself. Question then research and scrutinize everything I say."

"Yeah, yeah... I do, Max – I do!"

"Cool, cool... good to know. And hey, the most insane thing about the heliocentric model is that it insinuates that we experience summer when the Earth is furthest from the Sun – during aphelion. And we experience winter when we are closer to the Sun – during perihelion."

"What do you mean? That doesn't make sense! How could we be warmer when we are further from the Sun? Are you sure you have that right?"

Max confidently replied, "Sure have. Look it up. Just research it. It's what the heliocentric model claims. I don't just make this shit up – you know!"

"Okay... fair enough, mate. It just sounds strange – that's all. And they didn't teach us that sort of stuff at school. Did they?"

"Exactly! Could you just imagine if we were taught to stand further away from a heater if we wanted to warm up; then to stand closer if we wanted to cool down? Because it would be considered nonsensical, and most people – and even kids – would roll their eyes at the very suggestion. But, that's what heliocentrism proposes. As it implies that we experience summer when the Sun is further from the Earth—and that's just pure bullshit!"

"That's lunacy, Max!"

"It's beyond lunacy," Max quickly agreed. "And heavily indoctrinated globe Earth believers relentlessly defend the absurdity by arguing that the axial tilt of the Earth explains the anomaly. However, a mere tilt of even ten-thousand kilometres could never compensate for the five-million-kilometre disparity during perihelion and aphelion."

"I highly doubt it too, Max."

"But, it gets even worse! Do you want to hear some more bullshit? I've got more – it's almost neverending."

Sam reached over to lower the sound of the radio. "Absolutely... go for it, Max. You know, the more I hear, the funnier it gets."

He was eager to learn; because it was now more than apparent that the heliocentric model was just hogwash. And rather sad, to say the least, Sam realised that humanity was foolishly catfished into accepting a model of the world around them that was pure fantasy since its conception – many hundreds of years ago.

"It sure is funny, but I just wish it wasn't true, Sam!"

"Anyway, despite attempting to determine the mean distance of the Earth to the Sun with absolute certainty; it has been widely hypothesised and debated over the centuries; and by some of the smartest people to walk this Earth. As suffice to say, how could anyone really know with absolute assurance?"

"So, how did they work out the distance, Max?"

"Well, as far as I can ascertain, the science is rather flimsy, to gin with, astronomers cleverly devised a method of measurement called distance and motion parallax. They then mixed it up with nomenclature – or jargon – by attempting to triangulate the location of the Sun and the stars with a bunch of equations. In essence, as part of the trickery, they presumptively assumed that Venus is the same size as the Earth. In effect: their assumptions were whimsically attained by guesswork rather than using the scientific method. Because their first mistake was assuming that Venus was the same size as the Earth before proving it."

Max briefly glanced at Sam, "You still with me there, bud? You haven't dozed off under those dark sunglasses, have you?"

"No, no... go for it! I'm with you... I'm all ears... keep going," straightening himself into the seat.

"Well, as I was saying... and then in the 1500s, another Jesuit priest, the somewhat famous Nicolaus Copernicus, claimed that the distance of the Earth to the Sun was 3-million miles (approx. 5-million kilometres). Followed by Tyco Brahe, and then Johannes Kepler, who later estimated the Sun to be 13 million miles from Earth."

"Then comes along Isaac Newton. Who on his first attempt, said the Sun was 28 million miles away, then adjusted it to 54 million miles without suspicion by the masses. Who during that era could barely write their name – let alone comprehend the complexity of calculus, trigonometry and astronomy."

"And did you know that Issac Newton once said... '*It matters not whether we reckon it, 28 or 54 million miles distant – for either would do just as well!*'"

"Really? Newton said that?" Sam replied, raising his eyebrows.

"Yep... no shit, Sam! Then another guy named Johann Franz Encke estimated the Sun to be 95 million miles away, and then some dude named Robert Stawell Ball claimed it was 92 million miles away from Earth. But the math still worked, regardless of the distance to the Sun. Because equations can be reverse-engineered and skewed to suit any model without representing the true nature of reality. And many physicists openly admitted it. Including; Newton, Copernicus, Poincaré, Hoyle, Cohen, Hawking, and even Einstein. All famous physicists, astronomers, and theologians who, until their dying days on Earth, questioned the mainstream narrative—because deep down inside, they knew it was bullshit!"

Sam remarked, "How convenient! And you're right; it seems as if they built a mathematical model to suit their agenda!"

"Absolutely; it's just nonsense at best! The religion of 'heliocentrism' or 'paganism' relies on mystical mathematics to describe reality, but as Tesla said, it has no merit with natural phenomena. Just like the magical 'goldilocks zone', where it is suggested that Earth perpetually orbits the Sun at an ideal distance, and thus keeps us – not too hot, and not too cold: just right!"

Max elaborated, "And don't forget; apparently all caused by a cosmic accident that occurred by pure coincidence and fluke, enacted by a big explosion billions of years ago. But, as we both know, the theory is based on a hypothetical construct, which they hoodwinked everyone into believing. Again, with advanced theoretical math to support their fanatical concepts. It's a religion at best!"

"That doesn't sound like science to me, Max! I could easily construct a mathematical model to show that I have six red Ferraris in my garage. But, it doesn't make it true!" he joked.

"Exactly, mate," Max snorted. "And you know, that's the only way to explain the globe Earth model, as opposed to the core of one's senses and natural science, that proves that we are not 'upside-down', and hurtling through space on a revolving 'pear' shaped oblate spheroid; as once described by an astrophysicist. Who ironically has never been to Outer Space to verify the shape of the Earth for himself; but thinks it's friggin pear-shaped!"

Max relished any opportunity to debate with atheists who would cling to the Big Bang theory, like a child clinging to an outworn teddy bear when defending their dogmas—appreciating that hard-core atheists were often far more obsessive about their beliefs than religious extremists.

Paradoxically, atheists also hold a false misconception that the Big Bang theory debunks intelligent design or divine creation. Although ironically, many headstrong atheists are unaware that the theory was, in fact, founded by the Catholic Jesuit priest, Georges Lemaître. Therefore, in essence, the Big Bang theory is religious by design. And more than likely intended to continue the worship of the demigods and the fallen angels – where it is biblically described that one-third, or 'thirty-three' percent of the stars were expelled from Heaven and here now reside on Earth. And with Lucifer in charge, wickedly they fell with hate. Their grand aim: to disrupt mankind.

Blindly evident, by the naming of the planets and the wandering stars; where Satan was granted his namesake planet: Saturn. And even the Goddess Venus was revered by assigning her with a divine planet, amongst many others.

In fact, the Catholic Church who owns the world's largest binoculars that point to the sky, even bizarrely named their multi-million-dollar observatory – Lucifer!

"Max, I don't know where you get all this info, but it's rather fascinating, to say the least."

"Neither do I, Sam," he chuckled.

Observing the GPS map on the dashboard, excitingly, Max said, "It looks like Miguel's place is just up the road here," activating the turn signal, veering off the highway via the exit ramp.

"*The best possessions of man are his senses; and, when he uses them all, he will not be deceived in his survey of nature. It is only when some one faculty or other is neglected or abused that he is deluded. Every man in full command of his senses knows that a level surface is a flat or horizontal one; but astronomers tell us that the true level is the curved surface of a globe! They know that man requires a level surface on which to live, so they give him one in name which is not one in fact! Since this is the best that astronomers, with their theoretical science, can do for their fellow creatures – deceive them – it is clear that things are not as they say they are; and, in short, it is a proof that Earth is not a globe.*"

WILLIAM CARPENTER

38

They arrived at Miguel's property late morning—tall, fresh alpine trees surrounding his secluded rural estate; the driveway entrance protected by a high-fenced gate secured by a large padlock.

Max sent a text message to notify Miguel of their arrival, where he appeared minutes later riding a quad bike, with two Australian Blue Heelers running alongside. The dogs barked to let the strangers know who's the boss as they ran toward the gate. Their tails now wagging with delight, after Miguel settled them down by simply commanding them with a few direct words.

He met Miguel online, and they became close friends, where they would constantly discuss the Flat Earth theory for hours on end. With a particular focus on whether snipers account for the Coriolis effect when they fire their artillery.

Entering the ranch-style home, Miguel hospitably brewed a freshly percolated coffee, where they sat under a bullnose veranda discussing his tour of duty as a sniper with the U.S. Marines. The hour passing in no time before Miguel offered to show his prized collection of rifles that were securely locked away in a tall gun safe.

"Gentlemen, the supposed Coriolis effect is believed to be the result of the force generated by the Earth spinning from west to east," said Miguel with his still evident Texan accent. "So, this would mean that anything independent of a revolving Earth should be affected."

"But that doesn't happen... right, Miguel?"

"Spot-on, Max! Yet, birds, bugs, planes, and even artillery – such as the U.S. Navy railgun – which can shoot a target 100-miles away, are unabated in flight in any direction whatsoever. The official explanation claiming that everything hovering over our Earth moves within our atmosphere, as what could be defined as surface friction. Essentially, they reckon the atmosphere somehow magically grips the planet as it spins!"

"So, why do some people say that snipers need to account for Coriolis, Miguel?"

Miguel was instantly triggered by the very thought. "Max... many of these people haven't even picked up a God damn gun in their entire lives – let alone fired one!"

Entering the passcode and unlocking the safe, he turned to Max and asked, "So I would like to know why so many non-experts in the field of shooting sophisticated long-range weapons systems are all of a sudden 'experts' when defending their bias?"

"I've noticed that too, mate. I don't have an answer; apart from that, some people like to defend their beliefs."

"They certainly do, Max. But, it would be like me – a trained U.S. Marine – going to a hospital and telling a bunch of surgeons the exact procedures for brain or heart surgery!" Miguel shook his head in disgust, "Who does that... but a lying fool!"

"Exactly, Miguel!"

Miguel took the Ruger Precision Rifle from the gun safe and said while relocking it, "Can't be too secure when it comes to gun safety."

"Absolutely... 100%... definitely," replied Max, looking at the rifle in awe. A rare moment for him, as it had been a long time that he'd seen a gun in real life.

He then entered the code to unlock another safe and grabbed several boxes of 308 calibre bullets; again, relocking the safe.

Miguel continued, "I have a brainteaser conundrum for those who believe that we are spinning at 1,000 miles per hour at the equator," he confidently spoke.

"You see, gents, I have challenged countless people who claim that our Earth is spinning to provide experimentation and documentation of their results. And I have a $20,000 cash bet challenge on the table for anyone smart enough to teach me how to fire long-range weapons that I've trained with for over five years during my military career!"

Max and Sam listened intently whilst admiring the rifle's features, and just as Max envisaged from the many discussions that he had with Miguel online, he was an interesting character. A little rough around the edges in his demeanour, as you'd expect from a hardened U.S. Marine, but a gentleman at heart and probably the nicest guy you could ever meet via the internet by chance.

Miguel teased, "This should be an easy-peasy cinch for them. Because all they have to do is show me the exact mathematical calculations to use when aiming for a target in these three very different scenarios. I've got the precise calculations right here on my smartphone, ready to present to any 'ball Earth' defender," reaching into his pocket for his phone—his rifle hitched over his shoulder.

He said, "Picture this, fellas!" as he proceeded to read out the scenarios to his long-standing challenge:

Scenario 1: Sniper in Washington State acquiring a target at 1,500 metres away facing East, while the Earth is spinning West-to-East at 1,275 kph (792 mph). Elevation is Sea Level. Wind velocity 20-mph going North. Stationary target. 50 calibre Sniper rifle.

2: Sniper in West Africa acquiring a target at 1,200 metres away facing West, while the Earth is spinning West-to-East at 1,550 kph (963 mph). Elevation is Sea Level. Wind velocity 10 mph going South. Stationary target. 50 calibre Sniper rifle.

And finally, 3: Sniper in Ecuador acquiring a target at 2,000 metres away facing North, while the Earth is spinning West-to-East at 1,650 kph (1,025 mph). Elevation is 20 metres—wind velocity 40 mph going East, stationary target, 50 calibre Sniper rifle.

"Far out... that sounds impossible, Miguel!" exclaimed Sam. "How could any sniper be expected to randomly do that type of math before shooting at a target?"

"You've got it, Sam... it's God damn impossible, alright! And the Marine sniper manual has no mention of the Coriolis effect. Whereas the FMFM 1-3B Sniping (U.S. Marine Corps) manual for Marksmanship Training explains that the effect of the path of the bullet is dependent on the elevation, weather, wind, a stationary or moving target, range, the height of the sniper and target, the atmosphere, and even light conditions."

He took a breather, then said, "But, you know... there's not one mention of the fictitious Coriolis force! You see, a sniper must know the general principles of perspective, the vanishing point, delineation, and the geographical surroundings of the intelligence operations."

Miguel clicked ten bullets into the double-stack magazine, then slid a bullet directly into the chamber as he continued to ramble on, hardly allowing either Max or Sam to get a word in.

Miguel explained, "Every bullet spins out of a rifle barrel in a perfectly straight-line trajectory called a 'line of departure'. It then follows the long bore of the rifle in a perfectly straight line, that is, until the bullet leaves the barrel – which is cut or swaged with a spiral groove pattern, lengthwise along the barrel of the firearm. And when the bullet is met with wind resistance, its weight causes the bullet to drop in mid-flight during the trajectory as it spins through the air causing a Magnus effect; caused by ridges inside the barrel."

"And I should also mention that all rifles fire a straight-line trajectory until the weight and the spin of the projectile causes the bullet to fall and thus appears to travel in an arc. Not, the bullet 'hugging' the terrestrial surface of the Earth in flight as it spins... as some globe theorists suggest!" gasping in frustration.

Sam asked, "And what about people who claim that bullets arc and hug the Earth in flight due to gravity, Miguel?""

Miguel shrieked, "What is this blasphemy people speak of...

that a bullet flies in a rainbow arc out of a rifle due to gravity? What kind of acid are these globe lovers taking before handling a weapon? As there would be no such thing as a sniper being able to hit a target one-thousand metres away, especially if they had to compensate for the imaginary gravitational pull of a bullet... or the imaginary spin of the Earth!"

"Yeah, that's exactly what I thought, Miguel." Sam then queried, "By the way, what type of weapons did you use during your tour of duty?"

"I've mastered several weapon systems. Everything from an M-16 to a Mini 14, Mp5, Uzi 9mm's, shotguns, 240 Golf machine gun, SMAW 83mm warhead rocket launcher, mortars, and grenade launchers. Oh... and I also trained with platoon snipers and fired long-range sniper rifles," he proudly boasted whilst holding the Ruger.

"Wow... you're like a real-life Rambo!"

Miguel smirked, "Not quite," clicking the loaded magazine into the rifle.

"And gentlemen, at no stage do any of those weapon systems require an adjustment for the alleged 'Coriolis Force' to account for the imaginary spin of the Earth. Never in my entire military weapons career did I ever hear the words 'Coriolis effect'. Much less train our Marines to calculate for this big pile of bullshit!"

"Did you say that's for every one of those weapons, Miguel?" asked Sam. "Including the grenade launcher?"

"Yes – that's correct, Sam. You got it. And it includes weapon systems like mortars and artillery shells that are fired up at an angle and thus have a greater arc of trajectory in flight. Where those rounds also fly straight out of the barrel until met with wind resistance, weight, mass, and density – which ultimately causes the round to fall to the Earth. Just like everything else falls to Earth!"

"Okay. That makes sense," replied Sam – impressed by his reply.

"Just think about this; if the Earth is spinning – as they say it does – and we are trying to fire a weapon system, then we would have to account for the direction we are facing when firing. Meaning, if the Earth is spinning west-to-east, as presumed, then I would have to make a different adjustment for all four directions, including; north, south, east, and west—amongst many other real-life variables."

Miguel unfolded the bipod stand attached to the rifle and set it down on the ground laying down beside it, then pulled back the bolt to load a bullet directly into the chamber.

"Put on your protective gear, fellas. This is going to be loud," aiming at the target positioned approximately 100 metres away – whilst making minor adjustments to the dials on the scope to line up the cross-hairs with the bullseye.

The shot let out a deafening boom, followed by a slight ting that sounded a split second later, letting them know that Miguel had accurately hit the metal target.

"Bullseye!" he bragged, still laying on his belly with the rifle remaining in aim.

Miguel was in his element. Where you could tell by the look on his face that holding a gun; well, it kind of suited his style—almost like it was meant to be.

Placing his pointer finger over his lips, Miguel whispered, "Shh... I'm a sniper dressed in full camouflage gear, wearing my ghillie suit, and hunkered down into the grass. I've got enemy forces surrounding me; they are approaching from three different directions," as he convincingly pointed around at the imaginary targets in the woods.

"The terrorist targets are closing in fast, and they are big friggin dudes with big fuckin guns coming toward me in lockstep! I have very little time to engage, but I've lined 'em all up in my scope and got 'em in line of sight. And I'm gonna take 'em all down... one by one. They are goners! I'll pop 'em all... any day of the week. No problemo!" as Max and Sam gave each other a look of concern.

Miguel smiled, quickly snapping out of combat mode and said, "In all seriousness, does anyone actually believe that at that moment, a sniper is pulling out a calculator, protractor, and a compass to compensate for Coriolis? And to then make the necessary adjustments for the variables necessitated for each direction to which he must shoot?" as he pretended to write mathematical equations into the air.

"Haha... again, that would be friggin impossible. That is unless snipers are also mathematicians."

"Exactly, Sam. You begin to understand just how ridiculous the notion is, especially after you consider that mainstream science tells us that everything inside the Earth's atmosphere moves in lockstep with the spin of the Earth; and that we don't feel the Earth spin because of the conservation of momentum."

For the sake of his neighbours, Miguel considered screwing in a silencer to the barrel of the gun that he proudly machined to precision within a thousandth of an inch in his shed; that practically resembled an engineering workshop with a lathe, milling machine, and all—deciding against it.

Miguel pointed for Sam to lay down beside the Ruger, "Here... take a shot, Sam. Just line up the target, relax, exhale your breath, then shoot. Take your time," he advised.

After lining up the target through the scope, another loud boom echoed the sky. Sam smiled, proud as punch that he'd hit the target on his first shot.

Miguel shook his head in admiration. "Nice shot, Sam! Pull the bolt back, and keep firing."

Without hesitation, Sam took another shot at the target and reloaded – firing several more rounds, then jumped up, grinning from ear-to-ear.

"That was bloody awesome. Best stress relief I've had... in a friggin long time," Sam smirked—hyped up with adrenaline.

After clipping in another magazine and resighting the target with another shot, Miguel said, "It's your turn, Max. Just point and shoot. You know the drill. Go for it, big buddy!"

Within moments, another thunderous bang reverberated the sky. Max continued firing until the cartridge was spent, hitting the target on every shot; as Sam took a photo of him hunkered down beside the rifle, beaming a huge smile.

"Nice work, Max... good stuff!" seemingly impressed with his guests, reloading the magazine, where they continued to take turns shooting at the target until all the rounds had been spent.

Miguel was making logical sense, and Max was now convinced beyond a shadow of a doubt, especially after personally viewing the Foucault pendulum in London, that the Coriolis effect was just more gaslighting to propagate the notion that the Earth is a spinning ball.

Miguel then explained how the Coriolis effect would also affect the NATO Sea Sparrow Surface Missile System and Railguns – which can accurately fire a line-of-sight projectile at a target from over 100-miles if it were, in fact, real.

"In addition, aeroplanes, hot air balloons, gliders, and other flying systems, do not account for the alleged spin of the Earth. So, why would a bullet speeding at 1,000 kilometres per hour need to?" he rhetorically asked.

Miguel laughed, "Globe Earth supporters never think further than the indoctrination they received at school. Coriolis is just a bogus made-up myth to support the heliocentric fairy tale. It's as simple as that!"

Max's only thought right now, was that he had to have Miguel as part of his manned expedition to the unknown world.

"So, what can I do for you gentlemen?" asked Miguel. "As I'm pretty sure you didn't visit me today, just to hear me talk about me!" he chuckled.

Max replied, "Well, Miguel – I wanted to know if you noticed anything strange during your deployment in Antarctica. You see, I've heard that there could be more land, and I'm thinking of forming an exploratory mission to find it."

Nonchalantly, Max asked, "You know, I was kind of wondering if you'd be interested in joining us?"

Miguel charged, "Are you God-damn crazy, Max!"

"I'm not crazy! Why does everyone keep asking me that? Just hear me out!" Max insisted.

"Max, you do know that's a suicide mission, right? How would you even know which way to go? And I hope you realise that the ice wall is freakin' huge!"

"What can you tell me about it, Miguel? Tell me more."

"As I said, the ice wall is freakin' huge! From what I witnessed, it's hundreds of feet high. And I've seen it with my very own eyes, so you better get your shit together if you're thinking of climbing that 'big beast' of a wall!"

"What else did you see, Miguel?"

"There's also a military presence. Guys with big guns! And military aircraft roaming the skies – looking for a random breach. And I hope you know that they somehow monitor that miserable place twenty-four-seven!"

"But, how could they protect the entire circumference of the ice wall? It sounds implausible to me, Miguel!"

"I'm not sure, Max! We were compartmentalised. They didn't tell us much. We just completed our tasks and went back to our warm shelters at night... or day... or whatever you'd bloody call it. It was cold and shitty, and there's no way in the world we wanted to explore that devilish ice block during our free time. You just lock yourself up at night and drink expensive Scotch whisky! The more, the merrier!"

"That's crazy, Miguel!"

"Crazy is a friggin understatement! So, do you still want to go, Max?" staring at him, eagerly awaiting a reply.

Max huffed, "Bugger that, mate! I'd probably need a warm heater attached to my side – 24/7! But anyway, I've got a plan to explore that white stuff without the huge risk! I'll fill you in with all the juicy details soon, Miguel."

"Okay, okay... it does sound interesting, Max, but just be careful—because, as you probably know by now, they don't like people snooping around down there. Oops, I meant to say, over there!"

"Anyway, we better get out of here. We've got a bit of a drive ahead of us. It was great to finally meet you, Miguel."

"Likewise, Max... take care, my friend," warmly shaking his hand—Miguel's dogs following his every step.

Shaking Migeuls hand, "See ya later, Miguel. Thanks for the stress relief. It was the best!" blown away to have experienced the opportunity to meet a real-life sniper who had served duty.

He chuckled, "Anytime, fellas. And yeah, it sure was fun. Let's do it again. My house is your house – so you're both welcome around here anytime you need to get away from the city life."

Waving goodbye to Miguel, they drove through the gate as Max honked the horn whilst watching him lock the gate in his rear-view mirror.

* * * * *

Setting the cruise control to the signed speed limit as they drove home to Melbourne from Miguel's tree-lined property, they stopped at a highway roadhouse for a late lunch.

"Miguel's a top bloke, but he's friggin scary... isn't he?" said Sam, sliding into the booth and grabbing the menu.

"That's for sure! Exactly the type of guy we need on the mission. I reckon we should make him head of security. What do you think?"

"You're right. We do need Miguel. Do you reckon you'll be able to convince him, Max?"

"Too easy, Sam – no problem at all. He was shocked, but he seemed intrigued. Don't worry; I'll get Miguel on board. Especially once he sees proof of more land with his own eyes."

"What do you mean, Max?"

"Well, Sam – I've ordered a high-tech Unmanned Aerial Vehicle that is capable of helping us achieve our goal, and she's going to be delivered any day now. She's being shipped here from America, as we speak."

"No friggin way! What are you going to do with it?"

"We're going to send her far-far away from here in the hope to discover more land, Sami."

Sam smirked, "Hey, Max – has anyone ever mentioned before that you're a little bit crazy?"

Max smiled wryly, "Yeah... you know... as a matter of fact: maybe just once or twice."

They both burst out laughing as their burgers and hot chips were brought to the dining table.

Max took a bite into his burger, where he suddenly thought about the potentially dangerous situation that he just put Sam and himself into by visiting an eccentric man with guns—in the midst of secluded bushland.

39

Later that evening—Max snuggled up with Zoe in bed and thoughtlessly asked her without thinking his words through, "Could you just imagine the disagreements that Aristotle, Copernicus, Newton, Tesla, and Einstein would have had if they were all in the same room together?" and it didn't take long for Zoe to snap.

She shrieked, "Really, Max!" Is that what you're thinking about right now? Do we always have to discuss the shape of the Earth?"

Crossing her arms in frustration, she said, "I think that you are officially obsessed with this topic, Max! And you hardly spend any time with me anymore!"

"I'm so sorry, Zoe. But, you see... I'm kind of on a mission," he replied, as he thought it was probably as good a time as any to tell her about the plan that he began to devise while she was away in London.

"What do you mean by... *'I'm on a mission'*, Max?"

"Well, um, you know, this probably isn't the best time to tell you, Zoe, but I want to go on an adventure to find more land across this flat plane we live on. You know... kind of like a modern-day explorer. Just think about it; it's going to be fun!"

"What!!! Have you lost your bloody mind, Max? I can't believe what you have just said! You can't even explore the freakin' laundry to do some washing, let alone... explore the world!"

"Please hear me out, Zoe. It's not that crazy after all, especially after you see the plan that I've devised."

He tried to spoon his body against hers. "I can do it. I mean – we can do it!"

She impulsively elbowed him away. "What do you mean by 'we'? We're supposed to get married and make little baby Max's! Not find new land! How about we think of that plan, for just a moment?" wrapping herself up tight under the Egyptian cotton sheets.

But sometimes, Max just didn't know when to shut his mouth and foolishly suggested, "Well, we could always get married when we get there!"

She angrily snapped, "Where is this 'there', Max?"

"Umm... well, I don't know yet!"

Zoe was beyond annoyed, and with good aim, she swung her pillow, hitting him smack-bang in the head!

"I really think you should crash out on the couch tonight, Max!" turning her back, pretending to be asleep.

Lucky for Max, the couch was comfy; but he would rather be cuddled beside his feisty fiancé—returning to bed hours later.

She sensed his touch, and did not resist when he snuggled up close to her, as Zoe then turned to snuggle him tight around the waist.

40

There was a calm stillness to the night, and Max was back at his favourite local bar for a relaxing drink – or two – while Zoe was out catching up with her friends.

And upon entering the local watering-hole, Max was immediately greeted by his tall friend Shaun, who was casually leaning on the bar chatting to the friendly barmaid.

"You know what, Max?" asked Shaun, shaking his hand.

"Oh, shit!" he thought. "Not another bloody debate!" as he wasn't in the mood. Because most of the regulars at the pub had labelled Max as a 'Flat Earther', and many just couldn't accept his differing opinion about the world where he lived – and consequently had many disagreements with some of the patrons.

Shaun was one of the local patrons and Max gelled with him. A good bloke—big in size, spirit, and personality. And Shaun spent many a night deliberating whether the Earth is flat after initially ridiculing the concept as most people justifiably do so.

Growing up in Port Melbourne, he'd seen the dramatic changes in the area over the years. And as a professional fisherman, he was known around the traps for his record catch in Port Philip Bay, after snagging and catching one of the largest Mulloway caught in the Patterson River—measuring at over one metre in length and weighing over ten kilograms.

"What's up, Shaun?" signalling the barmaid for a beer with just a nod of his head, where she immediately began to pour Max's favourite brew from the beer tap.

"Well, you know, Max, I don't really care if you're one of those Flat Earther's. I still reckon you're a pretty cool bloke!"

"Um... thanks, mate," Max replied, shrugging his shoulders modestly. "Well... what can I say; even though you like big spinning balls, you know, I think you're a good bloke, too!" giving his friend a high-five as they both chuckled.

"Nah... what I mean is; I've given you a rather hard time about Flat Earth and I'm not sure why! You see, I've known you long enough to realise that you're inquisitive. I don't even know why I argued with you about it," leaning over to give Max a bear hug.

"It's cool... don't worry about it. I'm over it... it's no problem," wriggling himself away from the 6-foot, 7-inch giant-sized man.

"Yeah... but you're right!" replied Max. "You know, I'm also not sure why we argue so much about the shape of our Earth. I sometimes reckon that I'd be far more accepted around here if I dressed up as a pink unicorn – rather than be a Flat Earther."

Shaun broke out into laughter. "Far out, mate. I'm not sure where you come up with this shit, but I could never imagine you dressed up as a pink unicorn."

"Don't judge me! I can be whoever I want to be!" he joked.

Shaun nearly choked on his drink as Max cheekily smiled and downed his beer. Knowing him too well, the barmaid poured Max another pint while shaking her head at their strange conversation; now walking away from the two eccentric men to assist another customer.

"Anyway, thanks, mate... I appreciate your kind words. And I know this is a pipe-dream, but I just want to see a world where people get along with one another. Because there's an orderly logos at play in this world, and one of my goals in life is to help people acknowledge it."

"What do you mean by logos, Max? What does that mean?"

"Well, you see, logos can be conceptualised in many ways. But in a nutshell, it is the Greek word philosophically and theologically analogous for order, logic, speech, discourse, rationality, reason, divinity—and the way, the truth, and the life. The word made flesh. The soul of the universe, if you like. And rebelling against logos means rebelling against a higher order."

Max ranted on, "Because the concept of logos defines the way of life and the order of everything in the Universe. And logos is intuitively fashioned into all of nature, including us humans, animals, insects, fauna, and the fundamental physics of our Earth; where logos even specifies which way is up – and which way is down. And defines that what goes up must come down!"

"And there's also logos in the meaning of love. And not just the love for sentient beings and materialistic objects in this material world. But to appreciate and love the unique opportunity given to us to experience the joy and magnificence of life on Earth."

"That's pretty deep, Max!"

"Sure is, man. And I'm beginning to think that there's more to this world than we'll ever understand during our brief, limited lifetime here on Earth!"

"Me too. And between you and me, Max, I've been doing a lot of thinking about this world almost every day for the last six months. You see, I've been observing long distances during our charter fishing tours, and I reckon that the water across the bay is flat and level. There's simply no curvature... anywhere!"

Gently placing his hand on Max's shoulder, he confessed, "I think you've been right all along, and the truth was literally smack-bang, in my face! Because I'm literally on the water – you know, fishing nearly every single day – and the truth was always right in front of me. But I friggin denied it!"

"And, Max, one of my closest friends recently called me and said he could even see the mainland of Victoria from over 100 kilometres away while he was coming back to port on a cruise ship."

"Umm... yeah... you know, I tried to tell you the very same! Because apart from waves, or the ebb and flow of tides; water is always level at rest from shoreline to shoreline."

"I know, Max. And I just wish I listened rather than to mock you. Because for me, water was the biggest clue! Because I've never in my life seen water bend across the bay or the ocean."

"Spot on, mate. I'm glad you finally realised that I'm not so crazy after all!"

"Well, I'm not sure about that, Max," he chuckled. "But, yeah, it took me a while to unplug my brain from the matrix of lies. I'm actually kind of embarrassed about it! Pardon the pun, but it was a huge learning curve," motioning a curve with his hand.

Max smiled graciously, "Hey, it's all good. Don't worry about it! You know, I gotta admit that it also took me a while to connect the dots. But the truth was always in plain sight."

"But Max, there's just one niggling question that I can't quite wrap my head around, and that is; why would our governments lie to us about the shape of our Earth? Like... what's in it for them? Why don't they just tell us? Because it's more than obvious that the Earth is flat. It doesn't require a Nobel prize-winning genius to work it all out. It looks flat, and it feels motionless because it is. It's as easy as that!"

"Exactly, mate, it is rather easy when you think about it. But, you know, I'm not exactly sure why they would lie about it; that's a rather complex question. However, they tell us that all the land across this Earth has been discovered, but I reckon there's more land that's hidden out there somewhere, Shaun!"

Max elaborated, "And the extraterrestrial land is over yonder, and at a place where no man can freely go to explore."

Max invested a lot of thought into the reasoning of why governments would collectively withhold the truth from humanity and was now fired up.

"And do you really wanna know the truth?" he asked. "Well, here it is, big fella. In their grand aim to deceive the world, they now teach people the polar opposite to the truth. Think about it; they've inverted almost everything we know, and the lies are non-stop, 24-7!"

"If water is flat and level at rest. Then they say it curves!"

"If the Earth is stationary. They say that we are spinning!"

"If the Sun is close. Then they say it's afar!"

"If there is a God, they say we're related to friggin chimpanzees!"

"All whilst keeping us busy with nonsensical issues, where they bewilder humanity with garbage, fake news."

"It's sleight of hand! They make you look to the left while they pull a magic trick on the right. Humans have been stooged through trickery and tomfoolery – and no longer even trust their own natural senses!"

"But, why would they do that? What's the end goal?"

"I don't know, mate! It could even be a knowledge versus power kind of thing. Or maybe some people are just evil! However, what I do know, is that some people are bloody insane!"

"Yeah... that kind of sounds like my ex-wife. You practically described her down to a tee," Shaun chuckled.

"Well, I've almost had enough of all the bullshit on this Earth, Max! One of these days... I'm just gonna take my boat and sail it to the end of the Earth!" swigging down the remnants of his beer.

Laughing at his joke and placing his empty pint glass on the bar, Max said, "Anyway, good seeing you, big fella. I've got a busy day tomorrow, so I better get home for some shut-eye."

"You take care of yourself, Max. It was good seeing ya again, buddy," shaking his hand.

"Likewise. By the way, careful you don't fall off the edge of the Earth, Shaun!" Max mocked, reciprocating the joke Shaun used a long time ago when Max first told him about Flat Earth.

41

Three Kenworth semi-trailers loaded with shipping containers rolled their big wheels along the highway, heading towards a rural property near a coastal town approximately 300-kilometres west of Melbourne that Max specifically leased to accommodate the Odysseus reconnaissance mission.

It was a moment that Max had anticipated for many months; the Odysseus high-altitude pseudo-satellite had finally arrived at Melbourne's docklands. And after clearing customs inspection for illegal contraband, the containers were finally being shipped to Max's property, which offered a secluded place to experiment from the prying eyes of authorities. Always on the lookout and still somewhat paranoid after his incident with the black SUV many months earlier.

The long driveway led to a commercial building, once the premises for a leading Australian fruit cannery that had since closed its operations after going into involuntary liquidation – and although requiring some modification, the property conveniently hosted a private airstrip to accommodate Odysseus's short take-off requirements.

A mission-control room was established at the property, with multiple 65-inch LCD high-definition monitors installed spanning a large wall—each monitor to accommodate one of the twelve high-definition cameras awaiting to be synchronised with the Odysseus satellite. The elaborate configuration of monitors almost resembling a NASA mission control room; with eighteen LCD screens in total. The larger monitors to display live video footage, and the smaller monitors to present data in real-time from the various sensors onboard the pseudo satellite.

A seated observation area was constructed to offer the guest invitees a prime view of the television screens and a fully-stocked bar with beer taps – was ready to accommodate the "MissionX party".

Max's pipedream plan was beginning to come to fruition.

It had been his vision for quite some time, and Max finally formed a tentative team of individuals that were willing to join him on a manned expedition. But first, they required proof of confirmed sighting of unmapped land, by the soon to be launched Odysseus pseudo-satellite.

Coincidentally, in Greek mythology, it describes Homer's epic journey of exploration as Odysseus; the name of Max's newly acquired aircraft, nicknamed "Epica", now seemed more than fitting.

What began as a novel way to kill some spare time by debunking the preposterous Flat Earth conspiracy theory; his long-held beliefs about the cosmos was now at polar opposites. As Max could no longer entertain the thought – for even a moment – that he lived "down-under" on a planet hurtling through Space.

In his opinion, the concept was not only preposterous but also hilarious; and he would often find himself rolling his eyes whenever he saw a globe on an office desk, a store shelf, or during the beginning of the evening news.

The very notion; now laughable.

He appreciated that the debate about the shape of the Earth had never been settled, to begin with. And that it was a topic of discussion that flowed well into the 1960s until the Moon landing hoax presented the famous "Blue Marble" image of the Earth from Space to an overly trusting society. Who most likely, were still influenced by the effects of LSD; which probably rationalises why so many people believed that man landed on an ever-so-distant Moon in the first place!

Looking back in time and examining the archived news articles from the early 1900s, Max acknowledged that people had always questioned the heliocentric model. And a report he found online claimed that a group of parents threatened the head of the British Education Department under the impostor's act; for what they considered as disseminating treasonous doctrine that was corrupting their children – by teaching the eccentric philosophical viewpoint that our Earth is a spinning sphere flying through Space.

In fact, Max found hundreds of associated news articles and publications that verified that the topic was always contentious.

With countless esoteric books written by dozens of heliocentric debunkers, including William Carpenter, Lady Blount, Thomas Winship, and Dr Samuel Rowbotham, whom all relentlessly objected to the heliocentric model well into the late 1800s and early 1900s; before war plagued the world, consequently distracting society from such topics of discussion for many years.

Additionally, and somewhat surprisingly, Flat Earth was even referenced in the 1958 edition of Encyclopedia Britannica. Whereas, under the category "Firmament", it peculiarly documents and describes a dome covering the Earth at the outer edges of Antarctica; remarkably discovered following an expedition by the United States of America that departed from New Zealand in 1955.

Max was adamant to prove the globe Earth proponents wrong – who had ridiculed him over the years and was no longer ashamed to speak publicly about Flat Earth. Where he now told almost everyone about his newfound realisation. A flat, motionless Earth, just as it appears. With no doubt about it.

He would often think about the countless people that taunted him with ludicrous snide remarks during many heated debates on the topic, including, "Careful you don't fall off the edge of the Earth". Which, as strange as it may sound, became part of his motivation. Because Max didn't believe there was an end to Earth. And to the contrary, he thought there are other ponds beyond our own. And maybe even other worlds.

Or perhaps, it was due to his persistence – which many could perceive as pure stubbornness – that drove him to achieve his goal.

Or did he just want to share the truth about his newfound reality with the rest of the world?

Because the day he acknowledged the grand deception was the very day that Max's life changed forever.

Even more than his newfound riches.

Now far more connected with his "God-given" natural senses, which he nowadays trusted like never before.

Whereas, everything changed in Max's life—including his perception of people, animals, insects, and nature in general. He couldn't explain it, but Max was now connected with the universe at a new sensory level.

In fact, it changed his entire understanding of the cosmos.

With his more caring and unselfish manner, now even carefully stepping over insects with consideration and respect for their short but essential lifecycle on Earth.

Buddha stated that there are three things you cannot hide: *"The Sun, the Moon, and the truth."*

And Max was hopeful that if humanity somehow united, even for just one day—then, just as Jessica optimistically suggested months earlier: *that the truth would set us free.*

42

M ax had another crazy idea, but this idea was rather risky.
Because he was now considering the possibility – and the implications – of hacking into international television networks to stream live video footage of the Odysseus; and knew the task would require a team of deep-web hackers that had the capability to bypass complex systems without being traced.

Snapping back to reality after contemplating the legal implications of unlawfully breaching television networks – like a rogue villain – which would undoubtedly include criminal charges if he got caught. Max concentrated on the matter at hand, syncing the multiple monitors in the control room to Odysseus, and he knew the right man for the job.

Max met JP through a mutual business acquaintance, and although he was now happily retired, he was always ready to help a friend in need.

JP was a telecommunications engineer with extensive experience within various aspects of the industry. Having even commissioned many balloon-based satellites during his career, with one that crashed out of control into a group of cars whose passengers were spectating the launch in the Australian outback—as wild winds carried the satellite off-course just moments after being released from its tether.

Picking up his phone, he dialled JP.

"Hey, big buddy. How are you doing there, mate?"

"I'm great, thanks, Max. How's life treating you?"

"Flat out, JP."

"Ha-ha. Good one, Max. I like it!"

"Hey, JP – what are your plans this evening?"

"I was just chopping up some ingredients to cook up a stew."

"Really... a stew – do people still cook stews these days?"

"Umm... yes, we do, Max! And I'm actually going to cook it off-grid. I'm in the middle of nowhere right now, but I've got it all—a log cabin with solar panels, lithium battery back-up, rainwater, an organic garden, and even chooks that hatch me some fresh eggs. Not to mention the small creek down the end of my property with fresh Rainbow Trout; whenever I need it. Couldn't ask for more!"

"Sounds like a great setup."

"Sure is! Anyway, Max, let's not stay on the phone for too long. We don't want to fry our brains with that high-frequency mobile phone radiation," said JP, snorting as he laughed.

Max laughed, "Yeah, funny but true, JP. Well, I need your help with a small project, but I need to tell you about it face-to-face. Do you have time to catch up, mate?"

"Anything for you, Max. But first, I've gotta get a new axle for my 4WD. Because I snapped the bloody thing crossing a creek a few days ago, but hopefully, I'll have it fixed tomorrow. And if that's the case, then I reckon I can be in Melbourne by Friday."

"Sounds great, JP. Meet me at St. Kilda Marina. We'll have a bit more privacy on my boat, and I'll also organise some lunch."

"I can't wait to see your smiley face again, Max. I've got so much to tell you, as I've been researching a stack of new topics. I'll give you a call when I reach the city limits," hanging up the call.

* * * *

They finished lunch on the Zenith Star, then strolled toward the lighthouse at the tip of the Marina, where Max divulged his plan to JP.

Impressed, he asked, "So, how did you get into this Flat Earth thing anyway, Max? I mean, I know that you're a smart bloke and all, but I never thought you would be the type of guy who would pursue such an ambitious plan."

After being briefly distracted by the squawk from a flock of seagulls flying nearby, Max replied, "Hey, I'm just a normal guy who wants to know the truth about where he lives. No different to anyone else, really. And what started out as a hobby by intending to debunk the Flat Earth theory – has now become an obsession."

"Anyway, JP. I need you to do me a big favour."

"Yeah, no worries – shoot! That's why I'm here. Go for it!"

"Well, I've bought a surveillance drone and I need her cameras synced to some monitors."

"Too easy, Max. How big a surveillance drone are we talking?"

Max reached for his phone. "Here are the specs, mate."

"Holy shit, Max! She's freakin' ginormous!"

"Yeah, I know. Quite amazing, hey. And I need to have her airborne as soon as possible. So whatever you can do would be great."

"Consider it done, Max. Give me the time and the place – and I'll be there!"

"Awesome, JP. You're a bloody lifesaver, mate," as Max handed him a business card with the location of his property scribbled on the back, where they arranged to meet the following morning.

43

Max was convinced that our Earth is an extended flat plane that continues infinitely. With our Earth and all continents contained within a big pond; with the grand question constantly plaguing his mind, "Could there be other ponds beyond Antarctica similar to ours?"

And as the founder of many start-ups, he appreciated that due diligence, preparation, and continuous research would be crucial factors for a safe and successful human-crewed exploratory expedition.

And thanks to the pioneering adventurer, Rear Admiral Richard E. Byrd, Max now had a hunch in which direction to send the Odysseus.

Admiral Byrd was the first person to fly over the North Pole in 1926 and followed the adventurous feat by being the first person to fly over the South Pole in 1946-1947, coined as Operation Highjump. Where 5,000 men, 13 naval ships, and 33 aircraft, designed to launch from specifically engineered vehicles that piggy-backed the aircraft after reaching the Antarctic ice-wall.

Upon his return from the expedition, and during a speech on the Longines Chronoscope interview, Byrd was asked by an interviewer if there was unexplored land on this Earth which might appeal to adventurous young Americans.

In response, Admiral Byrd stated that there was more land beyond the poles and that this unfound land contained minerals and resources capable of fuelling Earth's requirements for hundreds of years. Byrd said...

"Ah yes, there is. And not up around the North Pole, because it's getting crowded up there now because they found out it's really usable not only to live in but militarily. But strangely enough, there is left in the world today, an area as big as the United States that's never been seen by a human being. And that's beyond the pole, on the other side of the South Pole, from middle America. And I think it's quite astonishing... that there should be an area as big as that, that is unexplored; so there is a lot of adventure left, at the bottom of the world."

Admiral Byrd also claimed that the Antarctic continent is surrounded by a belt of ice, with at least twelve hundred miles of deep-frozen seas. Where Max then recalled that Antarctica is also noted as the highest continent on Earth, with an average elevation of 2,500 thousand metres above sea level. He laughed in thought, "Well, no wonder why no one has seen the edge of this freakin' Earth!"

He reached for the map Roberto gifted him and wondered, "Hmm... what if Admiral Byrd was right, and there was more land to be discovered along the path he took many decades earlier?"

Interestingly, Max had never considered the premise of undiscovered land on Earth prior to hearing about the concept of a flat, stationary Earth.

Nor had he heard of the inspirational explorer, Dick E. Byrd, or many other notable adventurers for that matter, including the famous Swiss physicist and explorer Auguste Piccard—recognised for his thrilling hands-on approach to the scientific method, by exploring the stratosphere by containing himself in a pressurised capsule with his record-breaking high-altitude helium-filled balloon experiment in 1931. And if that wasn't enough, he later trumped the enormous feat by exploring the deepest oceans on Earth.

But the rabbit hole was far more sinister than eccentric men on a mission to explore; because Max stumbled across many clandestine operations initiated and conducted by militarized governments worldwide, provisioned by alphabet agencies concluding Operation Paperclip in 1942, including:

Operation Highjump in 1946-47: discovering the ice wall.

Operation Deepfreeze in 1955: exploring beyond the ice wall and attempting to reach the firmament.

Operation Fishbowl in 1962: bombing the firmament with high altitude nuclear weapons—a semblance to the ancient biblical story of the Tower of Babel. Where mankind attempted to reach God – for a battle 'til the end!

Operation Dominic in 1962: the further bombing of the firmament.

After achieving the goal of exploring beyond Antarctica via Operation Highjump and Deepfreeze, the Antarctic Treaty was established in 1959 to protect Antarctica on the premise to save the environment. In 2019, the treaty consisting of fifty-two signatory nations and, strangely enough, the only international treaty in history to have never been broken.

Who knows? Perhaps there was nothing nefarious about the covert expeditions at all. And maybe the subsequent establishment and the strict adherence of the international treaty was all for the sake of protecting the cute, fluffy little penguins!

44

It was just days prior to the scheduled launch of the Odysseus reconnaissance exploratory mission.

The Odysseus's array of solar panels – designed to charge the lithium batteries to propel the aircraft – were installed and tested. The solar panels embodied the majority of the wings, fuselage, and tail of the plane; and were capable of charging the batteries for continuous autonomous flight.

Epica was finally ready to be launched on her maiden voyage after many months of relentless effort and meticulous planning.

The multiple high-definition monitors were now respectively synced to the numerous cameras positioned on the Odysseus. Each camera strategically positioned to record a unique vantage point. With up, down, left, right, forward, and back – synced to the larger screens.

A preliminary test flight was conducted without hindrance. The aircraft was tested by flying for twenty continuous hours whilst streaming its data to the monitors and a backup hard drive. Everything worked to flawless precision after JP spent night and day – practically sleeping beside Odysseus – to ensure she was ready for her voyage.

Ingeniously, Jerry, who was now also enthusiastically assisting with the project full-time, synced the high-definition cameras to Max's smartphone via a basic app that they jointly developed, allowing Max to instantly select a particular camera view and zoom-in to view the terrain below with a simple tap of the screen. Even from the comfort of his own home.

His tech-team applied "MissionX" decals – depicting a stylish modern designed black and white logo to the fuselage and the three individual tails of the aircraft.

Later that afternoon, he called in to see his friend Andy, where they decided to head out for a steak and beer at Andy's local watering hole.

During the meal, Max presented Andy with the map that Roberto had brought him from Japan – by zooming into a photo of the map saved to his smartphone. Detailing the path where he was to send Odysseus and outlining his ambitious plan to travel across Antarctica once he had sighted more land.

Andy rhetorically asked, "Max, do you even realise how hard it is to get approval to fly across Antarctica, let alone complete the journey? You just can't go there to explore freely. And even if you could, it's so far away that you would need the biggest plane on the market – just to complete the trip!"

Andy ranted on, "The Antarctic Treaty will also prevent you from going to Antarctica without approval. So, how the heck are you going to get approval from the Australian Government for your trip? And I hope you know that entire teams have been arrested for trying to access Antarctica without approval and never heard from again. Just look it up!"

"And Max, while you're at it, look up the impossible red-tape and documentation that must be lodged in every country's official language. You have to overcome the various hierarchy each government has in place by the fifty-odd countries that protect the treaty. Even North Korea is a signatory – for God's sake! The legal work required is never-ending! And if just one of those countries is not satisfied with the application, the entire project goes down the drain!"

"Oh, and did I mention that you need to conduct environmental impact assessment studies? And apparently, you can't even take extra fuel past a certain point – whether for a plane, a snowmobile, or a boat! And countless documents need to be submitted and approved by Environmental Protection Agencies. And you even need to carry your personal waste in a sealed bag!"

"Really? It looks like you've looked into it, Andy!"

"Yeah, I have; I've postulated the journey many times, and I've done the research. It's a huge friggin exercise, and it's going to cost you a pretty penny – anywhere up to five million bucks just for approval. Even at the basic count of one-hundred thousand per country. Because, as you know – lawyers aren't bloody cheap these days!"

"It's a huge bloody gamble, Max! And I'd hate to be the one to break it to you, but it's more than likely that you won't even get approved to travel down there! You know, I reckon you're more likely to win the lottery, than to gain approval to travel around Antarctica!"

"Well, based on my research, we'll start by getting permission from the United Nations, and then the Australian Government."

"For God's sake, Max! Stop saying 'we'! I'm not friggin doing this! Don't try and coerce me into this bullshit!"

Max shrugged off Andy's reluctance and asked, "Anyway, what type of plane would we need?"

Andy laughed like a mad man at Max's perseverance.

"I've always loved your feisty nature, Max... you crazy Greek bastard! And of course, I'll join you. I was just messing with you! I'm not sure what I'll say to the missus – but I reckon I'll be able to get away for a week. And if I spoil her wildly the week before, then I may be able to get away for two!"

✶ ✶ ✶ ✶ ✶

Max arose early the following morning, with clear intent to contact the Office for the Australian Minister for Antarctica to begin his application in the hope to get approval to visit the enormous block of white ice that supposedly sits at the bottom of the Earth.

However, after sifting through the countless pages of the application form and reviewing the travel restrictions, Max concluded that it would be near impossible to get approval for an expedition.

* * * * *

Zoe now supported Max in every aspect of his mission.

In fact, he kind of wished he told her about the Odysseus sooner; rather than being secretive about the acquisition.

Later that night, she sat beside Max at his desk, where they excitingly prepared a guest list for the MissionX party.

Zoe typed the invitees' email addresses into a message.

She then blind-carbon-copied the recipients before clicking the send icon to invite Max's closest friends and acquaintances, so they could all view firsthand footage from the Odysseus firsthand.

They arose early the following day with twenty-two of the guests already accepting the invitation to attend.

Zoe was super excited; preparing for the extravagant event by jotting down suggestions for the menu, entertainment, and even her fashion choice—because she was about to host the most extraordinary party on Earth.

45

S am spent many a night keenly observing the stars and their zodiacal constellations with Jessica.

It was their new hobby, and they were now a steady couple.

But more than that, Sam popped the big question and they were engaged with a wedding on the way; trying to decide whether to make the event small and intimate – or make it a huge fiesta by inviting all their family and friends.

Sam proposed within months after meeting her, and without a second thought, Jessica swiftly answered, "Yes".

They synced since the moment they met, and if Sam could somehow turn back time—he would have probably proposed to her the very moment they met at the café months earlier.

Their lives had experienced a positive change, and they were both somewhat thankful to Max.

Because, although Sam initially adamantly resisted the notion that the Earth is flat, it changed his entire outlook of life when the realisation occurred.

And it was a huge revelation, whereas his extensive research studying esoteric topics and conspiracy theories for many years had finally meshed together.

Now decisively acknowledging that the world was hoodwinked into believing that they live on a spinning ball via a deceptive mystical matrix of mathematics and cartoon science – derived from "man-made" theories that display no basis with objective reality.

Jessica felt the same way, and the last thing they wanted to do was raise children in a world full of lies and deception.

So, they decided to step-it-up and make a change!

Sam diplomatically told his Director "where to go", sold his shares in the company he'd been with for over a decade, and looked forward to joining Max full-time and was anticipating seeing the results from the Odysseus. Assisting wherever he could, as he knew that Max was deeply vested in his project.

He also finally comprehended why the topic was so important to Max. As he now acknowledged, more than ever before, that our Earth is a special place. And although humans ambitiously dream of finding an exo-planet to escape to in the event of a cataclysmic event, there is no other body in the Universe that can support life —apart from this perfect realm that we live within.

And Sam now fully grasped more than ever before that the perfection to this world did not occur by mere chance. Appreciating that it was quite possible and, in fact, more than plausible that all life on Earth was created by a grand designer with supreme reason, intent and order. Akin to the apparent fact that a building, a car, a computer, or a wristwatch; are also designed and created for an intended end-user.

Now also acknowledging with a solid belief that the probability that humans are geocentrically positioned at the centre of the universe was more than likely the truth.

The awakening unleashed a new sense of wonder about the world where he lived.

Because Max was right, after all; discovering and freeing himself from the lies and knowing the Earth is flat and motionless was far more wonderous than one could ever envisage, and Sam felt far more satisfied with life.

His "new eyes" appreciating nature and all creatures on Earth at an inconceivable level. All by the simple revelation through self-discovery, and via Max's perseverance on the matter, where he finally acknowledged that he was not standing upside down and spinning around and around – on a ball!

And although he thought the concept of a Flat Earth was completely absurd when Max initially presented it to him during breakfast several months earlier. The idea that we live on a spinning rock that hurtles through Space; was not only easily debunkable when he finally let down his guard.

But blindly obvious – to be the polar opposite!

And Sam's future was looking bright.

Because Jessica carried a new addition to their family – and as a mother-to-be, she looked more radiantly beautiful than ever before.

46

It was precisely 12:22 am on a clear, balmy Thursday evening; when Max finally launched the Odysseus onto her grand maiden voyage.

Elated, he stood on the tarmac full of hope, wonder and awe as he watched the multi-million-dollar aircraft fly towards the unknown, where Epica glided away high into the night sky and was out of sight within several minutes.

Crossing his arms, he shook his head in thought and muttered, "Fuck it! It's just money after all!" acknowledging long ago that money wasn't everything. And he was prepared to invest almost his entire fortune to prove that the Earth contains more land to be discovered across the infinite plane that we live upon.

Because in his opinion, as long as he still had Zoe by his side, and they had enough money to sustain their lifestyle: the future was going to be grand!

Taking approximately ninety minutes to reach the designated cruising altitude of around 98,000 feet – or almost 30-kilometres above sea level; Max used his smartphone to monitor Odysseus's status, and was ecstatic that she was finally airborne.

The Odysseus was geared up with every possible enhancement after Max ensured that the engineering team installed a myriad of equipment onboard the aircraft; to detect any anomalies during her journey whilst maintaining payload specifications.

They also disengaged the concealed tracking device that JP discovered after scanning the aircraft with his high-tech equipment, capable of detecting the most minute radioactive signal. He then reversed engineered and configured the tracker to present misleading data from the aircraft, making it appear to be circuiting around the top-end of Australia to bamboozle any prying eyes.

After several hours of flight, the aircraft was now thousands of kilometres from basecamp, according to the data pinged back to mission control; the signal bouncing off the troposphere using Troposcatter knowhow – pioneered way back in the 1920s.

The Odysseus was finally recording continuous live-stream high-definition video from her extensive array of cameras to a dedicated computer server configured by Max's trusted technicians to document every detail of the voyage.

Sam was driving his Skyline to meet up with Max at the rural property the following day, where they arranged to stay onboard Max's boat, the Zenith Star—after, Captain Alex cruised and anchored the vessel less than 100 meters off the coastline, approximately 8-kilometres from mission control.

Veering his car down the long gravel lined driveway – where a plume of dust followed his trail – he parked beside Max's car and entered the vast warehouse.

Sam yelled out, "Coooeee!!!" upon entering the premises. His voice echoing throughout the building.

His calling was welcomed by Max speaking in a Transylvanian accent, "Velcome to crazy town!" now laughing like a mad man into the microphone connected to the surround-sound speakers.

"Fuck you, Max! You scared the bloody crap out of me, ya cheeky bugger!" he chuckled, where Sam noticed Max standing behind the bar laughing at his playful prank, while cracking open two bottles of lemonade and placing them onto the benchtop.

He spent the afternoon showing Sam around the property, where they had lunch while watching live footage from the Odysseus on the large wall of monitors.

Sam was more than impressed with the operational setup, now wishing he had joined Max sooner to assist with the project. But, Sam was in "La la land" since meeting Jessica, and Max fully comprehended the scenario.

They boarded the Zenith Star later that evening.

After settling in, they live-streamed the footage of the Odysseus onto the LCD monitor, whilst sipping on cognac and smoking cigars and stuff until the early hours of the morning, falling asleep soon after.

He arose mid-morning to a television screen displaying static white snow; while Sam was still warmly wrapped up in a blanket sleeping on the adjacent couch.

It was as if Odysseus had disappeared off the face of the Earth.

Max pinged the aircraft using the smartphone app, but there was no signal. All communications to Odysseus were lost!

He patiently waited for the signal to resume – but to no avail.

"She's friggin gone!" he angrily yelled out, waking Sam from his deep slumber.

"Who's gone, Max?" rubbing his eyes from sleep.

"The Odysseus! She's friggin gone!" replied Max, still fumbling with the phone app, trying to restore communication with the aircraft.

"What! How do you know?"

"We've got no signal, Sam! Nothing! Zilch! Niente! Tipota!" he sombrely responded.

Out of character, Max then smacked the television in his attempt to reach his beloved aircraft – Epica.

But there was still nothing!

He smacked the television again – this time even harder; before accepting that she was lost, where he then angrily punched the wall with his fist.

After tirelessly sifting through the recorded footage for hours on end, Max excitedly yelled out in Greek, "To evrika!" as he'd finally found what he was looking for; and it was a real, eureka moment!

Sam high-fived, Max; shaking his head slowly in admiration because he knew Max had a knack: to make things happen!

47

The Mission-X party was in full swing. Beer taps were flowing, and cocktails were being shaken and poured as Marcus cranked up the music after he volunteered to be both the barman and disk-jockey for the night.

Max's guests were all merrily socialising and enjoying the party atmosphere.

The aroma from the pizza oven and the outdoor barbeque spit-roasts wafted throughout the building, where the guests soon after helped themselves to the delicious buffet selection while the food was still hot.

Pierre was lavishing it up, chatting with Shaun about the expansive waters – where they both acknowledged that water is flat and level – as they shared stories about their fishing triumphs; bragging and trying to outdo each other – on who had caught the biggest fish.

Pierre smiled and winked at his bubbly wife, Leisa – happy to see that she was enjoying herself; who was laughing and chatting with Zoe and Jessica, like long lost friends, even though they had just met hours earlier.

Sam, Roberto, Miguel and Alex – were mingling with two overly dressed venture capitalists, who appeared odd wearing their expensive tailored suits amongst the casually dressed crowd.

The eager venture capitalists – associated with the billionaire investor, Jordan Jones – attended the function with the scope of securing the mining rights to rare and valuable commodities that Max could potentially find during a crewed expedition. After he had told them under a strict non-disclosure agreement about the

potential resources and minerals to be discovered; including lithium, indium, and gallium. Commonly used to power and illuminate many digital devices including smartphones. And Jones, as
well as his advisors, were more than keen to invest in any future
expeditions.

Andy sat at the bar chugging back drinks, where he was in deep
thought; anticipating viewing the footage that Max was about to
present. And was considering the consequences of briefly leaving
his family to join Max on his journey; if, by chance, there was, in
fact, undeniable proof of undiscovered land.

Max kept the Odysseus high-altitude pseudo-satellite a
well-guarded secret; that is, apart from disclosing the acquisition
and his audacious plan to just a few close friends and colleagues
working with him on the project. Whereas, the last thing Max
needed was for the media to get wind of the story, and to mockingly portray him as an insane Australian man who believed that
the Earth was flat.

Jessica directed the guests to be seated at the observation area,
while Jerry and JP made final preparations to the audio-visual
equipment to present the Odysseus – and the video footage Max
recorded – to a group of selected family, friends, and colleagues.

The rousing, feisty song, "*I Told You So!*" by the captivating
musician, Conspiracy Music Guru, boomed from the speakers as
Max took centre-stage on the podium.

The guests rowdily cheered and applauded.

Casually dressed in blue jeans with an untucked white linen
shirt and tan slip-on leather shoes – Max looked fit and healthy,
like never before; after losing several kilograms by working out at
the gym almost every week with Sam.

Lightly tapping the microphone after switching it on while the
music faded away, Max jubilantly said, "Welcome, everyone. It's
great to have you here this evening. I hope you're all having a great
time," cheerfully speaking into the microphone.

The guests now cheered and applauded even louder.

"Firstly, Zoe and I would really like to thank you for joining us, as we know you had to travel some distance to attend this event. So, we greatly appreciate it."

Max glanced around at the familiar faces in the crowd before continuing. "Many of you have known me for a very long time, and you probably thought that I was going crazy – when I first mentioned that the Earth is flat!"

He chuckled, "You know, I really can't blame you!" where they collectively laughed at his candidness.

"Yeah, yeah… okay! C'mon, now… settle down, ladies and gentlemen," gesturing with both hands to quieten down the crowd while beaming a cheeky smile.

"Because I'm about to present video footage that I captured with my latest purchase. Let me proudly present, Epica: the Odysseus high-altitude pseudo-satellite," as a photo simultaneously appeared on the large screen; where the crowd were now silenced and left in awe by the sheer size of the aircraft.

He clicked to load the next slide of his presentation which outlined his journey thus far. Where he flicked through several photos in sequential order, explaining the slides as they appeared on the screen.

The first slide was of a photo of Max pointing to the Odysseus as he stood on the runway in Virginia – whilst pulling a funny face.

The second slide was of him handing a multi-million-dollar cheque to Jeremy – with a not so smiley face.

Followed by a photo of the trucks leaving the docklands.

The fit-out of the mission control room.

The assembly of the Odysseus.

The expansion of the runway.

And then finally, video footage of the Odysseus – taking off for her maiden voyage.

The monitors – ingeniously daisy-chained together to form a cinema-sized screen – now displayed footage of a level horizon with no visible curvature of the Earth, at an altitude of almost 100,000 feet.

The crowd erupted into cheer and applause!

But the grand highlight of the night was when Max presented video footage and extraordinary evidence of a strange-looking island – ironically shaped like a banana, just like Elena had once joked about!

And Max secretly and securely held the primary coordinates to conduct a human-crewed expedition to visit this newly discovered land.

After witnessing the "banana" shaped island on the big screen, the guests were momentarily left gobsmacked; looking around at each other in disbelief.

When they realised that Max had successfully achieved his ambitious goal to find more land, they erupted with cheer and delight, giving him a standing ovation as Marcus pumped up the volume to one of Max's favourite songs, *I Want to Break Free*, by Queen.

It was now game on!

And that's when the party started!

"Question everything, and if someone tells you not to question it; then question it – even more!"

BILLY ZIG

AWESOME QUOTES
FROM AWESOME MINDS

"The surface of all water, when not agitated by natural causes, such as winds, tides, earthquakes etc. is perfectly level. The sense of sight proves this to every unprejudiced and reasonable mind.

Can any so-called scientist, who teaches that the earth is a whirling globe, take a heap of liquid water, whirl it round, and so make rotundity? He cannot.

Therefore it is utterly impossible to prove that an ocean is a whirling rotund section of a globular earth, rushing through 'space' at the lying-given-rate of false philosophers."

— William Thomas Wiseman, "The earth an Irregular Plane"

* * * * *

"Is water level, or is it not?' was a question once asked of an astronomer. 'Practically, yes; theoretically, no,' was the reply. Now, when theory does not harmonize with practice, the best thing to do is to drop the theory. (It is getting too late, now to say 'So much the worse for the facts!') To drop the theory which supposes a curved surface to standing water is to acknowledge the facts. Whenever experiments have been tried on the surface of standing water, the surface has always been found to be level. If the earth were a globe, the surface of all standing water would be convex. This is an experimental proof that Earth is not a globe."

— William Carpenter, "100 Proofs the earth is Not a Globe"

* * * * *

"Rivers run down to the sea because of the inclination of their beds. Rising at an altitude above sea-level, in some cases thousands of feet above the sea, they follow the easiest route to their level – the sea.

The 'Parana' and 'Paraguay' in South America are navigable for over 2,000 miles, and their waters run the same way until they find their level of stability, where the sea tides begin.

But if the world be a globe, the 'Amazon' in South America that flows always in an easterly direction, would sometimes be running uphill and sometimes down, according to the movement of the globe. Then the 'Congo' in West Africa, that always pursues a westerly course to the sea, would in the same manner be running alternately up and down.

When that point of the globe exactly between them was up, they would both be running up, although in opposite directions; and when the globe took half a turn, they would both be running down!

We know from practical experiment that water will find its level, and cannot by any possibility remain other than level, or flat, or horizontal – whatever term may be used to express the idea. It is therefore quite out of the range of possibility that rivers could do as they would have to do on a globe."

— *Thomas Winship, "Zetetic Cosmogeny"*

* * * * *

"Whoever heard of a river in any part of its course flowing uphill? Yet this it would require to do were the earth a Globe. Rivers, like the Mississippi, which flow from the North southwards towards the Equator, would need, according to Modem Astronomic theory, to run upwards, as the earth at the Equator is said to bulge out considerably more, or, in other words, is higher than at any other part. Thus the Mississippi, in its immense course of over 3,000 miles, would have to ascend 11 miles before it reached the Gulf of Mexico!"

— *David Wardlaw Scott, "Terra Firma"*

* * * * *

"The upper surface of a fluid at rest is a horizontal plane. Because if a part of the surface were higher than the rest, those parts of the fluid which were under it would exert a greater pressure upon the surrounding parts than they receive from them, so that motion would take place amongst the particles and continue until there were none at a higher level than the rest, that is, until the upper surface of the whole mass of fluid became a horizontal plane."

— W.T. Lynn, "First Principles of Natural Philosophy"

* * * * *

"But as such declination, or downward curvature, cannot be detected, the conclusion is logically inevitable that it has no existence.

Let the reader seriously ask whether any and what reason exists in Nature to prevent the fall of more than 400 feet being visible to the eye, or incapable of detection by any optical or mathematical means whatever.

This question is especially important when it is considered that at the same distance, and on the upper outline of the same land, changes of level of only a few yards extent are quickly and unmistakably perceptible.

If a man is guided by evidence and reason, and influenced by a love of truth and consistency, he cannot longer maintain that the earth is a globe.

He must feel that to do so is to war with the evidence of his senses, to deny that any importance attaches to fact and experiment, to ignore entirely the value of logical process, and to cease to rely upon practical induction."

— Dr. Samuel Rowbotham, "Zetetic Astronomy, Earth Not a Globe!"

* * * * *

Children are taught in their geography books, when too young to apprehend aright the meaning of such things, that the world is a great globe revolving around the Sun, and the story is repeated continuously, year by year, till they reach maturity, at which time they generally become so absorbed in other matters as to be indifferent as to whether the teaching be true or not, and, as they hear of nobody contradicting it, they presume that it must be the correct thing, if not to believe at least to receive it as a fact. They thus tacitly give their assent to a theory which, if it had first been presented to them at what are called 'years of discretion,' they would at once have rejected. The consequences of evil-teaching, whether in religion or in science, are far more disastrous than is generally supposed, especially in a luxurious laisser faire age like our own. The intellect becomes weakened and the conscience seared."

— *David Wardlaw Scott, "Terra Firma: The earth Not a Planet Proved from Scripture, Reason, and Fact"*

✷ ✷ ✷ ✷ ✷

"A sphere where people on the other side live with their feet above their heads, where rain, snow and hail fall upwards, where trees and crops grow upside-down and the sky is lower than the ground? The ancient wonder of the hanging gardens of Babylon dwindle into nothing in comparison to the fields, seas, towns and mountains that pagan philosophers believe to be hanging from the earth without support!"

— *Lacantius, "On the False Wisdom of the Philosophers"*

✷ ✷ ✷ ✷ ✷

"I confess that I cannot imagine how any human being, in his proper senses, can believe that the Sun is stationary when, with his own eyes, he sees it revolving around the heavens, nor how he can believe that the earth, on which he stands, is whirling with the speed of lightning around the Sun, when he feels not the slightest motion."

— *David Wardlaw Scott, "Terra Firma"*

* * * * *

"Modern astronomical teaching affirms that the world we live on is a globe, which rotates, revolves and spins away in space at brain-reeling rates of speed; that the Sun is a million and a half times the volume of the earth-globe, and nearly a hundred million miles distant from it; that the moon is about a quarter the size of earth; that it receives all its light from the Sun, and is thus only a reflector, and not a giver of light; that it attracts the body of the earth and thus causes the tides; that the stars are worlds and Suns, some of them equal in importance to our own Sun himself, and others vastly his superior; that these worlds, inhabited by sentient beings, are without numbers and occupy space boundless in extent and illimitable in duration; the whole of these interlaced bodies being subject to, and supported by, universal gravitation, the foundation and father of the whole fabric.

To fanciful minds and theoretical speculators, the so-called 'science' of modern astronomy furnishes a field, unsurpassed in any science for the unrestrained license of the imagination, and the building up of a complicated conjuration of absurdities such as to overawe the simpleton and make him gape with wonder; to deceive even those who truly believe their assumptions to be facts."

— *Thomas Winship, "Zetetic Cosmogeny"*

* * * * *

"The distance between the Red Sea at Suez and the Mediterranean Sea is 100 statute miles, the datum line of the Canal being 26 feet below the level of the Mediterranean, and is continued horizontally the whole way from sea to sea, there not being a single lock on the Canal, the surface of the water being parallel with the datum line.

It is thus clear that there is no curvature or globularity for the whole hundred miles between the Mediterranean and the Red Sea; had there been, according to the Astronomic theory, the middle of the Canal would have been 1,666 feet higher than at either end, whereas the Canal is perfectly horizontal for the whole distance.

The Great Canal of China, said to be 700 miles in length, was made without regard to any allowance for supposed curvature, as the Chinese believe the earth to be a Stationary Plane.

I may also add that no allowance was made for it in the North Sea Canal, or in the Manchester Ship Canal, both recently constructed, thus clearly proving that there is no globularity in Earth or Sea, so that the world cannot possibly be a Planet."

— David Wardlaw Scott, "Terra Firma"

＊ ＊ ＊ ＊ ＊

"One hundred and eighteen miles of LEVEL railway, and yet the surface on which it is projected a globe? Impossible. It cannot be. Early in 1898, I met Mr Hughes, chief officer of the steamer 'City of Lincoln.'

This gentleman told me he had projected thousands of miles of level railway in South America, and never heard of any allowance for curvature being made. On one occasion he surveyed over one thousand miles of railway which was a perfect straight line all the way.

It is well known that in the Argentine Republic and other parts of South America, there are railways thousands of miles long without curve or gradient. In projecting railways, the world is acknowledged to be a plane, and if it were a globe the rules of projection have yet to be discovered. Level railways prove a level world, to the utter confusion of the globular school of impractical men with high salaries and little brains."

— Thomas Winship, "Zetetic Cosmogeny"

＊ ＊ ＊ ＊ ＊

"If the earth be the globe of popular belief, it is very evident that in cutting a canal, an allowance must be made for the curvature of the globe, which allowance would correspond to the square of the distance multiplied by eight inches.

From, The Age, of 5th August 1892, I extract the following: 'The German Emperor performed the ceremony of opening the Gates of the Baltic and North Sea Canal, in the spring of 1891. The canal starts at Holtenau, on the south side of Kiel Bay, and joins the Elbe 15 miles above its mouth. It is 61 miles long, 200 feet wide at the surface and 85 feet at the bottom, the depth being 28 feet. No locks are required, as the surface of the two seas is level.'

Let those who believe it is the practice for surveyors to make allowance for 'curvature' ponder over the following from the Manchester Ship Canal Company (Earth Review, October 1893) 'It is customary in Railway and Canal constructions for all levels to be referred to a datum which is nominally horizontal and is so shown on all sections. It is not the practice in laying out Public Works to make allowances for the curvature of the earth."

— *Thomas Winship, "Zetetic Cosmogeny"*

* * * * *

"We are told that though the earth has the appearance of being a vast plane, with the Sun moving high above and over the earth, that what we see is a deception; it is an optical illusion – for it is not the Sun that moves, but the earth, with 'the sea and all that in them is,' in the form of a globe, whizzing with terrific rapidity round the Sun, located millions of miles away – its mean distance being assumed to be 91 millions of miles, and that the earth travels at the rate of 68,000 miles an hour, or 19 miles every second."

— *Lady Blunt, "Clarion's Science Versus God's Truth"*

* * * * *

"It is in evidence that, if a projectile be fired from a rapidly moving body in an opposite direction to that in which the body is going, it will fall short of the distance at which it would reach the ground if fired in the direction of motion. Now, since the earth is said to move at the rate of nineteen miles in a second of time, 'from west to east,' it would make all the difference imaginable if the gun were fired in an opposite direction. But, as, in practice, there is not the slightest difference, whichever way the thing may be done, we have a forcible overthrow of all fancies relative to the motion of the earth."

— *William Carpenter, "100 Proofs the earth is Not a Globe"*

✳ ✳ ✳ ✳ ✳

"In short, the Sun, moon, and stars are actually doing precisely what everyone throughout all history has seen them do.

We do not believe what our eyes tell us because we have been taught a counterfeit system which demands that we believe what has never been confirmed by observation or experiment.

That counterfeit system demands that the earth rotates on an 'axis' every 24 hours at a speed of over 1000 MPH at the equator.

No one has ever, ever, ever seen or felt such movement (nor seen or felt the 67,000MPH speed of the earth's alleged orbit around the Sun or its 500,000 MPH alleged speed around a galaxy or its retreat from an alleged 'Big Bang' at over 670,000,000 MPH!).

Remember, no experiment has ever shown the earth to be moving. Add to that the fact that the alleged rotational speed we've all been taught as scientific fact MUST decrease every inch or mile one goes north or south of the equator, and it becomes readily apparent that such things as accurate aerial bombing in WWII (down a chimney from 25,000 feet with a plane going any direction at high speed) would have been impossible if calculated on an earth moving below at several hundred MPH and changing constantly with the latitude."

— *Marshall Hall, "A Small, Young Universe After All"*

✳ ✳ ✳ ✳ ✳

"It will be seen that my reasons for thinking that the earth is round are rather precarious ones. Yet this is an exceptionally elementary piece of information. On most other questions I should have to fall back on the expert much earlier, and would be less able to test his pronouncements. And much the greater part of our knowledge is at this level. It does not rest on reasoning or on experiment, but on authority. And how can it be otherwise, when the range of knowledge is so vast that the expert himself is an ignoramous as soon as he strays away from his own speciality? Most people, if asked to prove that the earth is round, would not even bother to produce the rather weak arguments I have outlined above. They would start off by saying that 'everyone knows' the earth to be round, and if pressed further, would become angry. ... This is a credulous age, and the burden of knowledge which we now have to carry is partly responsible."

— *George Orwell*

QUOTES FROM
PHYSICISTS & PHILOSOPHERS

"In order for the earth to be at rest in the center of the system of the Sun, planets, and comets, there is required both universal gravity and another force in addition that acts on all bodies equally according to the quantity of matter in each of them and is equal and opposite to the accelerative gravity with which the earth tends to the Sun...And thus celestial bodies can move around the earth at rest, as in the Tychonic system."

— *Isaac Newton, Physicist*

* * * * *

"I have come to believe that the motion of the earth cannot be detected by any optical experiment."

— *Albert Einstein, Physicist*

* * * * *

"...to the question whether or not the motion of the earth in space can be made perceptible in terrestrial experiments. We have already remarked...that all attempts of this nature led to a negative result. Before the theory of relativity was put forward, it was difficult to become reconciled to this negative result."

— *Albert Einstein, Physicist*

* * * * *

"Briefly, everything occurs as if the earth were at rest..."

— Henrick Lorentz, Physicist

$* * * * *$

"There was just one alternative; the earth's true velocity through space might happen to have been nil."

— Arthur Eddington, Physicist

$* * * * *$

"The failure of the many attempts to measure terrestrially any effects of the earth's motion..."

— Wolfgang Pauli, Physicist

$* * * * *$

"We do not have and cannot have any means of discovering whether or not we are carried along in a uniform motion of translation."

— Henri Poincaré, Physicist

$* * * * *$

"A great deal of research has been carried out concerning the influence of the earth's movement. The results were always negative."

— Henri Poincaré, Physicist

$* * * * *$

"This conclusion directly contradicts the explanation...which presupposes that the earth moves."

— Albert Michelson, Physicist

"The data [of Michelson-Morley expirment] were almost un-believable...There was only one other possible conclusion to draw — that the earth was at rest."

— *Bernard Jaffe, Physicist*

* * * * *

"We can't feel our motion through space, nor has any physical experiment ever proved that the earth actually is in motion."

— *Lincoln Barnett, Historian*

* * * * *

"Thus, even now, three and a half centuries after Galileo...it is still remarkably difficult to say categorically whether the earth moves..."

— *Julian B. Barbour, Physicist*

* * * * *

"Such a condition would imply that we occupy a unique position in the universe, analogous, in a sense, to the ancient conception of a central Earth. This hypothesis cannot be disproved, but it is unwelcome and would only be accepted as a last resort in order to save the phenomena. Therefore we disregard this possibility.... the unwelcome position of a favoured location must be avoided at all costs.... such a favoured position is intolerable. Therefore, in order to restore homogeneity, and to escape the horror of a unique position... must be compensated by spatial curvature. There seems to be no other escape."

— *Edwin Hubble, Astronomer*

* * * * *

"There is no planetary observation by which we on Earth can prove that the earth is moving in an orbit around the Sun."

— *Bernard Cohen, Physicist*

* * * * *

"Thus, failure [of Michelson-Morley] to observe different speeds of light at different times of the year suggested that the earth must be 'at rest'...It was therefore the 'preferred' frame for measuring absolute motion in space. Yet we have known since Galileo that the earth is not the centre of the universe. Why should it be at rest in space?"

— *Adolph Baker, Physicist*

* * * * *

"...The easiest explanation was that the earth was fixed in the ether and that everything else in the universe moved with respect to the earth and the ether...Such an idea was not considered seriously, since it would mean in effect that our earth occupied the omnipotent position in the universe, with all the other heavenly bodies paying homage by moving around it."

— *James Coleman, Physicist*

* * * * *

"It doesn't matter how beautiful your theory is, it doesn't matter how smart you are. If it doesn't agree with experiment, it's wrong."

— *Richard P. Feynman, Theoretical Physicist*

* * * * *

"Space isn't remote at all. It's only an hour's drive away if your car could go straight upwards."

— *Fred Hoyle, Astronomer*

www.ingramcontent.com/pod-product-compliance
Lightning Source LLC
Chambersburg PA
CBHW030654260626
47157CB00007B/2642